GHOST HUNT 2

GHOST HUNT 2

MORE Chilling Tales of the Unknown

BY JASON HAWES AND GRANT WILSON

WITH CAMERON DOKEY

✸ PARACHUTE

PRODUCED IN CONJUNCTION WITH PARACHUTE PRESS

(L)(B)

LITTLE, BROWN AND COMPANY
NEW YORK • BOSTON

Little, Brown and Company

Hachette Book Group
237 Park Avenue, New York, NY 10017
Visit our website at www.lb-kids.com

Little, Brown and Company is a division of Hachette Book Group, Inc.
The Little, Brown name and logo are trademarks of Hachette Book Group, Inc.

The publisher is not responsible for websites (or their content) that are not owned by the publisher.

First Paperback Edition: September 2012
Originally published in hardcover in September 2011 by Little, Brown and Company

ISBN 978-0-316-09958-5 (hc) / ISBN 978-0-316-22042-2 (pb)

10 9 8 7 6 5 4 3 2 1

RRD-C

Printed in the United States of America

I dedicate this book to my daughters, Samantha, Haily, and Satori, and my twin sons, Austin and Logan. I love you more than life itself and thank you for every minute you have allowed me to be your father and your friend. You five have made every day of my life truly the best one could ever hope for.

To my wife, Kristen, whom I love endlessly. Since we met in seventh grade, you have never stood in front of me or behind me; you have always been beside me, helping me find my way.

To every member of TAPS, past, present, and future. You are the backbone of this group and what it has accomplished. It has taken sacrifices from us all to push this field ahead.

Last but not least, this book is dedicated to all the people who invest their time in this field. From the skeptics to the believers, from the hunters to the researchers—you are all part of this powerful and unstoppable movement. You should all take a bow for what you have accomplished.

—JASON HAWES

I dedicate this book to my amazing children, Connor, Noah, and Jonah, and to all the future ghost hunters out there. To all children who decide not to be afraid of the dark, but rather to embrace it and own it. To those who boldly conquer ignorance with imagination and intelligence. May you take my torch and carry it farther than I ever could. And, of course, to my lovely wife, Reanna, the very pillar of my life.

—GRANT WILSON

TABLE OF CONTENTS

INTRODUCTION

We started our first **Ghost Hunt** *book
with a simple question:
Do you like ghost stories?*

Well, it looks like you do. We have received so many letters
from readers saying how interesting and spooky the stories are,
and many of you have even tried your own ghost hunt investigations. Awesome!

We are so happy to be back with *Ghost Hunt 2: MORE Chill-
ing Tales of the Unknown*. The stories are all based on real cases
that we investigated. All the strange events you will read about
in here really happened.

As we were working on this book, we wanted to give you a variety of the kinds of investigations to read about. And we have to admit that we think these stories are even spookier than the ones in the first book.

"The Ghosts of Alcatraz" takes place in the most famous prison in the country. It's a tourist attraction now and no longer used as a jail. Many people have claimed it is haunted. Walking through the dark halls was scary enough, but the sounds we heard coming from the empty cells were even scarier!

"It's Just a Dream" may be one of the most interesting cases we've ever investigated. In that story, a woman has terrifying nightmares. In her dreams, a dark figure is trying to harm her. That sounds bad, right? But what's worse is that the nightmares come true.

"Restless Spirit" and "Ghost Town" have twists that will surprise you. "Runaway Ghost" and "The Beast in the Dark" might make you feel a little sad for the spirits. "Play Dead" might make you smile.

And "Cries in the Night" may just be the scariest story ever. See if you agree.

Don't forget to go to www.GhostHuntBooks.com so you can see and hear some of the evidence from the cases for yourself.

Then check out the *Ghost Hunt* Expert Guide in the back of the book. It has some advanced tips and two quizzes that will show you whether you've got what it takes to be a real ghost hunter. But we know that you do!

As we always say:

On to the next one!

JASON HAWES and GRANT WILSON

CRIES
IN
THE
NIGHT

"*Where are you? I can't see you!*"

Lyssa stumbled along the rocky seashore. Dense fog wrapped around her with a cold and clammy embrace, so thick that she couldn't see where she was going. Lyssa could hear the waves pounding against the shore, but she couldn't see the water through the hazy vapor. She also couldn't see the other members of the TAPS team, but she knew they were nearby. She had been walking right next to Jason, but the fog had rolled in so fast—all it had taken was a few steps in the wrong direction and they had become separated.

Now she was all alone.

Lyssa waved her flashlight around, trying to see where she was going. But the light showed only the cold, white mist.

"Help us! Somebody, please save us!" she heard a voice cry out. She tried to turn toward the sound and almost lost her balance on the sharp, uneven rocks. She didn't recognize the voice, and she couldn't tell where it had come from.

"Jason, is that you? Where are you? I can't see you!" Lyssa called.

No answer. She stared into the darkness. There was a light! It appeared to be floating on the water. *Is it a ship?*

Lyssa began to go forward again. She walked slowly, trying hard not to slip on the shifting rocks beneath her feet. If she could just get down to the water, maybe she could find Jason and the others.

"Aaaaaah!"

Lyssa's ankle turned on a large stone. With a sharp cry, she lost her balance and fell to her knees. The flashlight flew from her hand and went skittering away. Pain shot through her from slamming into the jagged edges of the rocks. She toppled over onto her side and lay still for a moment. She could feel the sharp edges of the rocks digging into her body.

Her skinned arms and palms felt sticky—there was some bleeding from her scrapes. She pushed herself upright. Then she flexed her foot and stretched her arms in front of her. At least nothing felt broken.

Careful not to lose her balance again, Lyssa got to her feet. Every part of her body felt battered and bruised. The mist surrounding her was really getting to her. Beyond the pain from the fall, Lyssa had to admit to herself that she was just plain scared.

Lyssa swallowed hard to keep from crying. Where was the team?

"Aiiieeeee!" A sudden scream cut through the night. Lyssa's heart leapt into her throat.

"Help! Somebody, please! Help! Help! HELP!" a voice cried out. It sounded like a little boy's.

Then the air around Lyssa seemed to explode with sound. There were voices everywhere in the fog, shouting and calling out words that Lyssa couldn't understand. And the whole time, there was the sound of the waves, pounding furiously against the shore. Then a deep, weird groaning filled the air.

Something's being pushed to the breaking point, Lyssa thought.

But what is it? What?

Earlier that day...

"Got something?" Grant asked.

Lyssa paused in sorting through the TAPS mail.

One of her jobs as the chief interviewer for TAPS (The Atlantic Paranormal Society) was opening the mail. Lyssa actually liked that part of her job a lot. It meant she was the first person to see anything new and interesting. Today, one particular envelope caught her eye. The name and address were written by hand.

That looks like a kid's handwriting, Lyssa thought. It was big but not sloppy.

"I'm not sure yet," Lyssa answered. She took her letter opener and slit the top of the envelope. Inside were several sheets of binder paper with more of the same handwriting on it. Lyssa pushed the rest of the mail aside and spread the letter out on top of her desk.

The TAPS office was in an old house in Rhode Island. What used to be the living room was now the main work area. Jason Hawes and Grant Wilson had desks along one wall. They faced each other on either side of a brick fireplace. Sitting face-to-face made it easy for the two TAPS founders to talk over cases.

Lyssa's desk was next to technical manager Jen Shorewood's. The final two members of the TAPS team, identical twins Mike and Mark Hammond, shared a big worktable along the back wall. Mike was the team's evidence examiner. Mark was the researcher. Both were tall and serious-looking, with straight brown hair and dark brown eyes. It was really hard to tell them apart.

Grant got up from his desk and leaned over Lyssa's shoulder so they could read the letter together.

Dear TAPS, the letter began.

I hope it's okay for me to write. I don't know what else to do. (I want to ask for your help.) Not for me. Well, not just for me. It's mostly for my grandpa.

"Interesting start," Lyssa said.
"Yeah, it is," Grant confirmed. He pulled up a chair and sat down beside her. "Let's keep going."

Grandpa George lives in Maine. Sort of out in the middle of nowhere, right by the ocean. I go to see him every summer. It's just the two of us for most of August. That's the way we like it.

But there's one thing we don't like. It started when I turned nine. I'm eleven now. You probably want to know that, huh? Also my name, which is Tom Kelly.

Anyhow, I'm writing because of the voices and the lights, out on the water. We only hear and see them one night a year.

"Okay, now it's *really* interesting," Grant said.
Lyssa nodded, her eyes still on the page.

It happens the fifteenth of August. Screams. People yelling for help. There are crazy lights, and sometimes Grandpa George and I think we hear a bell. There are lots of other sounds, too, but we've never been able to figure out what they are.

The first year, Grandpa George and I tried to help. But we couldn't, because of the fog. It was so thick we couldn't see the water. It's hard to get to the ocean from Grandpa George's house. There are lots of big sharp rocks going down to the water. It's dangerous to climb on them, even in the daytime.

We even called the Coast Guard. They couldn't do anything, either. Not that night. That's how thick the fog was.

The Coast Guard came the next morning. They didn't find anything at all. They didn't really believe me. I think they thought I was making the whole thing up. They didn't even believe my grandpa! He told them he heard the sounds, too. I guess they thought he was just covering up for me because I'm his grandson and all that.

But Grandpa George did hear the sounds. He saw the lights. I didn't make it up. Not any of it.

Anyhow. That was the first time.

"The first time," Grant murmured.

Lyssa turned over the first page. The letter went on.

So then a year went by. Grandpa George and I thought maybe that was it. Just some weird and freaky thing, you know? But it happened the next August 15, too, just like before. And now the date is coming up again. I wasn't sure what to do, but then my best friend, Tony, told me about TAPS. As soon as he did, I knew I wanted to write you.

Please come to Grandpa George's house. Please help us figure out what's going on. Grandpa George won't admit it, but I think he's upset. He doesn't like to hear the people screaming and knowing there's nothing he can do to help them.

But maybe you can help. I think maybe you're the only ones. Because you want to know the truth. Those people on the water? I'm pretty sure they died. I think they died a long, long time ago. Can the ocean be haunted?

Please come as soon as you get this letter.

Sincerely,

Your new friend (I hope)

Tom Kelly

P.S. Here's Grandpa George's address. I drew you a map on the back of this page. I'll wait outside for you after dinner on the fifteenth, just in case you come.

Lyssa sat back. "Wow."

"Let's take a look at the map," Grant said.

She turned over the second page of Tom Kelly's letter. On the back was a well-drawn map. It showed a hill and the ocean. At the foot of the hill were lots of big rocks. At the top, there was a house with a road snaking up toward it. The address was written in big block letters. There was a mark at the bottom of the hill where Tom Kelly would be waiting.

"Check that out," Lyssa said. "*X* really does mark the spot."

"What's the date today?" Grant asked.

Lyssa checked the bottom of her computer screen.

"Oh my gosh, today's the fifteenth!" she said. "That doesn't give us much time."

Grant stood up. "Hey, Hammond," he called out.

On the far side of the room, both Hammond twins turned around. "Yeah?" they said in unison.

"Mike," Grant said, his voice brisk. "Please get me driving directions to this address." He read it out loud. Mike grabbed a piece of paper and jotted it down. "We need the travel time. Mark, I'd like you to look on a map and get me the name of the closest town. Find out whether or not there's a historical society. A lot of small New England towns have one."

"On it," the twins said, once again in unison. They swiveled back to their respective laptops at precisely the same time.

"How do they *do* that?" Lyssa asked.

"I'm pretty sure they practice at home," Jen said. "I keep meaning to set up a camera and catch them in the act."

"What's up?" Jason asked. He walked over from his desk to stand beside Grant. "You're giving a lot of orders all of a sudden—you think you're the boss or something?" he teased.

"You know it," Grant answered with a grin. "But I did say please." He picked up Tom Kelly's letter and held it out to Jason. "Read this. We can talk on the road."

"Aye, aye, Captain." Jason saluted.

"You came," Tom Kelly said. "I wasn't sure you would. I mean, I hoped—I mean—wow!"

Tom Kelly looks like everybody's best friend, Lyssa thought. He had bright red hair, freckles across his nose, and bright green eyes. He was wearing a pair of well-worn jeans and a plain white T-shirt.

"Of course we came," Jason said. He stepped forward to shake Tom's hand. "I'm Jason, and this is Grant."

"I know who you guys are," Tom said. "I looked it up on the Internet. You started TAPS."

"That's right," Grant said. "We did. And this is the TAPS team." Quickly, Grant introduced the rest of the group, ending with Lyssa. "Lyssa is the one who spotted your letter."

"Cool," Tom said. "Thanks."

"So," Lyssa said, "how does your grandfather feel about us coming?"

Tom made a face.

Busted! Lyssa thought.

"I haven't told him yet. Grandpa George is used to being on his own. He's used to fixing things himself. He doesn't like to ask for help."

"So you did it for him," Jason suggested.

"Yeah," Tom said. "And for me, too. I mean—it's kind of hard to describe. It just feels wrong to sit up in the house and not do anything. I want to figure out what's going on."

"We do, too," Grant said. He looked up, to where a small house with weather-beaten shingles stood on top of the hill. "But first I think we'd better go meet your grandfather."

"I appreciate your visit," Grandpa George said when they went up to the house to meet him. "But we're fine on our own. Tom shouldn't have asked you to come."

He shot his grandson a look that was stern but also full of love. George Kelly reminded Lyssa of a piece of old leather, thin but still strong. *And I guess we know where Tom got his red hair,* she thought. Grandpa George's hair wasn't as bright as Tom's, but it was still pretty red.

"Since we're already here, Mr. Kelly," Jason said, "we would really like the chance to experience whatever happens tonight.

We understand that it all happens down by the water. So we won't need to bother you."

"Well, you did come a long way," Grandpa George said slowly. "And I've got to admit I am concerned about tonight. A person doesn't like to hear others in distress and have no way to help them. It's just not right... So I guess my grandson here did what was best. Maybe we could use your help."

"Thank you," Grant said.

"You'd better take a look at the shore while it's still light out," Grandpa George said. "Otherwise, you'll have trouble for sure after it gets dark."

Sometime later, the group was at the water to check it out. "Okay, you guys," Grant said as he and Jason stood side by side facing the team with their backs to the ocean. "No two ways about it, this investigation is going to be a challenge. And challenge number one is getting down to the water."

Between the TAPS team and the ocean was a big field of jagged rocks. They weren't quite big enough to be called boulders. But they were big enough that walking across them was going to be tough. The light was already fading fast.

That meant the TAPS team was going to have to cross the rock field in the dark.

"According to Grandpa George, it stays rocky all the way down to the water. But right at the shoreline, the rocks are smoother and smaller—sort of a pebble beach. That will be easier to walk on. But it's still slippery, so even there we have to watch our step."

"What about equipment?" Mark asked.

"Audio only," Jason said. "Handheld. Or actually…" He lifted up an audio recorder that was hanging on a strap around his neck. "There isn't time to get down to the water and set up equipment. And it's probably too wet anyhow."

"Document and tag everything you can for the voice recorders," Grant continued. "Remember, the sound of the ocean will always be in the background."

"Got it." Lyssa nodded.

"We'll work in pairs," Jason went on. "Lyssa, you're with me. Mark is with Grant. Jen with Mike. Stay together as much as possible. If the fog rolls in, things could get pretty tough out there, guys."

"Um, Jason," Jen said.

"What?"

"I think you'd better look behind you."

Both TAPS founders turned. The entire team stood silently for several moments. At the edge of the water, a band of white fog was slowly creeping forward. It looked to Lyssa like long fingers reaching out for the land.

"Looks like Mother Nature's going to provide her own version of going dark," Grant said. "Okay, team. Let's get started."

Lyssa staggered her way across the rocks. They were big and jagged and hard to climb. Her feet kept slipping. Jason clambered along beside her. Even with his long legs, he was struggling. Jen and Mike had turned off to the right, Grant and Mark to the left. Lyssa and Jason were going straight down the middle to the ocean.

How much farther? Lyssa wondered. The sound of the waves crashing against the rocky beach filled her ears. But Lyssa couldn't see the water through the thick fog.

"This is Jason," she heard him say for the benefit of the audio recorder. "I'm with Lyssa. We're walking toward the water. The fog is coming in pretty good now. It should reach us any minute."

He turned his head to look at Lyssa. "You okay?"

"Sure," Lyssa said. "Absolutely." She took a few more steps, her eyes on the white wall of mist ahead of them. Reaching, grasping, inching ever closer and closer. Once the moisture surrounded her, it would feel like being stuck in a cloud—but with no way out.

Lyssa shuddered. She hated the feeling of being trapped. She knew Jason did, too.

"Okay," she admitted. "Well, to tell the truth, I'm not looking forward to being in the fog."

"Just stay focused," Jason advised. "Remember, fog can't actually hurt you, no matter how creepy it is in the movies. When in doubt, just listen for the sound of the water."

"Okay," Lyssa agreed. She felt a breath of cool, damp air move past her face. And then the fog surrounded them. Lyssa and Jason struggled through it. The mist made the rocks even more slippery and dangerous.

Oof! Without warning, Lyssa pitched forward. Her hands hit against the stones.

"Are you all right?" Jason asked at once.

"Fine," Lyssa said as she tried to catch her breath. "I think my shoe's untied. I must have tripped over the laces. Go on, I'll be right behind you."

"You're sure?" Jason said.

"Sure," Lyssa replied.

Jason continued toward the water. He vanished into the mist after just a few steps. Lyssa balanced as best she could, trying to get her shoe tied. Her fingers were clumsy with cold. The laces were wet. Finally, Lyssa gave up bending over. She turned around and sat gingerly on one of the stones. It took three tries before she could get the laces tied.

Finally! Lyssa thought. She stood up.

The fog was all she could see. Lyssa was all alone. She could feel the panic rising in her chest. *Remember what Jason said,* she told herself. *When in doubt, listen for the water.*

But which way was it? It seemed to Lyssa that the sound of the ocean was all around her now. *Think!* she told herself. What had she done? *I went to tie my shoelace. I sat down.*

Lyssa swung around. Back in the direction she thought the ocean was. She strained to hear...Was the sound of the waves louder that way? She honestly couldn't tell.

"This is Lyssa," she gasped for the recorder she was wearing. "I'm alone in the fog. I've lost Jason. I can't see anybody else. I don't know where they are. I'm going to try calling for help."

Lyssa pulled in a breath to shout. Before she could, she heard a cry.

"Help us!" a voice cried out. *"Somebody, please save us! Help. Help! HELP!"*

"Jason, where are you? I can't see you!" Lyssa shouted out.

She wasn't sure, but she thought the other voice was coming from the water. Lyssa staggered toward the sound. Her foot slipped. Lyssa lost her balance and went down, hard.

She lay on her side, trying to steady her breathing. Trying to beat back the pain and fear that she felt. Slowly, carefully, Lyssa got to her feet.

But she was in a nightmare world now. The sounds of fear and panic were all around her. She could hear voices screaming for help. Lyssa heard what sounded like a bell ringing wildly. Something groaned, like an enormous animal in pain.

"This is Lyssa," she said once more for the recorder. "There are all these sounds. I can't tell what's making them. I can't—"

Crrraaaacckk! Booooommm!

"We're lost!" Lyssa heard a voice cry out. *"We're going down."*

"No," Lyssa cried out. *"No!"*

The walkie-talkie in Lyssa's jacket pocket suddenly crackled. "Lyssa, this is Jason. Can you hear me? Come back." In all the confusion, the pain of her fall, she'd forgotten all about the walkie-talkie.

She fished it out with trembling fingers. "Jason," Lyssa said. "Where are you? Can you hear the voices?"

"I hear them," Jason replied. His voice sounded grim even over the walkie-talkie. "Hold on, Lyssa. I'm heading your way. Keep talking into the walkie-talkie so I can find you."

"Okay," Lyssa said. The bell was ringing nonstop now. Lyssa could still hear many different voices, all crying out together. "This is Lyssa. I'm waiting for Jason. I'm hearing all these sounds. I can't see what's going on. If only this fog would clear, just a little."

All of a sudden, Lyssa saw a light coming toward her. "I think I see you, Jason," she cried. "Is that your flashlight?"

A moment later, he was at her side.

"What's going on out there?" Lyssa gasped. "Could you see it?"

"No," Jason said. "I'm hoping the fog breaks up at the water. It does that sometimes. I want to get down there to see if we can see anything. Can you walk?"

"Yes," she said. Jason took Lyssa firmly by the arm to help her along. Together, they slid across the rocks.

"There!" she cried suddenly. "A break in the fog! Did you see it?"

"I saw," Jason said. "I think we're getting close. The rocks are getting smaller."

A moment later, the big rocks ended. Lyssa felt large, smooth pebbles under her shoes. The sound of the waves crashing onshore was very loud now.

"Jay! Lyssa! Is that you?" she heard Grant's voice cry.

"We're here!" Jason called back. "Can you see anything?"

"Nothing," Grant said. He and Mark appeared farther down the beach. "There was a big break in the fog a couple minutes ago. We got a clear view out to sea. There's nothing there, Jay."

"But I heard it," Lyssa protested. "I heard somebody say, *'We're going down.'* There has to be a ship of some kind."

"I guess now we know why the Coast Guard had trouble believing Tom and his grandfather's story," Jason said.

"Maybe there *is* a ship," Mark said quietly. "Or was."

Ghost ship, Lyssa thought.

"Come on," Grant said. "Let's get back to the house."

"That ought to do it," Jen said an hour or so later. She finished wrapping a bandage around Lyssa's knee. "I bet you'll be sore for a few days. You really took a tumble."

"I did, but it's okay," Lyssa said. She stood up, doing her best to ignore the sharp stabs of pain. "Come on. Let's go join the others."

"It all sounded so close," Jason was saying as Jen and Lyssa walked into the living room.

"That's a good way of describing it." Grandpa George nodded. "It never occurred to me there weren't really people out there who needed help." He spotted Lyssa and got up to make room for her on the sofa. "How are you feeling?" he asked.

"I'll be just fine," Lyssa told him. "Please don't get up, Mr. Kelly."

"Nonsense," Grandpa George answered. "You sit right down. Tom."

"On it," Tom Kelly said. He shot to his feet, grinning at Lyssa. "Grandpa made hot chocolate. His hot chocolate is the best, even better than my mom's."

"Hot chocolate is my absolute favorite," Lyssa said. She took a seat on the sofa. Tom vanished into the kitchen. A moment later, he returned with a mug of steaming hot chocolate. He handed it to Lyssa. Then he went to stand beside his grandfather.

"So," he said, "you believe us, don't you?"

"Absolutely, we believe you," Jason said.

"Do you know what it is?"

"Not for certain," Jason answered.

"What do you think it is, Tom?" Lyssa asked.

"I think it's a shipwreck," Tom said. "It has to be, right?"

"It sounded that way to me," Lyssa said. "I'm sure I heard a bell. And there was this big cracking sound. Like something breaking. Something big."

"Ship's mast, maybe?" Grant suggested.

"All these things are possibilities," Jason admitted. "But I think we shouldn't get too far ahead of ourselves. We need to review the evidence and do some research. Mark can visit the historical society tomorrow. See if there's anything there that could help explain what we all heard."

"Can you think of anything, Mr. Kelly?" Lyssa asked.

"Well"—Grandpa George scratched his chin—"there have been shipwrecks over the years, of course. There's a big sandbar just offshore."

"Why isn't there a lighthouse?" Mark asked.

"The big ships never put in here," Grandpa George said. "It's just not deep enough. But if a storm came up, it could blow a ship off course. That could be very dangerous."

"I was just wondering," Tom said, "how come you have to wait for morning? Why can't we listen to the evidence now?"

"Because it's late, Tom," Grandpa George said with quiet authority. "These folks drove all day to get here. They're cold and tired. And Lyssa is hurt."

"I'm just as curious as Tom is," Lyssa spoke up. She looked at her fellow team members. "Let's just listen to the audio, okay?" she said.

"Cool," Jen answered. "I just need a few minutes to get set up."

"We've lost the mast!" the voice on the audio shouted. *"We're doomed! We're going down!"*

"That's the last of it," Jen said. She punched off the playback and the room fell silent. One by one, she had played back the evidence from the audio recorders that the team had worn that night. They all painted the same picture: a ship going down, full of desperate people fighting for their lives.

"Those poor people," Lyssa said.

"There's something about the voices," Grant said. "I can't quite put my finger on what I mean. Did anybody else notice it?"

"They sound like they're in a movie," Tom said excitedly. "You know, like *Pirates of the Caribbean.*"

"That's it!" Lyssa said. "All those voices have English accents."

"That might give Mark a place to start at the historical society," Grant said. "Lots of ships sailed from England, I know, but not all of them."

"Sure," Jason agreed. "Still cuts down the number of ships we have to investigate."

"Let us do it!" Tom burst out. "Me and Grandpa George. I like investigating stuff. Ask Grandpa. He'll tell you."

"It's true," Grandpa George said slowly. Lyssa thought she could almost see the older man thinking over his grandson's suggestion. "Tom's like me that way. I've spent a fair amount of time over at the historical society, and I'm familiar with the collection. Maybe we *could* help. If you tell us what we're looking for."

"I've got a theory," Mark said. "This whole thing started the year Tom turned nine, right? Why don't you try looking for a ship with a nine-year-old on board? Ship records should show things like that."

"Why would somebody that young be on a ship?" Jen asked.

"Several reasons." It was Grandpa George who replied. "He could have been a cabin boy or even a stowaway. Or maybe the captain's son. Perhaps the ship was carrying settlers, like the *Mayflower*. Whole families came on ships like that. A baby was even born on the *Mayflower*."

"Oh, man, this is going to be totally awesome!" Tom exclaimed.

Grant smiled. "Sounds like you two are the perfect pair to take this on."

"Hey, check this out," Lyssa said a couple of weeks later. "It's a letter from George and Tom Kelly. I wonder what they discovered, if anything."

Grant grinned. "Only one way to find out. Go ahead."

Lyssa opened the letter. There was Tom's big, neat handwriting, just like before.

"Read it, Lyssa," Jason said.

"Dear TAPS," Lyssa read aloud.

This is Tom and George Kelly. You remember us, right? LOL Anyhow, we've been going to the historical society almost every day since you left. It took a while, but we think we may have found something really cool.

"This sounds good," Mark commented.

Lyssa looked up at Mark with a smile and continued to read the letter.

There were *lots* of ships. And some of them had better records than others. But just yesterday, we think we found her. (Grandpa George says you always talk about ships as if they were girls. Do you know why?)

Anyway, there was a ship called the *Amelia Rose*. She was heading for Boston in 1801. There were lots of families on board. One of them, the Pattersons, had a son who was nine. His name was Jeremiah.

So we think Mark was right. Maybe what happened has something to do with my turning nine. We never heard the ship before I was nine. Maybe Jeremiah wanted to tell me something because I'm his age. I know we'll never know for sure. Still, Grandpa and I keep thinking about Jeremiah and all the other people on the *Amelia Rose*.

We decided we want to do something to remember them. We haven't figured out what yet. But we've got almost a whole year to come up with something. Grandpa George and I want to invite all you guys to come back. We want you to be a part of whatever we finally decide.

"Oh, man," Mark said. "Can I just say this? I really like these guys."

"I think we all feel the same way," Jason said. "Is that all?"

"Pretty much," Lyssa said.

"Great! We could all use a little rest," Grant said.

RING RING RING…

Mark picked up the phone, and Lyssa heard him say, "TAPS,

how can we help you?" She watched as he then frantically grabbed a pen and starting writing.

"Hey, guys, you gotta hear this," Mark said as he hung up the phone.

"I know that expression," Grant said. "It looks like we're not getting a rest after all."

"Aye, aye, Captain," Jason said. "It looks like it's all hands on deck right now!"

*S*queak.

The strange, high-pitched sound wormed its way into Joe Hensick's brain. He groaned and pulled a pillow over his head to block out the sound. Joe didn't want to wake up. All he wanted to do was sleep.

Squeak.

Squeak. Squeak. Squeeeeak.

Joe rolled over.

Squeak. Squeak. Squeak. Squeak.

SQUEAK. SQUEEEEEEEAK!

"Ralph!" Joe bellowed. "For crying out loud!"

The dog didn't answer, but the squeaking stopped.

Joe rolled over once again—and fell off the couch with a *thump*. He landed flat on his face, right onto the hardwood floor. Joe was definitely wide awake now. He sat up, the blanket tangled around his legs.

I can't believe this is happening, he thought. For the third time in one week, he'd fallen asleep on the couch. *Too much studying.* That's what it was. He'd been sitting on the couch, reading his history book. And the next thing he knew, that squeaking was wrecking his sleep. Again!

"Ralph!" he called out. "Where are you, you lazy mutt? C'mere, boy."

Joe heard the click of nails on the wood floor. A moment later, his dog, Ralph, trotted into the room.

Ralph was some crazy, mixed-up combination of all sorts of different breeds. The Hensick family always had mutts when Joe was growing up. Ralph was just the latest in a long line, but he was the first dog Joe had ever had on his own.

He'd picked out Ralph at the animal shelter right before heading off to college. It made finding a place to live a little tougher, but Joe didn't mind. When it came to Ralph, it was love at first sight.

But the truth was that Ralph was the homeliest dog Joe had seen in his entire life. And he knew some seriously funny-looking dogs. Ralph was black and white, with a black head, tail, and back. He had a white belly and legs, and four gigantic black paws. One of his ears stood straight up; the other flopped over sideways. His tongue lolled out when he panted and drooled. He did that a lot.

"Hey, Ralph," Joe said. The dog had stopped halfway across the living room. He sat down, his black tail thumping. There was something in his mouth. "I'm not mad, I promise," Joe went on. "Come on, boy. Come show me what you've got."

Click. Click. Click. Ralph padded over to the couch and sat down. Joe squinted at the thing in Ralph's mouth and sighed. *Not again,* he thought.

"Okay, Ralph," Joe said. "Show me what you've got. Drop it. Drop it, boy."

Ralph dropped it right in Joe's lap.

Joe picked up the object by one ear. It was a plush bunny toy. And it was soaked with dog slobber. *Ew.*

"Gee, thanks," Joe said. He scratched Ralph behind his ears. "I guess I asked for it."

Joe stared at the bunny. When you squeezed — or bit — its middle, it squeaked.

Ralph loved squeaky toys. He couldn't get enough of them. And his favorite time to chomp on them was in the middle of the night, so Joe put the toys away when he went to sleep. He put them in the hall closet with the door shut tight.

That was the idea, anyhow. But for the third time this week, Ralph had somehow gotten the toys back out of the closet. Joe had no idea how the dog did it.

Joe untangled his legs from the blanket and stood up. Ralph stood up, too, his tail wagging.

"Okay, come on. Let's go check this out."

Joe set off toward the hallway with Ralph at his side. The closet was just to the left of the front door. Joe reached it and stopped and stared. Then he switched on the hall light to make sure he wasn't getting it wrong.

Just like the last three times this had happened, the closet door was closed. Joe was sure that Ralph hadn't opened the door and closed it again. The door opened out into the hallway, so there was absolutely no way the dog could have opened the door himself—unless he was secretly a werewolf and changed into a human. How else could Ralph use a doorknob?

"What are you, some kind of magic dog?" Joe asked.

Ralph thumped his tail happily.

I don't think so, Joe thought.

But at least the idea made him smile. Sort of. Because the truth was, this thing with the squeaky toys was starting to get a little weird. Ralph shouldn't have been able to get the closet door open. He should *not* have been able to get to those toys.

Okay, let's say he did, Joe thought. Suppose there was some trick to the closet door that only dogs could discover. Suppose Ralph could actually open and close the door on his own...

That still didn't explain one other extremely strange thing.

Joe had bought three squeaky toys at the pet store. Three and *only* three.

Now there were three plush squeaky toys lying in a heap in front of the closed closet door. And one in Joe's hand. The soggy one Ralph had been chewing on.

Joe shook his head. The math was too simple to get wrong. That added up to a total of *four* toys.

He looked at Ralph. "Can you explain this? How on earth did you get an extra toy?"

Ralph answered with a *woof.*

Joe shrugged and dropped the plush rabbit onto the pile. Instantly, Ralph made a dive for it. He came back up with the stuffed bunny in his mouth.

Squeeeakkkk.

Ralph gave Joe a hopeful look—as if to ask whether it was finally playtime.

Joe laughed. He couldn't help it. So there were four toys. Maybe Ralph had brought an extra one home from the park or something, and Joe just hadn't noticed. He might as well get some studying done since he was awake. But first, he decided to play with Ralph for a while. Then he would take a shower and make himself and Ralph a good breakfast. He planned to forget all about this weirdness.

That's what he told himself, anyhow.

An hour or so later, Joe was in the shower. Ralph was safely outside the bathroom door. Next to squeaky toys—and food—water was Ralph's favorite thing. Which was great when it was time to give him a bath, but not so great if Joe was the only one who was *supposed* to be in the shower.

Joe turned off the water. He slid the shower curtain back and reached for the towel on the nearby rod. *Scrambled eggs and bacon,* he thought. Ralph loved bacon.

Joe dried himself off and put on boxers and a T-shirt. With one hand, he hit the wall switch for the fan to help clear away the steam. With the other, he reached for his hairbrush. He glanced into the bathroom mirror.

Joe made a strangled sound. His hand froze in midair. He stared at the mirror, not seeing his face at all, but seeing something else instead.

The surface of the mirror was covered in small handprints. It looked like some wacky kindergarten art project.

He blinked, wondering if he was imagining it.

Nope, they were still there.

This was beyond weird. Who could have covered his mirror in handprints—and why? Was it a joke?

He blinked again. Was it possible that the prints were here yesterday and he hadn't noticed?

No, Joe decided. Not possible at all. The prints definitely were not there when he brushed his teeth last night.

That meant someone made them after he fell asleep on the couch.

An icy chill slid down Joe's spine.

What if someone was in the house last night? What if he, or she, opened the closet door—and gave Ralph an extra toy? And what if that same someone covered the mirror with handprints?

Slowly, trying not to notice the way his own hand trembled, Joe reached for the towel to wipe the prints away. He rubbed at the mirror. Then he rubbed again.

The handprints stayed right where they were. He couldn't wipe them off. Joe looked at them more carefully. The prints looked as if they were *inside* the mirror.

Joe felt the hairs on the back of his neck stand straight up. *Weird* didn't describe this. This was flat-out spooky.

Okay, calm down, he told himself. There had to be an explanation. Maybe the prints were somehow put there when the mirror was made.

Right, he thought. *So why haven't you seen them before now?*

First a dog toy that shouldn't have been there. And now these handprints. Was he imagining these things? Was he losing his mind?

Slowly, carefully, as if he expected the mirror to shatter at any moment, Joe reached out. He could hear Ralph whining outside the door. Joe chose a handprint. The one in the very center. And he laid his hand on top of it.

Well, at least that ruled out one possibility. He couldn't have made the prints himself. There was absolutely no way.

The hands on the mirror were way too small.

They had to be the handprints of a little child.

A strange, high-pitched electronic pinging sound echoed through the Hammond brothers' kitchen.

"Will you turn that thing down?" Mark asked his twin, Mike. "Every time your phone rings, it sounds like you're getting a message from outer space."

"I like my ringtone," Mike said. "It's not some stupid song, and I always know it's my phone."

"Well, are you gonna answer it or what?" Mark asked as the phone continued to emit the weird sound. "It's ruining my breakfast."

Mike put down the cereal box and picked up the phone. The caller ID read UNKNOWN NUMBER. Mike answered anyway.

"Hello?"

"Hammond," said a voice on the other end of the phone.

"Lucky guess," Mike said. "Which one? Whatever you want, the answer is *no* until you get it right."

"Mikey," the voice said. "Come on, man. It's me. I think maybe I need your help."

"*Joe?*" Mike asked. He sat down at the table with a *plop*. "What's the matter?"

There were only three people in the world who got away with calling Mike Hammond "Mikey." The first one was his mom. The second was Aunt Mona. Since she'd been dead for about ten years, she no longer did it very often. That left just one person: Joe Hensick. He had been the twins' best friend when they were growing up.

Joe had been there the first time Aunt Mona had come for a visit. She pinched Mike's cheek and told him how much he had grown, even though she had never seen him before. And *then* she called him Mikey. And to make it worse, she didn't call Mark "Marky." So Joe and Mark started calling him Mikey all the time. It made Mike furious. Finally he made them swear they would never do it again.

"Okay," Mark had said back then. "I promise."

"Me too," Joe agreed. "There's just one thing. I get to use the name only if I'm in real trouble. It will be a sort of secret code between us."

Mike had agreed to those terms, and Joe had never used the name Mikey again. Until now.

"Where are you?" Mike asked.

"I'm in Boston," Joe said. "I just got settled into my new house that I'm renting. Sorry, I've been meaning to call."

"Dude," Mike said. "You used the name. What's going on?"

"I think I may need you to tell me that," Joe said. "You guys are still doing the ghost thing, right?"

"Right," Mike said. "Wait a minute! You've got a ghost?"

"That's what I need *you* to tell *me*," Joe said again. "Come on, Mike. Keep up."

"Give me your new address," Mike said. He reached for a notebook. "Then tell me everything you know."

"The situation sounds unusual—and interesting," Jason said later that morning.

"So we can take the case?" Mike asked.

"*You* can take the case," Grant spoke up. "Jay and I are going to New York City, remember? We're checking out a possible haunted floor in an old hotel."

"Right," Mike said. "I forgot about that."

Grant smiled. "I don't see any reason why you and Mark

shouldn't take the case," he said. "Jen can go along. Lyssa's coming with us."

"Okay." Mike nodded. "I'll call Joe and tell him we'll be there tomorrow."

"Oh, man, you brought reinforcements," Joe said. "This is awesome."

Joe Hensick looked nice, Jen decided. He had brown eyes and dark brown hair that he wore just a little long.

"Come on in," Joe said. "I'll show you around."

"This is a great old place," Jen commented as she stepped across the threshold, carrying her laptop and a video camera. The house was made of brick and had smooth wooden floors.

"I like it," Joe said simply. "I still can't believe they let me have a dog."

"Where is he?" Jen asked.

"Probably eating a pair of shoes somewhere," Joe replied, then called, "Ralph! We've got company. Get out here, big guy."

A moment later, the ugliest dog Jen had ever seen bounded into the living room. There was something brown and fuzzy dangling from his mouth. Something with legs.

"What *is* that?" she asked. "Or maybe I don't want to know?"

Joe laughed. "That's Mr. Rabbit, his current favorite squeaky toy." He reached down and gave one of the dangling legs a tug. Ralph backed up, tightening his grip on the plush animal to play tug-of-war.

Squeeak.

"O-kaay," Jen said. "Got it."

Ralph took his rabbit to his doggie bed near the fireplace. He chomped on the toy, and the rabbit squeaked louder. Jen smiled. There was just something about a happy dog...

"Any new handprints?" Mike asked.

Joe shook his head. "Nope. They only appeared that one time."

"Have you ever noticed unusual activity anywhere else in the house?" Jen asked.

Joe frowned. "I don't think so. Just the prints on the bathroom mirror and the toys."

"Are they always new ones?" Mike asked.

"Huh?"

"The toys you find."

All of a sudden, Joe's face went pale. "Yeah," he said. "At first it was just one extra toy. But last night the ones I found were all new. I didn't buy any of them."

Mike frowned. "Well, either you've got someone who likes Ralph so much that they sneak into your house every night to give your dog new toys or—"

"Or there's someone—or some*thing*—already in the house with me," Joe finished. He took a deep breath. "This is getting very creepy."

Mike slapped Joe on the shoulder. "Don't worry. We're going to figure this out."

"He's right." Jen tried to sound encouraging. "That's our job."

Joe looked doubtful. "You sure you don't want me to stay?"

"Positive," Mark said. "We'll work better if we're here on our own. You've got somewhere to go, right?"

Joe nodded. "Yeah. I'll be at my friend Scott's place. Call my cell if you need me, okay?"

"We will," Mike promised. "You just get a good night's sleep."

Joe patted Ralph and told him to be a good boy. Then he grabbed his pack and left for the night.

Mike turned to the TAPS team. "Okay, guys. Let's get set up and see if we can find out who else around this place is into squeaky toys."

They set up quickly and were ready to get started. "And going dark in five, four, three, two...*one*. Kill the lights," Mike said.

Jen flipped down the light switch in the house's small dining room. The room went dark.

Still lots of outside light, though, Jen thought. The house was in

41

the middle of Boston, after all. There was a big streetlight just outside the front door.

"Okay," Mike went on. "Mark and I will take the hall and bathroom. I'd like you to stay in the Command Center, Jen. This is kind of a small place. No reason for the three of us to be tripping over each other."

"Sounds good." Jen nodded. "I put cameras and audio recorders in both the hall and the bathroom. Watch out for the recorders in the hall. They're on the floor. And I've got a camera on the closet, just in case."

"Great," Mark said. "Let's go."

"This is Mike. We're in the hallway," Mike said. He was setting a base level for the voice recorders. He glanced at his brother. "Are you getting any kind of a reading?"

"Nope," Mark answered.

Mark had an EMF detector in one hand. He held it out in front of him, moving it slowly back and forth.

"Let's check out the bathroom," Mark suggested.

"Okay." Mike nodded.

The two brothers walked down the short hall. The bathroom was to the right. Joe's bedroom was straight ahead, and the door was closed.

"The dog's in the bedroom, right?" Mike asked.

"Right."

Mark stepped into the bathroom first. Mike followed. It was kind of a tight fit. Like the other rooms in the house, the bathroom was small.

Mike shone his flashlight onto the bathroom mirror.

"This is Mike. We're in the bathroom now," he said for the recorder. "The mirror is clear. No sign of any handprints. I'm going to try and establish contact."

"Go for it."

"Hello," Mike said. "My name is Mike, and this is my brother, Mark. Is there anybody else here with us?"

Mike waited. He looked over at the EMF meter in Mark's hand. The readout was holding steady; just one light was glowing.

"If there is someone here, we'd really like to meet you," Mike continued. "We think you like dogs. We do, too, and so does Joe, the guy who lives here. If you like dogs, can you give us a sign?"

"Whoa!" Mark suddenly said. "Did you see that?"

In the darkness of the bathroom, the EMF meter suddenly flared to life. All of its lights came on at once. The brothers could hear Ralph begin to bark and scratch at the bedroom door.

Mike spun toward the sound. He stepped quickly into the hallway, sweeping the flashlight back and forth.

"What are you reading?" he asked Mark tensely.

43

Mark stared at the meter. "Nothing, now," he said. "It's dropped back down to level one. Anything out in the hall?"

Ralph continued to bark. The dog sounded frantic. *Let me out. Let me out. Let me out.*

"I think Ralph senses something," Mike said.

Mike opened the bedroom door. Ralph bounded out and ran straight into the living room. Curious, Mike followed him.

Mark stepped out into the hall. "What is it?" he called to his brother.

"I think you'd better take a look for yourself," Mike said. *Squeeeeak.*

"What gives?" Mark said.

"Sorry," Mike replied. "I couldn't help it. They're kind of . . . everywhere."

Mark came into the living room. He pointed his flashlight down to the floor. It was covered.

Every square inch of the wooden floor was covered with squeaky toys.

"And you didn't see anyone bring the toys?" Joe asked the next morning. He and Jen and the Hammond twins were sitting in his living room. They each had a large mug of coffee.

"No, they were just there," Mike answered. "We didn't see or hear any activity, but then one of our meters went crazy."

"Which can mean paranormal activity," Mark explained. "And Ralph went crazy, barking at the same time."

"So we let him out of your room," Mike filled in. "And that's when we found all the toys."

"Well, you *did* ask for a sign," Jen reminded them.

Joe gave them a shaky grin. "I'd say you got a pretty big one." He gazed around the living room and shook his head. "I just counted seventeen new squeaky toys."

He smiled at his dog, who was chewing on a fuzzy pink pig.

"Ralph thinks this is all great."

"Well, it's not the worst haunting we've ever seen," Jen admitted with a smile.

"Did you get anything on the cameras?" Mike asked her.

"Nothing definite," Jen said. "I'll show you." She cued the laptop to play back what the digital video cameras had recorded during the investigation.

On the screen, Mike and Mark entered the bathroom from the hall, and the lights on the EMF meter Mark carried lit up all at once.

Jen paused the playback.

"Okay," she said. "You see the time?" At the bottom of the screen, a readout displayed what time the events occurred:

12:32 AM. Jen tapped on the keyboard for a moment. "Now, here's what was going on at that same time out in the hall."

For the first few minutes after the brothers stepped into the bathroom, the feed from the hallway cameras showed nothing at all. Then, from out of nowhere, there was a sudden streak of something moving. But they couldn't tell what it was. It just looked like a blurry streak.

"Wow!" Joe exclaimed. "What is that?"

"Good question," Jen said. "But look at the time."

Once again, the bottom of the screen showed 12:32 AM, from the hall cameras this time.

"So at the exact same time the EMF went crazy..." Mark began.

"*Exactly,*" Jen finished. "That—whatever that is—was going on out in the hall. It's too bad we didn't have cameras set up here in the living room."

Mike was staring at the laptop screen. "Can you get a still image out of that?" he asked Jen. "Clean it up at all?"

"Give me a minute," Jen said. Her fingers worked rapidly on the keyboard.

Joe took a big gulp of coffee. On his doggie bed, Ralph rolled over with a sigh.

"Do you think that's a ghost?" Joe asked.

"Hard to say," Mike admitted. "I'd definitely lean toward

some paranormal explanation, though. It's just too big a coincidence. The EMF spike and whatever that is happening at the exact same time."

"Whoa!" Jen suddenly exclaimed. "Okay, guys, check this out."

She played back the video again. For several seconds, there was absolute silence.

"It's still hard to be a hundred percent sure," Jen warned. "The image isn't clear enough for that."

"Okay, I buy that," Mike said. "But look." He leaned over, pointing at the screen. "Those have got to be stripes. I mean, it really looks like—"

"A little boy's shirt," Joe said.

"You know what this means, don't you?" Mark asked. He rubbed his hands together in anticipation. "It's research time."

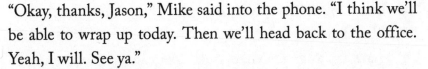

"Okay, thanks, Jason," Mike said into the phone. "I think we'll be able to wrap up today. Then we'll head back to the office. Yeah, I will. See ya."

"Jay and the rest of the team say hi," Mike said as he ended the phone call. "New York is going well, but he thinks they have to be there another day or so. I think we'll be done first."

The twins, along with Jen, were still at Joe's house, where

Mark had just done some online research. Now Mike turned to his brother. "So, what have you got?"

"Plenty," Mark replied. "About thirty years ago, this house was owned by a guy named Steve O'Leary. Steve had a young son named Paul, who died in this house from pneumonia. He was eight years old."

"How do you find out this stuff?" Joe asked.

Mark smiled. "Steve O'Leary was a firefighter. He got a special award for bravery not long before his son died. So when Paul passed away, the newspapers covered it. One of them even ran a picture. According to the article, it was Steve O'Leary's favorite photograph of his son."

Mark turned the laptop so everyone could see it. On the screen was a photograph of a young boy. He had on a pair of blue jeans and a blue-and-white-striped shirt. He was kneeling down with his arms around a dog's neck. Paul O'Leary was grinning, as if it was the happiest day of his life.

"Wow," Joe said softly. "Oh, wow." He cleared his throat. "So, what do we do now?"

"That's up to you," Mike said. "We can keep on trying to make contact. If it really is Paul O'Leary's spirit, maybe we can find out what he wants."

"I think we already know that," Joe said quietly, his eyes on the image of the boy. "He just wants to play with a dog."

"How are things going with your friend Joe?" Grant asked a couple of weeks later. Grant was reviewing that month's case files.

"Great," Mike replied. "Mark and I are heading to Boston this weekend to visit him."

"So he and the spirit worked things out?"

"So far, so good," Mark spoke up. "He struck a bargain. Paul can have as much playtime with Ralph as he likes during daylight hours, but not after bedtime. So Joe is getting sleep. And Ralph is getting as many toys as a dog could want."

"Sounds like a win-win situation." Jason chuckled.

"You know what?" Mike said. "I really think it is. And it also goes to show that thing you guys are always saying: Ghosts are still people, just like us."

"Well, maybe not just like *you*," Mark said with a laugh.

THE GHOSTS OF ALCATRAZ

The boat carrying the TAPS team rocked up and down on the choppy waters of the San Francisco Bay. Mist sprayed up from the water onto Lyssa's face. She grabbed hold of a railing and looked out into the distance. A small island covered by thin fog loomed directly ahead. Through the haze, Lyssa could see trees and a road carved into the side of the island. As the boat got closer, Lyssa made out more details. There were a tall lighthouse and a water tower. Behind them was a huge, wide gray building.

"There it is," Mike said. "Alcatraz. Also known as the Rock. The most famous prison in American history. They say it's impossible to break out of it."

Lyssa could now make out the razor wire spiraling over the tops of the fences surrounding the buildings.

"Is it really?" she asked.

"Well, even if someone was able to get out of their cell, get around all the armed guards, and somehow climb over the walls, they would still have to swim across the San Francisco Bay. Which is near freezing half the year," Mike said.

"And they also say there are sharks in the bay," said Jason. He broke into a smile. "But I don't know how true that is."

Lyssa scanned the water, looking for any fins skimming the surface. All she saw were small waves foaming up around the boat.

"But it hasn't been used as a jail since 1963, when it was closed down," Mark continued. "Now it's open to the public. It's actually a national park. Over a million people visit each year."

"It's not like any park I've ever been to," his brother said. "Before flying out here, I read a few blogs by people who've visited Alcatraz. They were pretty spooked by what they saw."

"Grant and I have always wanted to investigate this place," Jason said. "Can you imagine being trapped in there? It's a small dot in the middle of nowhere."

"Yeah, I can't believe we're finally able to check it out for ourselves," said Grant. "We've heard a bunch of interesting claims."

Lyssa had heard stories about Alcatraz since she was a kid.

She was just as excited as the rest of the team to investigate the place. But as the boat approached the island, she couldn't help thinking about how scary it looked. She glanced back once more toward land and got a quick shiver. She imagined the prisoners being locked up in their cells, staring at the wall every day, just as she was doing. But they knew there was no way out!

The captain stopped the motor, and the boat gently slid into the dock. Lyssa took a deep breath. The walls of the prison towered up ahead. Could anyone still be trapped behind those prison walls?

Shrugging it off, Lyssa grabbed a box of gear and scrambled out of the boat. The rest of the team followed. On the dock, they met a man with a bushy beard and thick glasses.

"Welcome to Alcatraz," he said in a booming voice. "I'm Frank. I'll be your guide today."

"Thanks for allowing us to come investigate," Jason said.

"I'm excited that you're here. Over the years, I've heard so many strange stories," Frank said. "I would love to find out if they're true. Load your gear into the van over there, and I'll drive you up to the top."

After a quick drive up a steep road, Frank stopped the van in front of the entrance to the prison. Lyssa stared up at a huge iron gate. It had to be at least twelve feet tall. It was in the middle of the brick wall that surrounded the entire prison. Through the gate was a yard. Past that was the entrance to the main building.

"Lead the way, Frank." Grant gestured for their tour guide to go first.

As Frank led them into the yard, Lyssa lagged behind a little. The ground was very hard, and each step vibrated up to her shins. She felt as if something were holding her back, as if there were energy around the building pushing her away. She felt almost as if she were walking in her sleep. She barely realized when the team had reached the building. But as soon as she walked through the entrance, she snapped back to reality.

The team went through a caged room with heavy doors on both sides. It reminded Lyssa of a trap to catch wild animals. Frank explained that the cage was originally a holding area for visitors so guards could make sure no one was bringing in anything to help the inmates escape.

When Frank led them into the main hall, Lyssa saw rows and rows of bars stretching out in front of her. She stared into the cells around her. They were all the same. Flat metal beds, single toilets, bars on windows. Above her head, she could see inside the cells on the second level. They were the same as well. There was barely enough room inside a cell for a person to walk three steps in any direction.

"This is what we call Broadway," Frank said. "A little prison humor, I guess. This is the main hallway. All the new prisoners were led through this hall when they arrived. As soon as a new inmate entered the prison, the older prisoners would yell at them. Call them names and throw whatever they had at them."

Lyssa gazed down the hall. She estimated that the walk would take several minutes.

"That must have been terrifying for the new inmates," she said. Jen nodded in agreement.

"Absolutely, especially for the ones who had never been to jail before. I'm sure it was the first time they realized what was in store for them."

Frank started walking slowly. The team followed.

"What kind of claims have people made about this area?" Lyssa asked. "What paranormal things have people reported?"

"Noises. Footsteps. Shadows."

Lyssa looked from side to side. Each cell had one light, giving the rooms a sickly yellow color. "Do the sounds come from inside the cells?"

"Not exactly."

"Then from where?" Jen asked.

"Most people say they hear the noises coming from or leading to D Block," Frank said, waving his hand toward some stairs.

"What's D Block?" Mark asked.

"The inmates at Alcatraz had nothing to lose. So they were brutal at times—using weapons or causing riots. When a prisoner was violent, he was punished by spending time on D Block,"

Frank explained. "Most prisoners who were sent there started to behave better when the punishment was over. No one who came out wanted to be sent back. Follow me, I'll take you there."

Frank led the team up a narrow set of stairs and down a short path. He stopped in front of a green door.

"D Block is through here. It was a solitary confinement area, which means prisoners were alone," Frank explained. "They were only allowed to leave their cells for one hour once a week. Inside the cell there was no light. No way to tell if it was day or night. Think about that for a minute. You know that feeling of waking up in the middle of the night, and you have no idea what time it is? You know that panic you feel in your chest before you calm down? Now imagine that happening all the time. A prisoner in one of these cells had no idea when he was going to be let out. It must have felt like they would be there forever."

Everyone looked at each other and shook their heads. They could only imagine being stuck somewhere like that. It would be awful!

Frank showed them into D Block. The doors for each cell were open. Lyssa noticed these cells were much smaller than the regular cells. The steel floors inside looked very cold. There were no beds. The cell was more like a locker for a person than a room.

"What kinds of activity have people seen in D Block?" she asked Frank.

"Much of the activity revolves around cell fourteen for some reason. Some visitors on my tours will walk in and get dizzy and sick to their stomachs. I had a visitor once, a grown man, run straight out to Broadway, his face totally white. He had gone into cell fourteen alone. When he was able to talk again, he said that first he felt a tap on his shoulder, and when he turned around, there were two glowing red eyes. A voice growled into his ear the words *you're mine*. I don't believe just anything people tell me, but I could see this man wasn't fooling around."

"Have you ever experienced something like that yourself here in D Block?" Jen asked him.

"Nothing like that. But I have seen big shadows that look like they're going in and out of the cells. I was never able to figure out where they came from." Frank shrugged.

Next he took the team back through Broadway and down more steps to what seemed to Lyssa like a dungeon with brick archways and a brick floor. The ceiling was low and the air was muggy. Everything about Alcatraz made Lyssa feel uncomfortable, as if it were closing in on her. She checked out the rest of the team. Everyone's shoulders were raised high — she could tell they were uneasy being down there, too.

"This is the Citadel," Frank said. "This space was originally used as solitary confinement until it was decided that being here was cruel and unusual punishment. That's when they built D Block. Down here it was like you were forgotten. Like you didn't exist. No time out of your cell at all. No letters from the outside. No food except when the guards remembered to bring it. If you take a close look at the walls, you can see where prisoners carved their names. They weren't allowed to have any sharp objects, so it's anybody's guess what they used. Some say they carved into the stone with their own fingernails."

"Has the same type of activity that happened on D Block happened here?" Mark asked.

"Not quite the same. I've heard voices when no one else was around—and I mean no one. After all the visitors leave, I always walk through the prison to make sure no one was left behind. I always call out to see if anyone is down here. Twice, I heard someone answer, but when I checked, no one was there…"

"What did the voices sound like? Could you hear actual words?" Lyssa asked.

"At first it just sounded like mumbling," Frank said. "So I called out again. Then I walked toward the sound. Then the voice got louder…almost like a shout. Honestly, I can't really be sure about the words. But I know I heard a voice. No doubt about it, it was a human voice."

"Could you tell if it was male or female?"

"It was a man's voice. Very gruff."

When Frank finished speaking, the group stood for a few moments, not moving at all. It was so silent that Lyssa could hear everyone breathing.

"It gets so quiet down here," she said out loud.

"Exactly," Frank said. "Follow me. I have one more place to show you."

Frank took the team to a spiral staircase and led them up.

"This is the hospital ward," he said, and kept walking.

The wing was big. In a strange way Lyssa was getting used to the cramped spaces of Alcatraz. But now, being in such a large hallway was jarring. The sound of the group's footsteps bounced off the walls. It made Lyssa feel as if someone were following her. She peered into each room as she passed. The ones right in front of her were still caged in with bars, but they were much bigger than the cells on Broadway. Some had nicer beds and sinks. One even had a bathtub. Some of the rooms farther on had no bars at all. Those rooms had sinks and cabinets, and a few had benches along the walls, like the waiting room at a doctor's office.

Out of curiosity, Lyssa walked over to the nearest cell. She tried to swing the door shut. But it was very heavy, and it squealed as she pulled. Jason tried moving another one, and it made a loud noise, too. Frank told them that since the doors were out of use, they had rusted.

"What kind of reports have you heard about the hospital ward?" Lyssa asked.

Frank took a deep breath. He started rubbing his hands together. He seemed nervous.

"Something happened to me here that I won't ever forget. I take tour groups through the prison. Usually I take fifteen to twenty people. But I never take more than twenty. One time a while back I was leading a tour, and right before going into the hospital ward, I did a head count. Twenty people exactly. On the way out, I counted twenty-one. I thought I must have counted one person twice. So I counted again. Still twenty-one. At that moment I realized I was standing right in front of a man I didn't recognize from the group. He was wearing a white shirt, blue pants, and black shoes. The same clothes the prisoners wore. At first it didn't really click with me. But it hit me a second later. I scanned the tour group, looking for the extra man. But he was gone."

Lyssa looked around the room. They were standing in front of a room with an operating table.

"Where did that happen?" she asked.

"Right here. Right where we're standing."

Everyone in the team turned their heads around at the same time. The bars on the cells looked like bones crossing each other. But you could see right through the spaces into the cells. There was no place for a person to hide in the hospital.

Finally Frank began walking back to the stairwell.

"That's about it," he said over his shoulder. "I'll take you back to where you left your gear."

After the team set up Central Command, Mark and Jen went back to the hospital ward. They settled around the area where Frank had seen the extra man. Mark got busy setting up cameras and making sure they covered the whole hall. When Mark was finished, Jen pulled out a small gray metal tube.

"What's that? I've never seen that piece of gear before," Mark said.

Jen pointed the tube at the floor and flicked a button. Little red dots appeared next to her feet.

"Laser grid."

"Whoa! High tech. Very impressive. How does it work?"

"A laser is just a very focused beam of light," Jen explained. "So if a person—or a spirit—walked in front of the light, the little dots would go away."

"Cool," Mark said.

"I know," Jen said, smiling. "Way cool."

Jen's walkie-talkie clicked on. Jason's voice came through a moment later.

"Everybody ready? Good. Going dark in three ... two ..."

Mark looked around the hospital ward one last time. The paint on the walls was peeling off. Some areas had tile, but most of the tiles were cracked. And the bars on the windows made him feel like he was inside a machine. Everything, from the cracks in the corners of the room to the dust particles he tasted in the air, was very depressing. Mark couldn't imagine it being any more upbeat when it was in use either.

"... One. Going dark, people."

The lights went out. Mark blinked a few times to adjust. Then he took a seat next to Jen and waited. And waited. They watched the laser grid for any changes for a while. The dots didn't dim even a tiny bit. Then Mark walked down the hall and back, looking into each room. After about an hour, there wasn't much action. So Mark suggested trying something a little different.

"I know we always act respectfully when we know we're calling out a spirit. But you know sometimes we have to provoke them a little. I'm going to try that." He stood up. "Is there anybody here?"

Mark began to walk down the hallway. Jen got up and followed him. Mark didn't see anything different from the last time he walked down the hall.

"Oh, I get it. You're hiding out. Probably because you're scared," Mark said, raising his voice. "Well, I guess since there's really no way for you to get off this island, you might as well—"

Mark stopped short when he heard a high-pitched squeal behind him. His eyes opened wide, trying to see everything around him.

"What was that?" Jen whispered.

"It sounded like a cell door...Remember when Lyssa tried to move one before? Let's check it out."

They walked quickly toward where the noise came from, looking at doors on the way. The empty hospital ward was bleak. The cells seemed to come at them, the bars flying by like spinning bike spokes. The medical equipment in each cell reminded Mark of torture devices.

They were almost back where they started when Mark stopped in front of the cell with the bathtub in it.

"Jen. This is the fifth time I walked past this cell today. But it's the first time the cell door's been closed."

Mark reached out and grabbed one of the bars. The metal was warmer than he'd expected. The door was so heavy he needed to grab it with both hands. He pulled back hard. The door squealed as it opened.

"It's the same sound!" he said excitedly.

Mark stepped inside the cell, placing each foot carefully as he slowly walked toward the center of the room. His mouth was dry. Being in the middle of the cell made him feel lost, as if the walls were a mile away. He had a sick feeling that he couldn't get out. He saw the bathtub near the wall. It was white and stood out in the dark room. He spoke directly to the spirit.

"If you are here, we would like to communicate with you. Can you make the door move again?"

Mark watched the door closely. Jen was on the other side

doing the same thing. They waited like that for a few minutes, not blinking. But nothing happened. Jen joined Mark in the cell and looked around, trying to find something that might have caused the door to shut. But nothing seemed out of the ordinary.

At least until Jen got a weird look on her face.

"Mark...are you wearing cologne or something?"

"No. Why?"

"Do you smell that?"

Mark breathed in deeply. Out of nowhere a memory popped into his head. When he was a kid in school, the bathrooms had this pink powdered soap. The smell in the room was the smell of that soap.

"Yeah. It's just like soap. I absolutely smell that," he told Jen.

They examined the walls of the room first, then the ceiling, looking for an open air duct. But there were no vents in the room, so the scent wasn't coming from someplace else.

"If it's not coming from outside the room, it must be coming from inside," Mark said.

They searched for where the smell was strongest. After a minute Jen stopped in front of the bathtub.

"I think it's coming from over here," Jen said.

Mark went over to the tub. The smell was almost overpowering. His eyes watered a little and he had to breathe through his mouth.

"It's so strong," he said. "But there's nothing here. No soap, no water. This smell just came out of nowhere."

Mark bent down. He touched the porcelain tub. It was bone-dry.

The darkness in D Block was thick. The flashlight in Grant's hand was like a full moon on a pitch-black night.

"Frank said a lot of people felt dizziness and nausea in the area," Jason said. "Especially in cell fourteen. I think we should use the EMF detector. It's possible a high electromagnetic field reading is the cause of those experiences."

"Agreed."

They walked down the hall, watching the readout on the EMF detector. Even with the flashlight, it was disorienting walking down the dark hallway. Grant's eyes had trouble focusing. It was like trying to walk on a rolling log. The room was stuffy, and it was hard for him to swallow. When they reached cell fourteen, they stopped. The EMF detector was rising fast, going from a steady 1.5 up to 6 in half a second.

"That's really odd."

They examined the area, looking for any source of electricity that would cause the change in the reading. Grant got low, looking for where there might be an electrical wire or an outlet. There was nothing but solid concrete.

"I have no idea what's causing this EMF spike. But it seems like it's coming from the cell," he said.

Grant moved toward the cell door. A hand touched his shoulder.

He spun his head. Jason was pointing down the corridor.

"I just saw something...Something changed in the darkness. Maybe a shadow. It was moving a few cells down," he said in a hushed tone.

Jason walked toward where he pointed, still holding the EMF detector.

"Hello?" Jason said as he walked through the darkness.

Grant followed. He called, "It's okay to come out. We're not the guards."

They walked cautiously, asking the spirit to show itself. Finally they stopped where Jason saw the movement. They pointed the flashlight into the cell and around the hall. As Grant waved the flashlight, cracks in the walls lit up.

"Jason, do you think the flashlight could have caused what you saw?"

"I don't think so. It was a big thing, the size of a person."

"Well, whatever it was, I don't think it's here anymore. We're not getting any responses. The EMF is steady, too. I think we should go back to cell fourteen."

"Yeah, I think so, too. Let's stay focused," said Jason. "People say they've seen shadows and apparitions with glowing red eyes."

Back at the door to cell fourteen, Jason and Grant decided it would be better if only one of them went in at a time. The cell was just too small for two people. Jason volunteered to go in first. He took the flashlight from Grant and disappeared into the cell.

Grant turned to face the hall. He kept his ear toward cell fourteen to make sure Jason was okay. He could hear Jason moving around the cell and tapping the walls. At the same time he watched the hallway closely for any movement. If anything changed, he would be able to see it. And now there was no chance of it being caused by the flashlight.

But all of a sudden Grant felt something was off. Jason was being totally quiet in the cell.

"Jason? You all right?"

There was a scrambling sound from inside the cell.

"Grant! Get in here. NOW!"

Grant rushed into the cell and he instantly felt strange. He felt as if the walls were closing in on him. The cell was just so dark and he couldn't see Jason at all.

"Jason?!"

"Down here."

Jason flicked on the flashlight.

"Sorry. The light was reflecting into my eyes. But check this out."

Grant walked to where Jason was crouching down on the floor.

"When I walked in here, I felt the way Frank said a lot of the visitors feel. I got a little tense and queasy. And then I found this." He pointed the light to what looked like the base of a toilet. But it was sealed up. "And then my plumber side kicked in. I saw a small hole in the wall—see, right over there—so I looked through it. There's a sewer line running right behind this cell."

Grant took the flashlight and shone it through the hole. He put his head closer and got wind of a stale stench.

"I doubt the pipes are in use now, but they definitely were at one point," he said.

"Yeah," Jason said. "And the gases coming from them can be toxic. They can put a person on edge, especially in a small space. Think about it: that smell is so faint you wouldn't even realize you were breathing it in. But it could still cause a major headache. Maybe to some people it would even cause mild hallucinations."

"Like seeing glowing red eyes..." Grant said thoughtfully. "I think that's enough to call that claim debunked."

Jason put his arm out and touched the wall. The concrete had a chalky, powdery feel. He rubbed his fingertips together. He realized that without the flashlight on, the cell was exactly the way it was for the prisoners all the time. That was much more frightening to him than the claims of glowing eyes.

"Well, the sewer line definitely explains at least some of the visitors' claims," Grant said. "And *maybe* it explains that shadow you thought you saw. But what about the spike in the EMF reading? Think of how many prisoners must have been standing exactly where we are, going crazy bit by bit. Isn't it possible some of that energy remained in the cell?"

Jason stood for a minute, thinking it over.

"It's possible," Jason said. "And you're right about the EMF spike. *That* I can't explain."

Mike and Lyssa had been sitting at Central Command for hours. It was after midnight when the rest of the group met up with them.

"Really great stuff, guys," Mike said. "I can't wait to go over the footage tomorrow."

"Hopefully when we go over it, we'll pick up on something we've missed," Jen said. "So far we've all had personal experiences—phantom smells, doors closing, seeing shadows—but as far as we know, we haven't caught anything on tape. I'd really love to get some hard evidence."

"There's still the Citadel left," said Lyssa.

She thought back to her experience when she and the team investigated Fort Mifflin, a fort from the Revolutionary War.

There she went into a prison they called Casemate 11. It was a lot like the Citadel. It was also underground. Both were solitary confinement cells. Lyssa had seen a ghostly face of the inmate in Casemate 11, and that face would never leave her mind. She remembered how scared she was when she saw the face. The thought of being trapped in a closed space with a spirit again terrified her. But at least this wasn't her first time. She knew she could do it.

"If you all don't mind, I'd like to go down there to collect evidence," she said.

Jason and Grant looked impressed.

"Sure!" Jason said. "Mike, why don't you go with her? We'll stay here and monitor you."

Lyssa grabbed her favorite piece of equipment, the audio recorder, and Mike took the camera. Then they made their way down to the Citadel.

Just outside the archway leading into the Citadel, Lyssa stopped and looked through.

"Everything okay?" Mike asked.

"Just wanted to get a good look. Are you ready?"

"Yeah. You?"

"Yeah. Let's start." Lyssa calmly walked forward. A few feet into the Citadel she turned on the audio recorder. "Hello? Is anybody down here?"

Lyssa and Mike moved side by side. Every twenty feet or so

there was an opening in the wall that led into a different chamber of the Citadel.

"My name is Lyssa Frye. I'm not here to harm you or get you in trouble. I just want to talk."

Mike whispered to her, "I think we should check inside these cells."

"Okay."

They went into the closest one. The roof was lower than the hall, and Lyssa had to duck a little to fit in. It was very uncomfortable, and after only a few minutes her back began to ache.

She and Mike studied the walls. There were carvings everywhere. At the back of the cell, Lyssa sat down on the ground. She didn't want the sounds of her moving to mess up her audio recordings. Mike sat a second later and focused the camera on the entrance.

"Is there anybody here with us?" she called out.

She waited for a response.

"Lyssa...do you hear that?"

Lyssa closed her eyes to concentrate. She breathed slowly, feeling her lungs expand and contract. Then she heard it. A faint scuffle.

"Footsteps."

"I thought so, too," Mike whispered.

"It's coming from the hall. Let's check it out."

They got up and walked out of the cell.

"Whoever is here, please walk toward us," she called out.

They stood their ground, waiting to see what would happen. Lyssa's muscles were so tense she felt as if they would snap. Her fingers tingled. The footsteps were coming closer. And they were faster!

Closer, closer...coming right at her. Then they stopped.

"We'd like to communicate with you," Lyssa said loudly. "Can you make that noise again?"

Every second that passed was like a year. Lyssa knew there was a spirit present; she could feel it. Whoever it was stood only an arm's length away. Lyssa strained her neck forward, hoping to hear another footstep.

But what she heard instead made her jump back in shock.

It was clear as could be.

"NO!"

For an instant Lyssa couldn't focus on anything. She was too stunned. Lyssa rewound the audio recorder and played it back, just to make sure she wasn't imagining it. She heard herself say, "Can you make that noise again?" A few seconds of whooshing noises from the recorder followed. Then she heard it again.

Someone with a deep voice growling, saying, *"NO!"*

Mike was amazed. He kept staring at the recorder in disbelief.

"Lyssa, we can't stop now!" he said at last.

She nodded. Lyssa fast-forwarded to where she left off and began recording again.

"Who am I speaking with? Tell me your name."

Silence.

"How long have you been here?"

No answer. She continued to ask questions. After a while, it became clear that whoever responded to them before was not willing to talk anymore.

"Lyssa, I think we got more than enough for one night. Let's pack it in and go over this in the morning."

On the way out she took one more look at the Citadel. When she had walked in just a little while ago, she saw only an empty room. But now she had the awful feeling that there *were* prisoners in Alcatraz.

And they would be prisoners forever.

The next day in their hotel room, Jen and Lyssa were going over the evidence. Jen had her eyes fixed on a monitor, watching each corner for anything that went unnoticed the night before. Lyssa had headphones on and listened to the audio evidence. She wanted to go straight to the part she recorded in the Citadel, but she knew she had to listen to the whole recording first. A few times she thought she had caught EVPs, which are sounds made by spirits that can only be heard on an electronic recording. But when she played them for Jen, she always found a logical explanation for them.

Finally Lyssa reached the Citadel section. With the audio

equipment she had, Lyssa was able to clean up the recording. After replaying the growling *"NO!"* she had to take off her headphones. It was like a ghost speaking right into her ears. It made her feel uneasy.

"What did you find?" Jen asked.

"It's a VP."

"I think you mean an EVP. Finding a VP means you actually heard the sound at the time of the recording."

"I did hear it. Mike heard it, too; he can back me up. But last night we agreed not to tell anyone until I was able to clean up the audio. We didn't want to get anyone's hopes up. Here, have a listen."

Jen put on the headphones. Suddenly her face lit up.

"That's awesome! That might be the best evidence we've gotten yet."

She handed back the headphones to Lyssa. Lyssa continued to listen to the recording but stopped after only a few more seconds. She thought she found something. There was a soft sound in the background. She rewound the tape and listened again. There was something unnatural about the sound. It wasn't just normal background noise. Lyssa thought maybe she had caught an EVP. She rewound the tape and listened three more times. Then she said, "Jen, I think I just heard something better..."

Jen put the headphones back on. Lyssa stared at Jen, waiting for her to react.

Jen gasped and covered her mouth.

"Lyssa, we have to get everyone in here now!"

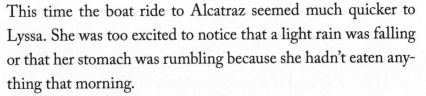

This time the boat ride to Alcatraz seemed much quicker to Lyssa. She was too excited to notice that a light rain was falling or that her stomach was rumbling because she hadn't eaten anything that morning.

They met Frank at exactly the same spot as last time. He took them quickly up the road and back through the main entrance. Frank led the team into an office, and everyone sat around a desk.

"Hi, Frank. We've got some interesting news for you," Jason said.

"Oh, really?"

"Really. Let's jump right in."

Mark and Jen explained their experiences in the medical ward, retelling how the door closed on its own and how the phantom smell of soap floated up from the empty bathtub. Frank seemed taken aback.

"Wow! That's really creepy stuff. Prisoners who had to go into surgery were scrubbed clean first in that tub."

"We didn't see any prisoners," Mark said. "But I think that's a real possibility of paranormal activity with the evidence we did find. There just aren't any other logical explanations for what happened."

Then Jason and Grant talked about their investigation of cell fourteen on D Block. They explained how gases from a sewer line might have made people feel dizzy or even imagine they saw things.

"But," Grant said, "we still couldn't find a reason for the EMF spike, which is strange."

"This is all very impressive," Frank said.

"Well, we haven't shown you everything yet. Lyssa, why don't you tell Frank what happened to you and Mike?" Grant said.

"Sure. Mike and I investigated the Citadel. Very shortly after we went down there, we started to hear footsteps. They were coming straight for us. It sounded just like a regular person walking up to us. We were able to catch it on tape."

She hit the play button. Frank nodded.

"I definitely hear that!"

Lyssa stopped the player.

"Then the footsteps stopped. I asked if the spirit could make the sound again. And we got an answer."

Lyssa started the recorder again. Right after the *"NO!"* came snarling out of the speakers, Frank sat straight up.

"That's the same voice!" Frank said. "I could swear that's the voice I heard."

"That's pretty amazing, but that's not all. At this point, I felt pretty sure we were in the presence of a spirit. So I asked a normal question. I asked what the person's name was. Listen closely."

Lyssa played the recording. She heard her own voice say, "Tell me your name." Then there was a murmuring, faint sound.

"It almost sounds like a message..." Frank said.

"Let me play it for you again. I'll turn up the volume."

She hit play. This time the sound came through loudly. A breathy voice said:

"Harry... Brunette. Three. Seven. Four."

Frank looked stunned. Lyssa rewound the tape and played it again.

"We looked up the prisoners' list. Prisoner number 374 was named Harry Walter Brunette."

A quiet fell over the room. Eventually Grant broke the silence.

"Then we did some more research. Harry Brunette was a bank robber and a kidnapper. He was even declared a public enemy by the FBI. When the police finally found him in New York City in 1936, there was a long shoot-out at his apartment. Eventually he was captured and brought here. With all this evidence, I have no problem saying Alcatraz is a haunted site."

Frank seemed upset.

"What's wrong?" Lyssa asked.

"I always sort of felt in my gut this place was haunted. But now with all this proof...well...is there anything to be worried about?"

"The inmates may have been dangerous when they were alive," Jason said. "But now, you have nothing to be afraid of. Seriously. From all we've seen, it seems they're just trying to communicate. These ghosts won't harm you."

Frank let out a relieved sigh.

"Good. Thank you. I really appreciate you coming all the way out here. I'll take you back down to the boat."

As the steel door slammed behind her, Lyssa smiled. She was glad to have found such hard evidence. And even happier to be escaping from Alcatraz.

RESTLESS SPIRIT

Ron and Dave Sandstrom crouched in a corner of their living room. It was the middle of the night. The boys knew they should be in bed, but there was something weird going on in the Sandstrom house.

Thirteen-year-old Ron was determined to find out what. Dave, who was only ten, insisted on tagging along. Because his older brother claimed he had seen a ghost.

Ron wasn't sure that he believed it, even though he saw it with his own eyes. But Dave was totally into ghosts. He was always reading anything he could about TAPS, The Atlantic Paranormal Society. He wanted to be just like its founders, Jason and Grant.

If the weirdness in the Sandstrom house really *was* a ghost, Dave was sure he could help.

The two boys waited for hours. First they waited for their parents to go to bed. Then they waited for them to fall asleep. Finally it was time. They snuck out of bed, grabbed the flashlights they always took camping, and tiptoed into the living room. There they crouched down behind the couch. Their goal was to get close to the fireplace...but not *too* close.

The fireplace was where Ron had seen *him*. The ghost.

"Did you really see something?" Dave asked now. He was trying to sound calm, but his voice trembled. He wasn't sure if it was from fear or excitement. Waiting for something to happen was a lot harder than he thought. Before tonight, Dave never realized that just *waiting* could freak a person out.

"I told you," Ron replied. "I saw a man wearing these weird old-fashioned clothes. Mom said she saw him, too. Only over by the front door."

Dave shuddered. "What about Dad?"

"I don't think Dad's seen anything," Ron said. "But he's the one who said we should start writing stuff down." He glanced down at Dave. "What's that thing those guys always say?"

"Documenting evidence," Dave said at once.

"Yeah. Okay. Whatever," Ron said. "That's what Dad said we should do. So that's why we're hiding behind the couch in the middle of the night."

"We're not hiding," Dave said. "We're *investigating*. Just like Jason and Grant. I bet *they* wouldn't go to bed and do nothing. If they thought there was a ghost, they'd try to find it."

"Yeah, you're right," Ron said. "They would."

Jason and Grant weren't do-nothing guys. They took action. Even Ron knew that. Because the truth was, he was interested in Grant and Jason's investigations, too. He just didn't talk about it all the time like Dave.

"What's the EMF meter doing?" Dave asked.

"What are you talking about? We don't *have* an EMF meter," Ron said.

"No, but you brought the compass, didn't you? It does the same thing. If it goes crazy, it means..." Dave said the next part slowly because he wanted to get it right. "It means the electromagnetic field is changing. So, if the compass goes crazy, it means a ghost is nearby!"

Ron shone his flashlight down at the compass.

"Nothing happening," he reported. "It's holding steady."

Dave leaned in so he could see it, too. Then, as the boys watched, the needle on the compass jumped! Dave gasped. It was just a little jump at first. The needle wiggled as if it couldn't make up its mind which way to go. Then it began to swing back and forth.

"Oh, wow," Dave murmured. "I don't believe this!"

"Is it getting colder in here?" Ron asked.

All of a sudden, Dave realized he was shivering. He'd thought it was just excitement. Now he knew it was something more. It was very cold in the living room. A whole lot colder than when they first got here.

"Whoa," he said. "You're right. That could mean a ghost has entered the area."

"Wait a minute," Ron interrupted. "What's that sound?"

Dave held his breath and listened *hard*.

That's when Dave felt it. The grip of icy fingers wrapping around his arm. Dave jumped at least a foot.

He tried to scream, but he couldn't.

His throat was totally closed up as if it were being squeezed shut by a giant fist.

The grip on his arm got tighter.

"Ron," he finally choked out. "The ghost. I think it's got me!"

"That's just me, moron."

Dave looked down. He saw that it was Ron's hand gripping his arm. He yanked his arm away, ready to give Ron a hard punch. But he stopped when he saw the startled look on his brother's face.

"Listen," Ron whispered. "I think I hear something."

Dave swallowed hard. He heard it now. He heard the strange sounds, too.

Step, drag. Step, drag. Step.

Step, drag. Step, drag. Step.

"Footsteps," Dave whispered. The room was freezing now. *This cannot be happening. It just can't be. I'm about to see a ghost!*

Step, drag. Step, drag. Step.

"That's the same sound I heard the last time," Ron whispered. "I think it's him. It's the guy!"

Step, drag. Step, drag. Step.

"I hear footsteps," Dave whispered. "They're coming closer!"

Step, drag.

Closer.

Step, drag.

Closer.

The footsteps came straight at Dave and Ron.

"Why's he coming this way?" Dave whispered. "Who is he? What does he want?"

"I don't know," Ron answered. "That's pretty much the problem."

Dave ducked lower behind the couch. "Where is he? Can you see him?"

"Of course I can't see him," Ron replied. "I'm behind the couch, just like you are. If we want to see him, we'll have to stand up."

No way! Dave thought. All of a sudden, he caught a glimpse of the compass.

"Ron, check it out. The compass is going nuts."

Step, drag. Step, drag. Step.

"He's right on the other side of the couch!" Dave cried.

Dave looked at his older brother. Ron was frozen in place. His mouth opened and closed like a fish out of water.

It's up to me, Dave thought. *Up to me to be brave, just like Jason and Grant.* Slowly, Dave reached up to grip the top of the couch. He stood up.

There was a man on the other side of the couch. A man who wasn't supposed to be there! Who could *not* be there!

In the dim light coming in from the front window, Dave could see that the man's face was pale. He had deep, dark eyes. They glowed eerily, locked on Dave's eyes.

Who is he? Dave wondered. *What does he want?*

Then, as Dave watched in frozen horror, the man lifted one arm and *reached for him.*

Dave screamed. The sound rang off the living room walls.

"Move!" Ron shouted. He jumped up to pull Dave back. "Now!"

The two brothers dashed frantically around the far side of the couch and ran across the living room. Dave darted into the hall. Ron shot past him and sprinted up the stairs toward their parents' room.

"Mom! Dad!" he yelled.

Dave stopped. All his senses were screaming at him to get away. But still, he turned around back toward that ghostly figure.

The man stood by the fireplace. Half in shadow, half in light from the window. He leaned against the mantel, as if he needed it for support.

He wasn't staring at Dave anymore. Instead, his head hung down. Dave heard him let out a great big sigh. Then, as Dave watched, the man lifted his head. His mouth twisted, as if he was in pain. On his cheeks, something glimmered.

Tears, Dave thought.

The ghost was crying.

"Okay, guys," Lyssa Frye said. She hung up the phone. "I think we've got a new case."

"What's up?" Jason asked.

Grant turned his desk chair. "Yeah. Tell us. What's the story?"

Jason and Grant were at their desks in the TAPS office. The rest of the TAPS team gathered nearby to hear about this latest case.

"I just got off the phone with a woman named Joyce Sandstrom," Lyssa explained. "She lives with her family just outside New York City. Her house is really old."

Quickly, Lyssa glanced down at the notes she took during the phone conversation. "It was built in the early 1770s."

Grant's eyes lit up. "Wow," he said. "That's before the Revolutionary War."

Both of the TAPS founders loved history. It was actually one of the things they loved best about investigating. To them it was a way to learn about the past and to connect with it.

"What does Mrs. Sandstrom say is going on, Lyssa?" Mark Hammond asked.

"Both Mrs. Sandstrom and her two sons, Ron and Dave, have heard footsteps in the house. In the living room and the front hall. They also report seeing a man standing by the fireplace. And once, they saw him at the front door."

"They've actually *seen* something?" asked Mike.

"Yep." Lyssa nodded. "The only person in the family who *hasn't* seen the ghost is Andrew Sandstrom, the father."

"How are the boys doing with all this?" Jason asked. "How old are they?"

Lyssa knew that Jason and Grant always took tips from younger people seriously. That's because kids are often more open to paranormal experiences. They often see ghosts when grown-ups see nothing at all.

"The boys are thirteen and ten years old," Lyssa answered. "According to their mother, they're doing pretty well."

She grinned. "Joyce told me her younger son, Dave, is into ghost hunting. He watches the show every week. Often, the rest of the family joins him. Dave is making a report for the team."

"Nice." That made Grant smile.

"The Sandstroms would like us to come as soon as possible,"

Lyssa continued. "I checked our calendar. We could go as early as Wednesday."

"Sounds good," Grant said. "Let's make it happen."

"We thought you'd want to have this right away," Dave said. He held out a file folder. Jason took it. Dave was sitting across from him. On the front of the folder, in big bold letters, it said:

CASE FILE #1
OUR INVESTIGATION
BY RON AND DAVE SANDSTROM

"Thanks, guys," Jason said as he opened the folder. Grant leaned in to read over Jason's shoulder. The TAPS team and the Sandstroms were all gathered in the family's living room. It was kind of a tight fit.

On the outside, the house seemed pretty big. Two floors, painted white with dark green shutters. Three windows looked out on the street from the upper floor. But inside, the rooms felt small, and the ceilings were definitely lower than Lyssa liked. She had a problem with tight spaces.

People were definitely shorter in the 1770s, she thought. *No two ways about it.*

Jason held up several sheets of paper. They were filled with bold, blocky handwriting. There was also a diagram showing the living room. All the furniture had been sketched in. The drawing also showed one set of footprints in red ink, another in black.

Lyssa turned to the two boys. "So you each drew your own footprints?"

Ron, the older brother, shook his head. "No," he said. "The black footprints show where *we* went — from the doorway to behind the couch."

"And the red footprints?" Jason asked.

"That's where the ghost walked," Dave said.

"We heard his footsteps," Ron added. "Kind of a scraping sound. It was hard to tell exactly where he was. All we could tell was that he kept coming closer."

"But then I stood up," Dave said. "And I *saw* him. He was standing near the fireplace." He pointed to a red *X* on the drawing.

Grant pulled another paper from the folder, a drawing of a man in old-fashioned clothing. He wore boots, pants that came just below his knees, and a long, black coat.

"Is this the man you saw?" Grant asked.

Dave nodded. "Except his clothes were dirty and torn up. It was kind of hard to draw that."

Ron pointed to another piece of paper. "That's where I wrote up our notes. So we wouldn't forget anything."

"This is excellent. You guys did a great job," Grant said.

"They did," Mrs. Sandstrom agreed.

"And you've seen the man, too?" Lyssa asked her.

"Yes. I saw him by the front door," Mrs. Sandstrom said. She shuddered. "He scared me. The strange clothing, the scraping footsteps, the look in his eyes...It was as if he wanted something, but I couldn't imagine what."

"Is that what you boys thought?" Lyssa asked.

"I'm not sure," Dave said slowly. "I thought the man just looked tired and sad."

Lyssa had one more question for their mother. "And you're sure you saw the same man as your sons?"

Joyce Sandstrom gave a quick laugh. "I wouldn't call myself *sure* about *anything* at the moment. But the boys and I compared notes. Everything matches up. We *think* it's the same man."

"Have you seen him anywhere else in the house?" Grant asked.

Mrs. Sandstrom shook her head. "No. Just near the front door and over by the fireplace. Nothing upstairs at all."

"Okay," Jason said. He shut the file folder with a snap and stood up. "Thanks for giving us such a great head start. We'll take it from here. Come on. Let's get set up."

"Are you getting any readings?" Lyssa whispered later that night.

She and Grant stood in the entrance to the living room. The room was very dark. This made the ceiling feel even lower.

The only lights in the room came from Lyssa's flashlight and the two red lights along the top of Grant's EMF meter.

"Nothing yet," Grant whispered. "Let's head into the living room. I want to check out the fireplace."

"Right behind you," Lyssa replied.

She followed Grant into the room. Jason and Mike were covering the hallway near the front door. Mark and Jen were in the Command Center in the back of the house, keeping an eye on both locations.

Grant held the EMF meter out in front of him. As he walked, he moved it slowly up and down and from side to side. The detector had a line of red lights across the top. At the moment, just the first two lights glowed.

The lights are probably on because of the TV set and DVD player, Lyssa thought. She knew the EMF detector reacted to an increase in the electromagnetic field, which could be caused by electronic devices.

Lyssa carried a voice recorder in addition to the flashlight. The team also had put voice recorders and video cameras in the room.

"This is Grant and Lyssa. We're in the living room," Grant said in a low voice into the recorder.

He went over to the fireplace. Lyssa walked around the edge of the room. Then she went over to the couch. She stopped behind it. She stood right where the boys had been the night they saw the man. Whoever he was.

"I'm going to try to make contact," Lyssa said.

"Go ahead." Grant nodded.

Lyssa cleared her throat. No matter how many times she did it, this moment always gave her a thrill—the moment she tried to talk to a ghost.

"Hello?" Lyssa called in a firm, clear voice. "My name is Lyssa Frye. The person with me is Grant Wilson. If there's someone here with us, can you give us a sign?"

She paused. *Slow down, Lyssa,* she reminded herself. *Remember to take it slow.*

Lyssa knelt where Ron and Dave had. She set the flashlight on the floor.

"If there's somebody here, can you try to move this flashlight? Just give it a push. It will roll." Lyssa stood up and stepped back toward the window. "Can you make it roll toward me?" She waited, her eyes on the flashlight. It didn't move. "Anything?" she asked Grant in a low voice.

Grant scanned the fireplace area with the EMF detector. "No," he answered. "Nothing."

"There are two boys who live in this house," Lyssa continued.

"Ron and Dave. Maybe you have seen them. The boys think you are sad. They want to find out why. They want to help you. Can you tell us what you need?"

"Whoa," Grant whispered. "Big energy spike. I think you're reaching him!"

A chill ran down Lyssa's back. The room was definitely colder.

"Oh, yeah," Grant said. "And we've got six lights now."

Grant stepped away from the fireplace, toward the center of the room. He held the EMF detector out in front of him. He was trying to see where the surge in energy was coming from.

Lyssa knelt to pick up the flashlight.

The second she touched it — the flashlight went out!

Lyssa gasped and straightened up. Was this the ghost's sign Lyssa had asked for earlier? Was the man about to appear?

"Lyssa," Grant whispered. "Listen. Do you hear that?"

She froze.

Step, drag. Step, drag. Step.

Step, drag. Step, drag. Step.

"Footsteps," Lyssa choked out. She fought back her fear. "Like someone limping. Dragging one leg. Where is it coming from? Can you tell?"

The room felt so cold now, goose bumps tingled up and down her arms.

"From the entrance to the room," Grant said. "Just like in the boys' drawing."

Step, drag. Step, drag. Step.

"That means he's probably heading for the fireplace!" Lyssa cried. "Better move, Grant! Get out of the way!"

Lyssa darted toward Grant. She grabbed him by the arm and pulled him toward her, behind the couch. Away from the fireplace.

Step, drag. Step, drag. Step.

The scraping footsteps kept coming.

Lyssa whacked the flashlight against the palm of one hand, desperately trying to get it to come back on.

"I just wish we could see something," she said.

Step, drag. Step, drag.

Then silence.

"They've stopped," she breathed. "The footsteps have stopped."

"At the corner of the fireplace," Grant whispered. "Right where they did before."

"So what do we do now?"

"Well, we were trying to reach out to him," Grant said. "I'd say we got a pretty big response, so let's keep it up. How about if I try?"

"Go for it," Lyssa said.

"Hello, my name is Grant," Grant said in a low, firm voice. "We heard your footsteps just now. It sounds as if you're having trouble walking. Are you injured?"

Lyssa wrapped her fingers around Grant's arm.

"Do you hear that?" she whispered.

"I hear it," Grant replied.

A sigh. One long sigh of weariness and pain.

Suddenly, Lyssa realized she was crying. Huge, hot tears rolled down her cheeks. No investigation she'd ever been a part of had made her feel this way.

She was in motion almost before she realized what she was doing. She moved around the far end of the couch to the coffee table. There was a straight-backed chair on the other side of the table. Lyssa remembered it because that's where she'd sat when she first met the Sandstrom family.

Lyssa walked to the chair and lifted it off the floor. Then she turned and carried it to the fireplace.

"Here," she whispered. "Won't you please sit down?"

"The flashlight went out," Grant told the TAPS team. "And the room got icy cold."

A hush fell over the long conference table. The team members leaned forward, eager to hear every detail. It was the next day at a nearby hotel. Time to review what had happened.

"We didn't see anything," Grant continued. "But there was energy all over the place."

"As soon as I put the chair down, the energy changed," Lyssa said. "The levels dropped back down. Not like the entity disappeared, but like he...relaxed somehow. I wondered if maybe he lived in the house at one time. If maybe that spot by the fireplace was his favorite corner."

"We couldn't see him," Grant said. "But we *knew* he sat down in the chair when Lyssa brought it over. Somehow, we could just tell. It was really pretty remarkable."

"All the action was clearly in the living room," Mike said. "Compared to you guys, Jay and I had a totally quiet night."

"Maybe the recorders picked up something," Lyssa suggested.

All eyes turned to Jen. She had her laptop all set up, ready to play back any evidence the cameras and voice recorders picked up the night before.

"I'll cut right to the chase," she said. "The video cams didn't pick up a thing. Except for all you guys, of course. Not so much as a shadow."

"Well, that's disappointing," Mark commented.

"Yes. That's the bad news. But here's the good news," Jen said. "Listen."

She pressed a key on the laptop and the audio began to play back. Lyssa leaned forward. She could hear what had to be Grant's footsteps and her own. Then came Grant's voice saying their names, setting a base reading for the audio recorders. She heard the conversation she and Grant had while investigating the room.

Then:

Step, drag. Step, drag. Step.

Lyssa jerked straight up in her chair. The footsteps had been captured on the audio recorder!

No one said a word.

And then they all heard a whispery voice from the laptop:

"My leg…so tired."

Lyssa felt her whole body begin to tingle.

"Man, oh, man," Jason said softly. "That's him. The ghost! We caught it on audio!"

Grant added, "I think he just explained the scraping footsteps, Lyssa."

"Unbelievable," Lyssa murmured. "Do you think he was walking all that time just looking for a place to sit down? He just wanted to rest?"

In silence, the team listened to the rest of the playback. Then Jen punched off the sound.

"You know, Lyssa, for somebody who *didn't* hear what that guy said, you did a pretty great job of coming up with just what he needed," Jen observed.

"I just wish we knew who he was," Lyssa replied.

"Actually," Mark Hammond chimed in, "I might have a little information. I think there's a pretty good chance he was a soldier during the Revolutionary War."

"Excuse me?" Lyssa exclaimed. "How on *earth* could you figure a thing like that out?"

"It's all in the research," Mark answered with a smile. He

opened a folder and pulled out a map. On it, he'd drawn several yellow lines.

"A couple of the biggest battles of the Revolutionary War were fought in this area of New York. In 1776, not long after the Declaration of Independence was signed."

"I didn't know that," Jen said.

"Things didn't go so well for the colonial troops," Mark went on. "They had to make a run for it."

"Did any of this happen near the Sandstrom house?" Lyssa asked.

"That's what I'm thinking." Mark nodded. "My research shows that the Sandstrom house was once the biggest farmhouse in the area. There wasn't really a town. The farmhouse would have been the only building for miles around."

"Which would have made it an ideal place to shelter wounded soldiers," Lyssa added. She sat back. "Wow."

"Don't forget the drawing that Dave did," Mark said. "It was pretty rough, but those clothes are right for the time period."

Lyssa's cell phone rang. She checked the number.

"That's the Sandstroms," she said. As chief interviewer, Lyssa often gave clients her number. She took the call.

"Hello? Oh, hi, Joyce." Lyssa listened intently for several moments. "Yes, yes, I understand that must be disturbing. Hang on just a minute. I'll find out."

Lyssa covered the phone. "It's Joyce Sandstrom," she said in a low voice. "She's been hearing the footsteps going back and forth between the door and the living room all day. She sounds very upset. She's almost crying."

"Tell her we're on our way," Jason said.

"Joyce?" Lyssa said into the phone. "Hang on. We're coming right over."

Lyssa walked into the Sandstrom living room and gasped. "The chair—it's gone!"

"What chair?" Joyce Sandstrom asked. Her face was pale and set. She appeared to be fighting back tears. "What are you talking about?"

"It's all right, Mrs. Sandstrom," Grant said. "Lyssa's talking about something that happened during our investigation last night. How about if the whole family comes into the living room? We can talk about what we found."

"Let's all listen to the audio evidence from the living room," Jason said. He set Jen's laptop down on the coffee table and powered it up. "I think that will help to clear things up."

Once again, Lyssa listened to the events in the living room. She watched the Sandstrom family as they listened, too.

"Wow!" Dave said when the audio was over. "That was *awesome*!"

"We totally agree," Jason told him.

"Do you think the guy actually sat down?" Ron asked.

"What do *you* think?" Lyssa asked.

"I say *yes*," Ron answered. "Because, when Mom moved the chair this morning..."

"He had to walk around all day!" Dave shouted. "He didn't have anyplace to sit down."

"So *that's* what you meant when you said the chair was gone," Joyce Sandstrom said. "I never even thought about it. I just put it back where it always goes when I straightened up the room."

"I'm sorry," Lyssa said. "I probably should have told you what I'd done. But even we had no idea how important it was."

"So," Grant said. "We think we gathered some pretty interesting information. The question is, what happens now?"

There was a moment's silence. Then Dave Sandstrom raised his hand.

"Go ahead, Dave," Jason said. "Tell us what you think."

"I think somebody should put the chair back," Dave said. "That way, the ghost will have a place to sit down."

"*I* think that's an excellent idea," Grant replied. "Who do you think those *somebodies* should be?"

Dave and Ron looked at each other. And smiled.

"Hey, check this out, you guys," Lyssa said.

She waved a large envelope in the air. It was several weeks later, after the TAPS team went to the Sandstroms' home.

"It's from the Sandstrom brothers. They sent a final case report."

The team gathered around. Ron and Dave had put their findings in a folder, the same way the TAPS team did. There was a label on the front of the report.

THE SANDSTROM INVESTIGATION: CONCLUSIONS

Lyssa flipped open the folder. Right on top was a sketch of the living room. The drawing clearly showed a chair, sitting to one side of the fireplace. It was circled in red. Underneath it was the report itself.

TO: JASON, GRANT, MIKE, MARK, LYSSA, AND JEN
FROM: RON AND DAVE SANDSTROM
RE: INVESTIGATION FOLLOW-UP

"Ever since we put the chair by the fireplace, the footsteps have stopped," Lyssa read aloud. *"We don't see or hear the limping man anymore.*

"We all talked it over and decided to leave the chair right where it

is for as long as we live in the house. And if we move out, we'll leave a note for the new people, explaining that the ghost needs a place to rest his leg."

"Oh, man," Mike said. "That is so cool."

"Thank you very much for helping us figure out what was going on. If you come to New York State, we hope you will visit us. This ends our report."

Lyssa smiled. "It's signed Ron and Dave Sandstrom."

"Wait a minute," Jen suddenly said. "I think there's some writing on the other side of the page."

Lyssa turned the page over.

"P.S.," she read. *"We're sorry you never got to see the ghost."*

"So am I," Grant said. "So am I."

"**M**om, I don't need a babysitter! I'm almost old enough to *be* a babysitter. Why can't I just stay by myself?" Charlie Hazelton glared at her mother. "I'm twelve," she said. "I mean, come *on*."

"Charlie, this is a new place. I don't think it's a good idea for you to be alone," Charlie's mother said.

From the way she said it, Charlie could tell that her mother hadn't made up her mind. Charlie still had a chance if she could talk fast enough.

"All you're going to do is run some errands, right? It's not like you'll be gone all that long."

"Most of the afternoon," Mrs. Hazelton said. "Which is long enough. I have to buy all the food for the housewarming party on Sunday. And it takes a while to get into town." Mrs. Hazelton sighed. "Sometimes I wonder what your father and I were thinking, moving way out into the country like this."

All of a sudden, her expression brightened. "Hey, maybe you should come along. You know, a shopping trip. Just you and me. Wouldn't that be fun?"

"Mom," Charlie said. "You're going to the *grocery store,* not the mall."

"Oh, all right." Her mother abruptly gave in. "I guess you can stay here by yourself. On one condition: stay away from the lake."

Charlie rolled her eyes.

"I really mean it, Charlie," her mother said. "You've lived in apartments your whole life. You didn't even learn to swim until last year. And we don't know how deep the lake is. I'm just not comfortable with you going down there on your own."

"I got my junior lifesaving certificate," Charlie reminded her. "Mom, I'm *twelve.* You know—almost a teenager." How many times did she have to say it before her mother got the point?

"There are stories about that lake," Mrs. Hazelton went on. Clearly, she wasn't really listening to Charlie at all.

"What kind of stories?" Charlie asked.

"I don't know," her mother said impatiently. "I've just heard that no one swims there. It's not safe. Now, either you promise not to go near the lake or you come with me."

"Oh, all right," Charlie said. "Honestly."

If I ever have kids, I won't treat them like babies, she thought. *It's embarrassing sometimes.*

Forget that. It's embarrassing all *the time.*

"Promise me," her mother said.

"Mom."

"*Promise* me," her mother insisted.

Charlie sighed. "I promise not to go near the lake," she said. "There! Okay?"

She meant to keep her promise. She honestly did. But her mom never said she had to stay inside. Right?

Right, Charlie thought. She stepped onto the front porch and closed the door behind her. She had lived here for exactly one week. Her parents dragged her away from her friends, her school...everything! So Charlie figured that she had a right to go exploring.

She walked down the porch steps and turned left. Her sneakers made soft swooshing sounds as she crossed the lawn. It was smooth and green, like a carpet. Charlie thought it was fake the first time she saw it.

She went around the corner of the house and headed for the orchard. It was pretty—if you liked rows and rows of apple trees. After the orchard came the meadow. It was on a hill, sloping down. At the bottom of the meadow was the lake.

The one that she was supposed to stay away from.

"I don't know what Mom's so worried about," Charlie muttered to herself. She stomped through the orchard. "It's not even a real lake. More like a pond. It's probably not even deep."

Still, to play it safe, Charlie stopped at the top of the hill. She could see the lake from there. Which was definitely *not* the same as breaking her promise. Mom never said that Charlie couldn't *look* at the lake.

The water looked quiet and peaceful in the summer sunshine.

Okay. It probably is *big enough to be called a lake,* Charlie thought. It even looked deep. But it didn't look dangerous.

The lake curved around in a funny shape, like an enormous kidney bean. The water was green and clear. The biggest willow tree Charlie had ever seen stood on the far shore. The tree's long, skinny branches draped down like a pale green curtain. Some of the tree's roots were actually underwater.

Charlie couldn't see the roots from where she stood. But her dad had told her about them.

A breeze came up. It ruffled the surface of the water, making it sparkle in the sun. Then there was a quick, blinding flash of light. Charlie cried out in surprise and covered her eyes.

When she uncovered them, she saw the little boy.

He looked as if he was about five years old. He wore a red

T-shirt and baggy jeans. He was standing about halfway down the hill, staring at the lake.

Who is he? What's he doing out here all by himself? Charlie wondered. *Does he live around here?*

No, she answered her own question. No one lived around here. The nearest neighbors lived over a mile away. And they didn't have kids.

"Hey!" she called.

The boy turned his head to look at her.

"What's your name?" Charlie yelled. "What are you doing around here?"

The boy didn't answer. Instead, he began to run.

He ran down the slope, toward the water.

"Wait up!" Charlie called. "I didn't mean to sound mad. I just..."

For such a little kid, he was running really fast. He ran down a steep, skinny path. He nearly tripped. But he kept running.

"Hey, watch out!" Charlie called. "Watch where you're going—or at least slow down!"

But the boy didn't slow down. He ran even faster, straight toward the lake. It was almost as if something was chasing him—or as if he couldn't stop.

Charlie didn't know why exactly, but something felt bad. The boy was so little. What if he couldn't swim? What if the lake was seriously deep? What if it really *was* dangerous?

What if he *was* being chased—by something she couldn't see?

Charlie forgot her promise to her mother and sprinted after the boy. She ran as fast as she could, but the hill was super-steep. It was hard to go fast without falling. She didn't understand how the boy could be running so quickly.

She forced herself to run faster. She felt a sharp pain in her left side. Her heart pounded hard. The boy was still running, almost to the edge of the water.

"Stop!" Charlie shouted. "I just want to talk to you. Please, stop!"

But even as she ran faster than she ever did before, she knew it wasn't going to do any good. The boy was too far ahead, and Charlie was never going to get to him in time.

And then the miracle happened. The boy stopped right at the edge of the lake. But Charlie couldn't. She was going too fast. She tried to stop, but the lakeshore was muddy. It grabbed on to her sneakers and held them tight.

Her momentum was too great and she plunged face-first into the water. Instantly, her shorts and shirt and running shoes were soaking wet and cold.

The water shot straight up Charlie's nose. It smelled like dead fish. She grasped at the bottom of the lake, trying to push herself up. But the bottom of the lake was soft and muddy, and her hands sank into thick, squishy mud.

Swim, she told herself. She knew how to swim. She tried to straighten and kick. But all she did was churn up mud. The water was a dark, murky brown. She couldn't tell where the top or bottom was. Slimy weeds wrapped around her leg. They were pulling her down, holding her under. Charlie's chest felt tight. She was almost out of breath!

Then, all of a sudden, her hands hit something hard. A big rock. Charlie pushed. Her head came out of the water. Charlie gulped air.

It's all right, she thought. *I'm all right.*

But she was going to be in so much trouble.

Her mom was never going to understand. She would think Charlie deliberately broke her promise.

But I didn't! Charlie thought. *I was just trying to help that little boy.*

The boy. Where was he?

With a great *whoosh* of water, Charlie staggered to her feet. She spun around. The boy was standing on the bank behind her.

"What are you doing here all by yourself?" Charlie asked. "Why did you run that way? Were you *trying* to scare me half to death? Are you all right?"

The boy didn't say anything. He just stood there, staring at Charlie with big, brown eyes. His skin was super-pale. As though he never went out in the sun.

"Who are you, anyway?" Charlie said. *"What do you want?"*

At that moment, a gust of wind came up. Charlie felt it lift the hair away from her face. It pushed her wet clothes tight against her body. She began to shiver uncontrollably. But not because she was cold.

The boy's hair. The boy's clothes. They didn't move at all.

But he did. He raised one arm. His hand was clenched into a fist. Then, slowly, one finger uncurled. His index finger. It pointed, straight at the lake. Then his whole body gave this funny sort of ripple. As if he were made out of smoke. But his finger never moved. It kept pointing at the lake.

Then, just like that, the boy was gone.

Charlie sat back down in the water.

She didn't care that her clothes were soaked. She didn't care about the trouble she was going to be in when she got home.

All she cared about was the image in her head. The little boy pointing at the water. And along with seeing the image, she heard a voice that seemed to be carried by the cold wind.

It circled around and around in Charlie's brain. Like it was looking for a way back out but couldn't find one.

Find me, the voice in Charlie's head said over and over and over. *Find me. I'm here.*

Find me.

Find me.

FIND ME.

It was the voice of a little boy.

"Let me be clear, right up front," Mr. Hazelton said. "I don't believe in ghosts."

"That's okay," Grant answered. His tone was friendly. "A lot of people—"

"Because I don't want you to think that's why we called you," Mr. Hazelton went on. "I don't want *you* to think it's because *we* think we actually have a ghost. We just want to check things out."

Lyssa bit down on her tongue to keep from smiling.

"Of course you do." Grant finally managed to get a word in edgewise. "As I explained when you phoned, we are here just to investigate. We don't come in with our minds already made up about what we might find. We never try to prove that there is a haunting. In fact, we try to prove there isn't."

"Good," Mr. Hazelton said. "Well, that's all right, then. We understand each other."

There was a pause. Now that he'd made his point, Mr. Hazelton didn't seem to know what else to say. He glanced over at his wife. She was sitting beside him on the couch. Their daughter, Charlie, sat next to her mother.

Jay, Grant, and Lyssa were sitting in chairs across from the Hazeltons in the family's living room. The rest of the TAPS team were outside unloading the equipment. There was a lot of gear. The team would be investigating both inside the house and out by the lake.

Charlie doesn't look particularly happy to be here, Lyssa thought. In fact, she looked like she would rather be someplace else.

"I'd like to ask Charlie a question, if that's okay," Lyssa said.

The girl lifted her eyes. They were a blue so dark they looked almost black. The expression in them seemed to ask Lyssa a question first: *Can I trust you?*

"Go ahead," Mr. Hazelton said.

"Charlie, you're the only one who has seen the little boy," Lyssa said. "Is that right?"

"Yeah," Charlie said. "I've seen him lots of times. I keep trying to tell *them.*" Charlie jerked her chin toward her parents. "They don't believe me."

"We're trying to believe you, honey," her mother said. "We know leaving all your friends back in Chicago was hard. It's not unusual to imagine things when everything is new and strange…" Mrs. Hazelton's voice trailed off.

"I saw him. He's real," Charlie insisted.

"The first time Charlie told us about the boy was after she did something she wasn't supposed to do," Mr. Hazelton put in. "So naturally we wondered if she was making it up. You know, telling a story to get out of trouble."

"I *explained* what happened—" Charlie began.

"I have a question for you, Charlie," Jason cut in quickly. The girl's eyes shot to his face. As always, Jason's expression was steady and calm.

"What?"

"Is the lake the only place you've seen the boy?"

Charlie nodded. "Uh-huh. I don't go near the water anymore. But I can see him from the hill. He isn't always there, though. Just sometimes. I think Roscoe sees him, too."

"Who's Roscoe?" Lyssa asked.

"Our dog. He comes with me when I go for walks. But sometimes he goes down to the lake on his own. Then all he does is just sit there and howl."

"Does he howl anywhere else?" Jen asked.

Charlie nodded. "Yeah, sometimes. Right outside my room. He always does it when the door to my room locks itself and I get stuck inside. That's pretty freaky, I have to tell you."

"Charlie," Mr. Hazelton said. His voice sounded worried and frustrated all at the same time. "Honey, we've been over this. Your door can't lock itself. It doesn't even *have* a lock."

Charlie shot to her feet. "Fine. Make me sound stupid. You're always right. I'm always wrong. But guess what?"

"Charlie," her mother murmured. But Charlie kept right on going.

"I think you know there's something weird going on around here," she said to her father. "You just don't want to admit it.

Because then *you'd* be wrong. Wrong about making us move here in the first place!"

Charlie swung around. Her eyes locked on Lyssa's. "That little boy is out there," she said. "I *saw* him. He needs us to find him. If you won't help him, I'll do it myself."

She dashed from the room. A moment later, the front door slammed.

"Charlie!" Mrs. Hazelton called, alarmed.

"I'll go after her," Lyssa said. She got to her feet. "Don't worry. I'll find her."

"Lyssa is our chief interviewer," Grant explained to Mr. and Mrs. Hazelton. "Sometimes kids tell her more when she talks to them on her own. So while she talks to Charlie, maybe you can give us some more details about what's been going on up at the house."

"All right. We can do that, can't we, Ray?" Mrs. Hazelton said.

"We can do whatever it takes," Mr. Hazelton said. His voice was grim. "But you just remember what I said."

"I remember," Grant said. "You don't believe in ghosts..."

"Okay," Grant said later that night. "Let's go over the assignments."

The TAPS team was in the Hazeltons' dining room. The

family's big dining table was now the TAPS Command Center. The Hazeltons were staying in a nearby motel.

One night. That's all Mr. Hazelton agreed to. Just one night to investigate.

"Jen and Mark, you'll stay inside the house," Grant went on. "Monitor the equipment and check out Charlie's room."

"Gotcha." Jen and Mark both nodded.

"Jay and I will take the far side of the lake. Mike and Lyssa will take the side closest to the house."

"Remember, this is the country," Jason said. "It's going to be dark out there, guys. Stay together. You're going to need to really back each other up. We've got a couple new pieces of equipment to help with that."

He pointed at the dining room table. At one end were backpacks and flashlights.

"Here's how it's going to work," Jason explained. "Each team will have one person carrying the flashlight and one carrying the audio recorder. You'll each have a backpack for supplies and the extra flashlight in case you need a backup."

"And if you get into trouble, use *these*," Grant said. He picked up a handful of shiny silver whistles on nylon cords. He handed them out.

"These are just like the ones that search-and-rescue teams use," Grant explained as the team put them on. "If something happens, blow your whistle. Don't just start shouting."

"Okay, flashlight check," Jason called out. "Grab your flash-lights and packs."

Jen picked up her flashlight, then moved to the light switch on the wall. "Ready?" she asked.

"Go," Grant said.

Click!

The light went out. The room was plunged into darkness.

"On my mark," Grant said. "One. Two. Three."

Three flashlights went on at once.

"Okay, everybody," Jason said. "We're now officially dark. Let's get busy. We've only got one night to find some answers for Charlie."

Lyssa and Mike followed Jason and Grant outside. The sum-mer night felt hot and thick. The sky was cloudy with no moon or stars. This far out in the country there were no streetlights. The only illumination came from their flashlights.

Lyssa aimed the beam a little ahead of her. She tried to aim it in between her and Mike so they both could see where they were going. The last thing the team needed was for someone to fall down and get hurt. That had happened to Lyssa before, and it wasn't fun.

The powerful flashlight made a wide beam of bright white light. But outside the reach of the beam, the night seemed to close in.

The group went around the side of the house and started through the orchard. *Jason's right*, Lyssa thought. *It's super-dark.*

The trees of the orchard stood silent as the TAPS team passed by. Not so much as a breath of wind moved through the branches.

"I'm a little spooked out here," Lyssa said to Mike in a low voice. "It's like the trees are alive."

"I really hate to break this to you, Lyssa," Mike whispered back. "They are."

Lyssa choked back a laugh. "Okay," she said. "You're right. But you know what I mean."

"Yeah, I do," Mike admitted. "It's like they're listening or something. But we shouldn't let our imaginations run away with us. Come to think of it, we shouldn't run at all. That is one steep hill ahead of us."

"Roger that," Lyssa said.

Up ahead, Lyssa could hear Jason and Grant talking in low voices as they walked toward the lake.

Lyssa knew the lake was right at the bottom of the hill. Not far, but the walk seemed to take forever. The team had to go slowly and carefully down the steep hill in total darkness. It seemed to Lyssa that the longer they walked, the thicker the air got. It was like walking through a heavy wool blanket.

We must be getting close to the water, she thought.

Finally, Jason and Grant stopped. Grant held his flashlight out in front of him. Lyssa followed the beam with her eyes. She caught the glint of water.

"This is it," Grant said. "We're at the lake. This is where we split up. Remember, stay together. And if you get into trouble, blow the whistle."

He slapped Jason on the back. "Let's go."

Without another word, the two moved off.

Lyssa and Mike were all alone.

"Let's go this way," Lyssa said. She pointed with the flashlight. "We can do this half of our side first. Then we can come back here to the middle and do the other part."

"Sounds good," Mike said. He pulled the white sweatshirt he wore over his head. "We can mark the spot with this." He draped it over a bush. "It should be easy to see. And it's not like I need it anyhow. Man, it's hot."

They started walking slowly, following the edge of the lake. Lyssa expected to hear the sound of water lapping the shore. She heard nothing. Everything was silent until Mike spoke.

"How do you think we should do this?"

"What if we walk a little way, then stop and try to make contact with the boy?" Lyssa suggested. "If nothing happens, we can walk a little farther, then try it again."

"That is just the right thing to do. You know how I know?"

"No, how do you know?"

"Because it was exactly what I was going to suggest!"

Lyssa couldn't see Mike's face in the dark. But she was sure that he was smiling. She always liked working with the Hammond twins. They knew that when things got scary, a little laugh really helped.

A few minutes later she said, "Okay. Let's stop here."

Mike held the recorder out in front of him. "This is Mike and Lyssa. We're down by the lake," he said. He was establishing a base reading for the recorder. "We're attempting first contact." He nodded at his partner.

"Hello?" she called out. "My name is Lyssa and this is Mike. We're here because we know you need some help. We know you're lost and need someone to find you. Can you help us do that? Can you give us a sign to show us where you are?"

She paused. She could hear Mike breathing quietly at her side. The sounds of crickets and frogs. But she didn't hear anything that sounded like a boy's voice.

"I got nothing. What about you?" she finally said.

"Same here," Mike answered quietly.

"Okay," Lyssa said. "Let's change location and try again."

They moved on. The ground beneath their feet grew swampy. Mosquitoes rose up in great clouds.

"Man," Mike said. Lyssa heard a *slap* as he tried to swat the bugs away. "Why didn't I think to put on bug spray? I'm getting eaten alive!"

"I think I put some in my backpack," Lyssa said. "Here. Take the flashlight a minute."

She held it out. The beam swept across the water. Lyssa stumbled back a step. She let out a sharp cry.

"Did you see that?" she gasped. "Did you see it?"

"What?" Mike said. He spun toward the lake. "What is it, Lyssa? What did you see?"

"A face," Lyssa choked out. "I saw a face in the water."

"Where?" Mike said. "Where is it? Show me!"

Lyssa swept the flashlight beam back and forth across the water.

"It was here. I know it was!" she cried.

"Take it easy, Lyssa," Mike said. "Slow down. Focus."

"I saw a face. A pale white face," Lyssa said. She continued to search the lake with the flashlight. But she took Mike's advice. She moved the beam more slowly.

"All of a sudden, it was just there. But I can't find it. It's gone now!"

"Okay. Hang on a minute," Mike said. "Hold the light steady and take the recorder."

He handed it over. Lyssa took it in one hand. She held the flashlight with the other. The beam shook. Her hand wasn't steady. And not just because the flashlight was heavy.

"Got it," Mike said. He pulled the backup light from the

pack and turned it on. Lyssa gave the audio recorder back to him. Mike tucked it under one arm. "Let's try again. Together, this time."

The two moved their flashlight beams back and forth across the surface of the water.

"Anything?" Mike asked.

"No," Lyssa said. "There's nothing now."

"Let's try getting a little closer," Mike suggested. "Our feet will get wet, but it's worth a try."

Together, they approached the water's edge. Lyssa was glad she had waterproof boots on. Her regular shoes would be soaked by now.

"Sweep to the right, then left," Mike said. "Ready, set, *go!*"

Together, the two TAPS team members swept their flashlight beams over the lake.

"Whoa!" Mike suddenly cried. "Did you see that? What *is* that? It looks like—"

"Like a hand. A bony hand sticking up out of the water," Lyssa said. She tried to swallow. But she couldn't. Her throat was too dry.

"I'm going out there," Mike said.

"You can't!" Lyssa cried. "We have no idea how deep it is. Please, Mike."

"I just want to get a little closer," Mike said. He took a few steps forward, into the water. He held the light out in front of him. "If I can get a better look, maybe I can—"

Lyssa couldn't let him go alone. She waded in after him. The water felt thick, and the bottom of the lake was slippery. Her front foot slid forward, went in deeper. Lyssa gasped as cold, slimy water crept up over the top of her boots, soaking her jeans.

"You okay?" Mike called back.

"Fine." She kept her eyes on the bony hand. She felt her heart beat faster. She really didn't want to find a body in the water.

"It's a branch," Lyssa said suddenly. She waded out to stand beside Mike. "From some kind of bush, I think. Look at it again, Mike."

Mike let out a long, slow breath. "You're right. It is a branch," he said. "Boy, do I feel dumb."

"At least you saw something that's actually there," Lyssa told him. "That's more than I can say."

The two turned and walked back to the edge of the lake. Mike handed Lyssa the recorder. He turned off his flashlight and put it in his pack. Then he took the recorder back.

"Let's try making contact again," he suggested. "If we still get nothing, we can turn around. We've almost reached the end of this half of the lake anyway."

"Good idea." Lyssa pulled in a deep breath, steadying herself. "Is there anybody out there?" she called. "I'm Lyssa and this is

Mike. We want to find you. Please. If you can hear my voice, give us a sign."

Nothing. Nothing at all. But then...

"Hey, do you feel that?" Mike asked. "The wind's come up."

"Yeah," Lyssa said. She shivered. "And it's cold."

"The temperature must have dropped ten degrees," Mike said. "Maybe that's the sign we've been asking for!" His voice sounded excited. "Charlie said she felt a cold wind when she saw the boy, didn't she?"

"Yes, she did," Lyssa answered.

"Are you trying to communicate with us?" Mike called out. "Are we getting close to where you are?"

For the first time, Lyssa heard the water of the lake. It slapped against the shore.

Like it's trying to get someone's attention, she thought.

Then she heard something else.

"What's that?" Mike asked suddenly. "What's that weird hissing sound?"

"I don't know," Lyssa said. An eerie sound, like whispering and hissing, filled the air.

"Shine the light over there," Mike said. He put a hand on Lyssa's shoulder and pointed. "That's the direction it's coming from."

Lyssa aimed the flashlight in the direction Mike pointed. Back and forth, she swung the light across the water. Then the flashlight caught a glimpse of green.

"There! Stop right there!" Mike cried.

"It's the willow tree," Lyssa said. "Wow! That's all the way at the end of the lake. I didn't realize we'd come this far."

Lyssa aimed the flashlight at the weeping willow. She'd never seen one so large. Its branches reminded her of long, green ropes. They swayed and whispered in the cold wind.

"What do you think we should do now?" she asked Mike. "Officially, that's Jason and Grant's side of the lake."

"Yeah," Mike agreed. "But I think we should investigate that tree anyhow. Maybe the wind came up just because it did. Or maybe there's something there."

"Come on," Lyssa said.

She lifted her foot to take a step. The flashlight went out.

She whacked it with the side of her hand. "Oh, come on. Not now!"

"I'll get the backup out again," Mike said. "Here, hold this." He thrust the voice recorder into Lyssa's hands. Then he froze. "What's that? Can you hear that?" he said.

Somewhere in the darkness, they heard an eerie howl.

"Roscoe," Jen called out to the dog. "What's the matter? Why are you howling? Where are you, boy?"

She and Mark were in the house, on their way to Charlie's room. They were halfway up the stairs when the dog began to howl.

"Maybe he misses the family," Mark said. "They did leave him behind."

"Yeah, and maybe it's something else," Jen said. She and Mark reached the top of the stairs. Jen shone her flashlight down the hall. The beam caught the glint of glassy eyes.

"He's right outside Charlie's room," Jen said. "Just like Charlie said."

The dog sent up another howl. It was a long, sad sound.

"Hey, Roscoe," Mark said. He held out a hand and moved cautiously down the hall. "Good dog. What's the matter, boy?"

Roscoe's mouth opened to reveal a set of sharp, white teeth. Then, totally without warning, he lunged.

"Mark! *Look out!*" Jen cried.

Mark threw himself sideways. Roscoe raced past him, heading for the stairs—and Jen. She flattened herself against the wall. Roscoe shot by, as though she wasn't there at all. He galloped down the stairs and vanished into the dark first floor.

"Mark!" Jen sprinted toward him. "Are you all right?"

"Fine," Mark said. "Just clumsy, that's all."

"I'm thinking it's a good thing you got out of his way," Jen said. "I wonder what that was all about."

"Something tells me the answer may be inside Charlie's room," Mark said.

"I'm with you on that," Jen said. She held out a hand and helped pull Mark to his feet. "Come on. Let's go check it out."

The door to Charlie's room opened easily, soundlessly. Jen and Mark stepped inside. The room was big. In the light of her flashlight, Jen could see a bed and night table on the left wall. Opposite them, on the right, she saw a desk and chest of drawers. Two big windows were just across from the door. The shades were up. The windows looked like two staring eyes.

Jen crossed the room to stand in front of the windows.

"I think you can see the lake from here," she said. "I can see flashlights moving around."

All of a sudden, she shivered.

"It's cold in here, colder than in the hall."

Mark blew a puff of air. It showed white, even in the darkened room. "Yep, it's definitely cold."

"Is there someone in this room besides us?" Jen raised her voice. "We want to find you. We know that you're lost."

"Can you give us a sign?" Mark asked. "Let us know if you're here with us."

The bedroom door suddenly slammed shut!

Jen and Mark spun toward it. The beam of Jen's flashlight danced crazily across the bedroom wall. Mark walked quickly to the door. He turned the knob, then pulled with all his might.

The knob turned easily. But the door wouldn't open.

"We're trapped," Jen said. "We're trapped inside."

"Well," Mark said. "Let's look at it this way: we asked for a sign. Looks like we got one."

"You're right. You're absolutely right," Jen said. She took a deep breath. Then another one.

"Are you trying to communicate with us?" she asked. "Is there something you want us to know? Are you trapped somewhere, too? Is that what you're trying to tell us?"

Whoosh! Crash! BANG!

As if to answer Jen's question, the room went wild. The window shades crashed down. Desk and dresser drawers shot open, then banged closed. The closet door flew back, then slammed shut. Over and over and over.

"What happened to you? Can you tell us?" Jen cried. "This was your room, right? Did you get lost by the lake?"

"You have to help us," Mark said. "We've only got tonight. After that, we'll have to go away. *We want to find you.* But first you have to let us out of this room."

The room fell silent. Jen held her breath. Then she felt Mark's fingers wrap around her arm.

"Look, Jen," he whispered.

The door to the room was slowly swinging open.

"Okay, everybody," Jason said the next day. The team was in the TAPS office conference room. "Let's go over the evidence we collected."

"I wish we could have more time!" Lyssa exclaimed. "I feel like we only just got started."

"I always feel that way," Mark said.

Mike poked his twin in the ribs. "That's because you're always behind."

"I'm sure we all wish we had more time on this one," Grant spoke up. "Still, I think we made some progress. We now have some pretty good reasons to believe that Charlie really did see and hear something."

"Even if her parents don't believe it," Lyssa muttered.

"They might change their minds when they hear *this*," Jen said. "Hold on a sec."

She tapped at her laptop keyboard. A moment later, a strange hissing sound filled the conference room.

"That's the sound we heard at the willow tree," Mike said at once. "I'd recognize it anywhere. That was one seriously spooky sound."

Jen held up a hand for silence.

"I'm Lyssa and this is Mike," Lyssa's voice came on. *"We want to find you. Please. If you can hear my voice, give us a sign."*

On the playback, they could hear the way the wind came up

so suddenly. The strange hissing and whispering from the willow tree got louder and louder. Then, over the noise of the tree, they heard something new.

"Did you hear that? What was that?" Mike exclaimed.

"It sounded like a voice," Mark replied.

"Did anybody catch what it said?" Mike asked. "It was kind of hard to make out."

"Jen, play it again, please," Grant said.

Jen tapped the keyboard again, and the sound cut out. She continued to type in commands. A moment later, it came back on.

Lyssa leaned forward, straining to listen. She and Mike didn't hear a voice last night. But maybe they caught an EVP— a sound the recorder could pick up but a human ear couldn't.

"...*lake*..." She thought she could make out the words now. "*Lake...find...*"

Then there was just the sound of the wind twisting the branches of the willow tree.

"That's it," Jen said. She killed the sound.

"Did anybody else hear the word *lake*?" Lyssa asked.

"Either *lake* or *rake*," Mark said. "I couldn't quite tell."

"*Lake* makes more sense," Lyssa said. "Mike and I were standing right on the shore of the lake at the time."

"It would also fit with what Jen and I experienced in Charlie's room," Mark said.

"And don't forget the boy appears to Charlie down by the lake," Jen added. "I think something happened there."

"Like what?" Lyssa asked.

"Well, when Mark and I were locked in Charlie's bedroom, we felt trapped. So I've been wondering if maybe somehow the boy got himself trapped." Jen looked at the others. "Does that make sense to anyone else?"

"Actually, it does," Grant said. "Mark, tell them what you found."

"I did some research when Mike and I got home last night," Mark explained. He slid a piece of paper into the center of the conference room table. On it was a picture of a boy.

"This is Ben Bristow," Mark said. "His family lived in the Hazelton house in the late 1980s. At the time this picture was taken, Ben was five years old. The same age he was when he went missing."

"Five," Lyssa murmured. "So young."

"Nobody knows quite what happened to him," Mark continued. "He simply disappeared one night. Right in the middle of a big storm.

"The newspaper stories I read said his mom went into his room. She knew he was afraid of thunder and lightning. But when she got there, Ben was gone. They started to search for him right away. But the storm made searching nearly impossible.

"It turns out the storm was famous around here. It was a really big hurricane. It shut down power all up and down the East Coast. Emergency crews in the area were out around the clock. They responded to the Bristows' call for help, of course. But no trace of Ben was ever found."

"Did they search the lake?" Lyssa asked.

"The reports don't say," Mark answered. "But they must have."

"The water would be pretty churned up because of the storm," Grant put in. "Lots of debris could make it difficult to see underwater. Maybe they just plain missed something."

Jason consulted his case notes. "*I'm here. Find me.* That's what Charlie claimed the boy's voice said."

"But how do you get trapped in a lake?" Mike asked. "There's nothing down there. No boat dock. Nothing."

"But there is," Lyssa said. "There's the willow tree."

"Just what I was thinking." Grant nodded.

"So what do we tell the Hazeltons?" Mark asked.

"We give them the results of our investigation," Jason said simply. "We let them listen to the evidence and make up their own minds."

"Once Mr. Hazelton hears the EVP, my guess is he's going to want to get to the bottom of this himself," Grant added. "Even though he doesn't believe in ghosts."

"Hey, check it out," Grant said a few weeks later. He came into the office with the day's stack of mail. "There's a letter here from Charlie Hazelton."

"What does it say?" Lyssa asked.

Grant opened the envelope and pulled out a couple of sheets of paper. He perched on the edge of his desk to read while the rest of the team gathered around.

"Dear Jason, Grant, Lyssa, Jen, Mike, and Mark," Grant read. *"Thank you for coming to our house. Thank you for believing me when nobody else would. Though Mom and Dad do, too, now. Sort of.*

"After you guys came back and made your report, my dad hired some guys. They explored the whole lake."

Grant looked up from the letter and grinned. "I told you so."

"Keep reading, smart guy," Jason said.

"I bet you can guess what finally happened," Grant continued to read. *"They found Ben Bristow."*

"Oh, wow," Lyssa said. "This is incredible."

"He was underneath the willow tree. Trapped beneath some branches and a really big root. There was a lot of mud. Maybe that's why he didn't get found the first time. I don't know."

Grant switched to a new page.

"I'm getting used to living in the country. It's not so bad, I guess. And I've finally persuaded my parents to let me go down to the lake whenever I want," Grant read on. *"But now that we found the*

bones, I don't see the boy anymore. And Roscoe's stopped howling. Big plus. Dad says it's all for the best. He says we should stop thinking about it—just put it all behind us. But I want to remember. At least for a while.

"Not how Ben Bristow died, of course. But what happened later. I want to remember that we helped to find him. Can you get a degree in helping ghosts? If so, please let me know. Dad says it's never too early to start thinking about college.

"Sincerely, Charlie Hazelton."

"No!"

With a cry of panic, Angie Larson sat straight up in bed. She pressed one hand to her chest. She could feel her heart pounding. It felt as if it were trying to slam its way right out of her body.

A dream. It's just a dream, she thought. Another one. She had them every night. They were always different, yet always the same. Every night, Angie woke up terrified.

But that wasn't the worst part. Even worse was what happened when Angie woke up. Her dreams, her *nightmares,* came true. Whatever happened in her dream happened again in real life. Angie couldn't stop it from happening no matter how hard she tried.

The dreams came true. Always. Every single time.

She had the first dream just a few nights after she moved into this house. Angie was taking care of the house for her friend Ellen while she was away. Angie was supposed to live here for a year. Ellen really needed her to keep an eye on everything, so Angie *had* to stay.

But after that first dream, Angie wished she could change her mind. She wished she could escape. In the dream, weird things happened *inside the house.* Angie walked into the living room and a window shade rolled up—all by itself. Next she was in the bathroom, and the water in the sink turned on, even though she hadn't touched it.

The dream had definitely creeped Angie out. But after she woke up, she told herself she was making too much out of it. Until she walked into the living room and the shade rolled up. Until she went into the bathroom and the water turned on all by itself. That's when Angie realized her dream was coming true.

Tonight will be different, Angie told herself. *I'll do what the sleep doctor told me to do.*

He'd said that when she had a dream, she had to write it down before she forgot it. Then she was supposed to turn on all the lights and watch TV—or do jumping jacks or sing a silly song. She could do anything, *except* what she had done in the dream.

Angie turned on the lamp next to her bed and reached for her pen and notebook.

I'll do what the doctor said, and this one won't come true, she vowed.

Angie hoped the doctor was right. She really, really did. Because tonight's dream had been the scariest one of all.

The shadow woman was in the dream tonight.

That's the first thing Angie wrote down.

The shadow woman. Angie thought of her that way because she never saw the woman's face. All Angie could tell was that she wore long dresses. And sometimes Angie saw something sparkling near her neck—maybe a necklace. Lately, the shadow woman appeared in Angie's dreams more and more. She seemed to follow Angie wherever she went—watching and waiting.

What does she want from me? Angie wrote in her journal.

Suddenly, Angie realized she was shivering. When did it get so cold? She pulled the blanket up to her chin.

Then Angie choked back a cry of fear. She remembered now.

Feeling cold. That's exactly how the dream had started. She was in her bedroom, sitting up in bed. She was writing in her journal, and she realized she was cold.

And in the dream she had pulled up her blanket. It was all happening exactly the way she'd dreamed it.

No! she thought. *No, no, NO.*

Angie knew she couldn't stay in bed one minute longer. She threw off the blanket and got out of bed. Beneath her bare feet, the wooden floor was icy cold. *I closed all the windows before I went to sleep. I know I did,* she thought.

She glanced over at the windows. Sure enough, they were

shut tight. But still she felt cold air sweeping through the bedroom.

That meant the draft was coming from another room. Angie took a step toward the bedroom door, then stopped. She had done this in her dream, too! She had gone out into the hall to see where the cold air was coming from.

She didn't want to do that now, but she was so cold that her teeth were chattering. She felt as if her blood were turning to ice. She had to find the open window or she would freeze. She *had* to go out into the hall.

The upstairs hallway was long and dark. Angie blinked. She couldn't believe it. Before she went to sleep, she'd put night-lights in every outlet. They should have been shining, lighting the hall. But every single light was out. The hall was so dark, she couldn't see a thing. She didn't know where the wall was—or the railing for the stairs. Slowly, carefully, Angie started down the dark hall.

She stayed close to the wall on her right. She brushed her fingers against it to keep her bearings. The air was even colder now. Angie could see her breath making white clouds—even in the deep darkness of the hall.

She stopped abruptly, a sob trapped inside her throat.

This was in the dream, too, she realized. And then she realized something else.

In the dream she'd been here, feeling her way along the pitch-black hall. And the shadow woman had been right behind her.

Angie's fear turned to pure panic. She wanted to turn around and look. She needed to see the shadow woman's face. But she was terrified of what she would see. And she was sick of being so scared.

Maybe I'll turn my head, just for an instant, Angie told herself. *Maybe there's no one there after all.*

She heard a soft, rustling sound. Like long skirts brushing against the floor.

Angie could feel the shadow woman there, standing just behind her. She dared a quick glance back over her shoulder. She saw only darkness—and something glittering, like a dark gem on a necklace.

"No!" Angie screamed. She tried to run—and felt her knees buckle under her.

Angie stumbled and fell. She hit the floor hard, landing on her side. Her hip hurt. She knew she should get up and run. But she was so terrified, she couldn't get her muscles to move.

That's when she heard the sound. It started low, then swelled until it seemed to fill the house.

Horrible, mocking laughter. A woman's laughter.

Frantic now, Angie pushed herself to her feet. Her legs felt weak, as if they were made of rubber bands. She stumbled down the last few feet of the hall, still using the wall as her guide. The rustling sound came closer. The laughter grew even louder.

Without warning, Angie's right hand met open air. She

teetered, windmilling her arms to keep from falling down the stairs. Her right hand smacked hard against the banister. Bright spots of pain danced before Angie's eyes. But she gripped the banister and held on tight.

The laughter stopped, as if it was a recording and somebody hit the off switch.

Angie started down the stairs. *One. Two. Three.* Clinging to the banister, she counted the steps as she made her way down. The house was silent now. The only sounds Angie could hear were her own breathing and the pounding of her heart.

At the bottom of the stairs, Angie could see an eerie glow. *That's the living room,* she thought. She started toward it.

She gave a little cry of fear as she remembered. In the dream she'd gone into the living room—to find out what had been causing the strange glow.

Do something else, she told herself. *Do anything else.*

But somehow she couldn't. It was as if there were a script that Angie had to follow and she couldn't change one line. In the dream she'd gone into the living room. She knew that was exactly what she had to do now.

Angie walked to the living room, then stopped in the doorway. The big sliding doors were open. The window shades were up, even though Angie always pulled them down at night. Light from the big streetlamp flooded into the room, bathing it in a cold, white glow.

Just a streetlight, she thought. *Not so scary.*

In fact, she didn't remember this from her dream. Angie felt herself relax a little. Maybe the nightmare was over. She could turn on the lights. Check out the rest of the house, and maybe even go back to sleep.

Then Angie's eyes were drawn to the fireplace. That's where the light was strongest. Above the mantel hung a portrait of a woman. Angie's friend Ellen, who owned the house, said that the woman in the painting was named Eloise Cavanaugh. Angie knew that Eloise was the first owner of the house.

Angie stared at the portrait. And she noticed something she hadn't before. In the painting, Eloise Cavanaugh was wearing a pin. It was a spot of color on the high collar of her black dress. The gem in the pin looked like a ruby, sparkling at her throat.

The shadow woman wasn't wearing a necklace, Angie realized. *She was wearing a pin.*

Just like the one in the painting.

Angie made a strangled sound. *That's her,* she thought. Angie remembered now. She remembered the pin. She could see it in her mind's eye. Pinned to the front of the dress the woman wore in the dream.

The shadow woman, the woman in Angie's dreams, the woman who *haunted* her dreams, was Eloise Cavanaugh.

Slowly, Angie walked to the fireplace. She gazed up at the portrait. Eloise's sharp blue eyes seemed to glare down at Angie.

"It's you, isn't it?" Angie whispered. "You're the one in my dreams. You hate me, don't you? But why? What have I ever done to you?"

CRASH! BANG!

Angie whirled around at the sudden explosion of sound.

CRASH! BANG! BANG! CRASH! BANG!

The sliding doors at the entrance to the living room slid open and closed with terrifying force. They smashed together, then hurtled back along their tracks to slam into their hiding places inside the walls. The whole room shook. The windows rattled.

And over it all, Angie heard laughter once again. Eloise Cavanaugh's laughter. Angie clapped her hands to her ears to shut out the sound.

"Stop it!" she cried. "Why are you doing this? Please, please, stop!"

CRASH!

With a final explosion of sound, the doors slammed shut. Silence filled the house once more.

Angie crossed the room until she stood before the closed doors. What would happen when she tried to slide them open? Was Eloise Cavanaugh waiting for her on the other side of the door?

Angie curled the fingers of her right hand into the little groove that was the handle for the door, then tugged. The right door slid open without a sound. Angie darted through it.

She ran as hard and fast as she could for the kitchen. She knew what she was going to do now. There wasn't a sleep doctor on Earth who could help with what was going on inside this house.

But Angie thought she knew who could.

She skidded into the kitchen. Her fingers grabbed the wall switch and turned it on. Angie blinked in the bright light. There! The newspaper article was on the kitchen table, right where she'd left it.

Angie snatched up the phone. She punched in the number listed in the article. Who cared if it was the middle of the night? Everybody had voice mail or an answering machine. They'd get the message. They'd come and help.

"Thank you for calling The Atlantic Paranormal Society," a pleasant young woman's voice said in Angie's ear. "Please leave a message, and we'll be in touch as soon as possible."

"Help," Angie said into the phone. "You've got to help me. I have these dreams... these terrible dreams. You've got to make them stop."

Lyssa Frye tossed her purse into her desk drawer and sat down. The light on the TAPS answering machine was blinking off and on.

Time to find out who needs our help today, Lyssa thought. She pressed the button to play back the messages.

There was only one.

Lyssa listened to the message once, twice, then started on a third time. And still she didn't write down a single word. Instead, she sat, her eyes wide open, tingles running up and down her spine.

As she listened to the message for the third time, Jason and Grant came into the office.

"Hey, Lyssa," Grant said. "How's it..." Lyssa swung around to face them, and Grant got a good look at her face. "Whoa."

He crossed the room quickly, with Jason right behind him.

"It's okay, Lyssa," Jason said. "Just tell us what came in."

"You guys," Lyssa said, finally finding her voice, "you really need to hear this one for yourselves."

"This team has a decision to make," Jason said a little while later. "We got a disturbing phone message overnight. It's clear the woman who called us, Angie Larson, is very upset."

"She's more than upset," Lyssa put in. "She's terrified."

"No doubt," Jason agreed. "But she says she's having bad dreams. The question is, is that really a case for us?"

"You spoke with Angie this morning, right, Lyssa?" Grant asked. "Did she explain why she called TAPS and not somebody else?"

"Yes." Lyssa nodded. Quickly, she looked at her notes. "For the past few months, Angie Larson has been having really scary dreams.

They began soon after she started living in her friend Ellen's house. She's staying there for a year while her friend is overseas."

"What kind of disturbing dreams?" Mark asked.

"All the dreams have one thing in common: They all take place *inside the house*. Sometimes, there are strange sounds. And strange things happen. Drawers open and close on their own. Lights flash on and off. That's freaky enough. But that's not what's really scaring Angie. The thing that scares her the most is what happens when she wakes up."

"So what happens when she wakes up?" Mark asked.

"There's really no other way to say it," Lyssa said. "The dreams come true."

"What?" Jen exclaimed.

"The dreams come true," Lyssa repeated. "If Angie Larson dreams about something, the exact same thing happens once she wakes up. Every single time. It's gotten so bad she's afraid to fall asleep at night."

"That *is* spooky," Mike said.

"I used to have nightmares when I was a kid," Grant said. "I woke up really scared, but my dad would say, 'It's just a dream.' And that always made me feel better." He shook his head. "It would be so weird to know that it's *more* than a dream, that all the scary things don't go away the second you wake up."

"Angie's dreams are getting scarier and scarier," Lyssa added. "She says there's a woman in the shadows—a woman who is after her, or at least that's what it feels like. That's why she finally called us last night. She's afraid the woman in the dreams means to do her harm."

Lyssa turned to Jason. "I think we should take the case. Angie Larson is frightened. She needs our help."

"She certainly needs help," Jason agreed. "I'm just not sure she needs *ours*. There are a million reasons for dreams. There may be nothing paranormal here at all."

"But how will we know that if we don't investigate?" Lyssa asked. "And we're not the first people Angie's turned to for help. She's been to a sleep doctor, and she's more frightened now than ever. My instinct is telling me there's something here, Jason. I think we should take the time to find out what."

Jason took a deep breath, then let it out slowly.

"Okay," he said, "since you feel that strongly about it. Check our schedule and find out how soon we'll be in Angie's area."

"I already did," Lyssa said. She flashed Jason a grateful smile. "We'll be close to Angie's house next Tuesday."

"Tuesday it is, then," Jason said. He stood up, signaling the meeting was over. Just as he did, the telephone rang.

Lyssa moved quickly to the phone on her desk. "Hello?"

"Lyssa?" said a breathless voice on the other end of the line.

"Angie?" Lyssa said. "Is that you? Are you all right?" She turned to face the others. *"It's Angie Larson,"* she mouthed silently.

"Fine. I'm fine," Angie's voice said. "It's just...please tell me that you're coming."

"Of course we are," Lyssa said. "But I'm afraid we can't get there until next week."

"No," Angie said. Lyssa could hear her voice rise. "That's not soon enough. You have to come now. Tonight."

"I'm sorry, Angie," Lyssa said. "But we've checked the schedule and—"

"Listen to me, Lyssa," Angie interrupted, her words tumbling over one another she was talking so fast. "I was so tired this morning that I fell asleep on the couch. I had another dream. You have to come..."

"I understand, Angie," Lyssa said firmly, "but we can't just drop everything. Other people need our help, too. Tuesday is the first day we can come."

"No, you *don't* understand," Angie insisted. "I'm sorry. I think it's my fault. You guys were in the dream I had, Lyssa. It was nighttime. I saw the date on my phone. The fifth. That's tonight."

"You have to come. You have to come *now*."

"Thank you. Thank you so much," Angie Larson said as she opened the front door. It was late that night. After Angie's frightened phone call, the TAPS team rearranged their schedule, then headed straight for Angie Larson's house.

In the glow of the porch light, Lyssa could see that Angie had shoulder-length blond hair and dark brown eyes. She looked tired and worried.

"Hi, Angie. I'm Lyssa," Lyssa said. She held out her hand, and Angie shook it. Her fingers were icy cold.

"I'm really happy to meet you," Angie said. Quickly, Lyssa introduced the rest of the team. Angie opened the door wider. "Everybody, please, come inside."

She stepped back so the TAPS team could enter the house.

"Go on into the living room," Angie said. "First door on the left."

The living room *looked* warm and cozy. Its walls were covered in creamy wallpaper. Floor lamps gave off warm light. But as she chose a place on the couch and sat down, Lyssa didn't *feel* warm and cozy. Across from her was a huge brick fireplace. Above it was a striking portrait of a young woman dressed in a simple black dress.

The woman's dark hair was swept back from her face. She had icy blue eyes. They seemed to be staring at Lyssa—almost as hard as Lyssa was staring at her.

"That's quite a painting," Lyssa said. "Do you know who she is?"

"Of course I do," Angie said. She sat up straight, as if she expected to bolt right out of the wooden chair she sat in. All the furniture in the room was old-fashioned and not very comfortable.

"That's the first owner of the house, Eloise Cavanaugh," Angie went on. "My best friend, Ellen, is Eloise's great-granddaughter. She inherited the house last year, after Eloise died."

"So you're the first person to live in the house after Eloise's death?" Jason asked.

"The first person who isn't a family member," Angie corrected him. "Ellen and her parents lived here for a little while."

"Did Eloise die in the house?" Grant asked.

"Yes." Angie nodded. "Ellen told me a little about her. Eloise died right here, in the living room."

There was a beat of silence.

"Eloise's husband, John, built this house for her when she was just a bride," Angie went on. "It's the first house they lived in after they were married. It was her pride and joy.

"But John was a very successful businessman. He wanted a bigger house right in the middle of town. So the couple moved, but Eloise was never happy about it. She always pined for her first home. She refused to let John sell it. She moved back here after he died."

Angie paused. "You'll probably think I'm losing it," she said. She gave a funny little laugh. "I pretty much think that myself. But lately, I can't help wondering... what if Eloise is responsible for what's been happening to me?"

"What makes you think that?" Jason asked.

"Lately the dreams are getting scarier and scarier," Angie answered. "Before, I just dreamed about the house. That was freaky enough! But now it's like there's someone in the dreams with me. Someone watching from the shadows all the time. But I can never get a good look at her face."

"Then why do you think it's Eloise Cavanaugh?" Grant asked.

"Because the one thing I can see is something glittering at her throat." Angie pointed at the portrait.

"The pin," Lyssa said.

Angie nodded. "At first I thought it was a necklace. But now I think it's that pin she wears. I'm sure of it now. The shadow woman in my dreams is Eloise Cavanaugh."

"What about your most recent dream? The one with the TAPS team in it?" Lyssa asked. "Where did that take place?"

"In the kitchen," Angie answered. "I can show you where."

"What happened in the dream?" Jason asked.

Angie shrugged. "We were all in there together. Everything was going crazy—the drawers and cabinets opening and closing."

"Sounds interesting," Grant said. "Let's get some equipment set up so we can start our investigation."

"You got it." Jen stood up and gestured to the Hammond twins. "Okay, guys, let's roll."

Several minutes later, Mike and Jen were in the kitchen,

installing cameras and audio recorders. "How cool is this?" Mike asked. "For once, we actually know right where to aim our equipment."

"It's definitely not the typical case," Jen agreed. "It's amazing that Angie can tell us exactly where to expect paranormal activity." From her position on the ladder, Jen adjusted one of the cameras. It was pointing at a set of kitchen drawers. A second camera was aimed at the cabinets just above them.

"Still, I really feel for Angie," Jen continued. "She's acting brave, but it's pretty easy to see she's scared to death."

"Can't say I blame her," Mike commented. He slid an audio recorder into place on the kitchen counter. "Okay," he said. "I think we're good to go."

At that moment Lyssa, Angie, and Grant walked into the kitchen. "I don't know how much more I can take," Angie was saying.

"What will you do if nothing changes?" Lyssa asked. "If you keep having the dreams?"

"There's only one thing I can do," Angie said. "I'll have to move out, even though I promised Ellen I'd stay. I can't go on living like this. I hardly get any sleep. I can't stand being so terrified all the time."

"If you do move and the dreams stop," Jen said, "that could be proof that they really are related to Eloise."

"I have a vacation coming up," Angie said. "I'm thinking of

spending some time with my sister. She has this great place on the coast, and—"

"Guys," Mark suddenly said, "I hate to interrupt, but..." He pointed to the opposite side of the kitchen; the silverware drawer was slowly sliding open. The doors to the cupboards right above it were already swinging back and forth.

And all in perfect silence. They didn't make a single sound. Not even a squeaky hinge.

"Angie," Lyssa said. "Is that—?"

"Yes." Angie nodded. Her face was pale but composed. "That's what I dreamed. That's it exactly."

For several moments, the TAPS team stood perfectly still, watching the activity in the kitchen. It showed no signs of slowing down. Back and forth. In and out went the cupboards and drawers in a bizarre and silent ballet.

"I don't know about anyone else," Lyssa finally said, "but I think someone is trying to get our attention."

"It worked," Jason said. "Whoever it is has definitely gotten mine!"

"All right," Grant said a short time later. "Here's how it's going to go down. Lyssa, you and I will take the living room. Jay and Mark will cover the rest of the downstairs. Mike and Jen, you take the second floor. Everybody, check back in here during the night."

"Roger that," Lyssa said. "Angie will be sleeping in the spare bedroom. That way, you guys can investigate her room. Mark and I set up several cameras in there, and audio as well."

"Excellent," Jen replied as she moved to stand by the light switch on the dining room wall. All the other lights downstairs were already out.

"Let's see if we can't figure out what's going on around here," Jason said. "On three. One. Two. Three...And we're dark."

Jen turned off the switch. The house was plunged into darkness and the team split up.

"This is Grant and Lyssa. We're entering the living room," Grant said in a quiet voice.

There was a recorder on the mantel just below Eloise Cavanaugh's portrait. Lyssa had put it there herself. She aimed her flashlight at Grant as he walked across the living room. He was heading right where she figured he would—to Eloise's portrait.

Even though the room was dark, Lyssa could see Eloise's face by the light of the streetlamp outside. Those blue eyes seemed to hover in the air. Watching. Waiting.

All of a sudden, Lyssa shivered. She remembered Angie talking about how cold it was in her dream.

"It seems a lot colder in here," Lyssa said. She knew that a drop in temperature could mean a spirit had entered the room.

"It is cold. I feel it, too," Grant said. "Why don't you try to establish contact?"

"All right." Lyssa swallowed past a big lump in her throat.

"My name is Lyssa, and this is Grant," she said. "We'd like to make contact with the spirit of Eloise Cavanaugh. Eloise, if you're here, would you give us a sign?" She thought about what Angie said had happened in the dream. "Can you make the window shade roll up?"

Lyssa paused. The air got even colder, and thick and threatening, the way it did right before a thunderstorm. Except this felt even worse, as if something terrible was coming toward them. Lyssa's chest felt tight. She could feel her heart begin to pound.

She forced herself to go on. "We don't want to disturb you, Mrs. Cavanaugh."

Maybe Eloise didn't like being called by her first name. The woman was quite old when she died. Maybe she expected more respect.

"We just want to understand what's going on. Angie Larson, the young woman living here, is very frightened. Can you help us help her? Can you give us a sign to let us know you're here?"

WHUMP!

Lyssa jumped at the sudden sound, then spun toward it. Her flashlight danced crazily across the living room wall. She was just in time to see the pull-down shade in the center window shoot up to the top of the window frame.

"Whoa," Grant said.

WHUMP! THUMP!

One by one, all the other window shades in the room began to roll up. They spun around and around, whacking against the tops of the window frames.

This time the sound was so loud that Lyssa wanted to cover her ears.

"This is just what Angie said happened in this room in her dreams," Grant said.

Lyssa could feel her breath coming in and out in short, quick gasps. When she exhaled, her breath made white clouds. Lyssa's fingers ached — either from the cold or from gripping the flashlight so tightly.

"What do we do now?"

Before Grant could answer, there was a scream from upstairs.

"No. *No. NO!*"

"That's Angie!" Lyssa cried as she spun toward the sound.

Lyssa raced out of the living room. Grant was right behind her. At the bottom of the stairs, they met up with Jason and Mark.

"Where's Angie?" Lyssa asked. She started up the stairs, calling out as she climbed. "Jen and Mike, are you with Angie? What's going on up there? Is everything all right?"

"It's okay. Everything's okay, Lyssa," Angie's voice called down. She appeared at the top of the stairs with Jen and Mike on either side of her. "I had another dream, and I..."

All of a sudden, Angie began to sob.

Lyssa rushed to Angie's side and put her arms around her.

"I saw her, Lyssa," Angie sobbed. "I really *saw* her this time. Eloise Cavanaugh. She was standing right beside my bed, looking down at me. She hates me. She hates me so much. I could see it in her eyes. She held her hands out."

"She held her hands out?" Lyssa repeated, puzzled.

"Yes." Angie took a deep breath. "She held them out and then she lowered them over my throat. She was going to strangle me. That's when I screamed."

Angie pressed her hand over her mouth to hold back another sob. When she spoke again, her voice was strangely quiet.

"Now I know what she wants. Eloise Cavanaugh wants to kill me!"

"That's not going to happen," Lyssa soothed her. "You're okay. We're here with you now."

"But you won't stay," Angie said. "And she'll try again. And sooner or later whatever happens in the dream will happen for real. I just know it. Eloise Cavanaugh is going to strangle me. And I won't be able to stop her."

"Come downstairs, please, everyone," Jason called out. "Let's regroup."

With one arm still around Angie's waist, Lyssa started down the stairs. Halfway down, she stopped.

"Listen," she said, her voice intent.

"What? I don't hear anything," Mark said.

"That's what I mean," Lyssa answered. "The window shades in the living room. They've stopped."

"You're right," Jason said. "You're absolutely right. Command Center. Everyone. Now."

"I'm trying to be brave. I honestly am," Angie said when they'd all gathered in the Command Center, in the dining room. The house was still dark. The only light in the room came from the row of computer monitors.

Angie sat in one of the dining room chairs, twisting her hands together in her lap. Lyssa knelt by her side.

"I'm scared. I'm just so scared," she said. "I'm not sure I can take much more of this. I just don't understand why Eloise hates me so much. I haven't done anything to her! All I'm trying to do is live in the house."

"Maybe that's just it," Lyssa said slowly. "Maybe it isn't *you* at all. Maybe it's just that Eloise thinks there's a stranger in her home."

Angie shook her head. "I'm no stranger. I'm Ellen's friend. I even visited this house when Ellen lived here."

"You're not a blood relation," Mark explained. "Which might be why Eloise thinks that you don't have a right to be here."

"But I love this house!" Angie protested. "I'll take good care of it, if only she'll let me." She gave a long sigh. "I wish I could tell her so."

"Maybe you can," Grant said.

"*What?*"

"As part of our investigations, we often try to make contact with a spirit," Grant explained. "Lyssa and I did this in the living room and got a pretty big response. We definitely got Eloise Cavanaugh's attention. And she's definitely got yours. Maybe it's time for *you* to try to get hers."

Angie sat still for several moments. Then she gave Lyssa's hand a quick squeeze and stood up. She didn't look so frightened now. Instead, she looked determined.

"You're right," she said. "Maybe it's time I had a talk with her."

"Outstanding," Grant said. "Let's give this a try."

A little while later, Lyssa and Angie were sitting side by side on the couch. The fireplace was directly in front of them. Eloise's portrait hung right above it.

Grant and Jason sat in chairs on either side of the couch. They had pulled the window shades down. The Hammond twins were back upstairs, continuing to investigate the second floor. Jen was in the Command Center, keeping an eye on everyone.

"Okay," Grant said. "Here's the way I'd like to proceed. Lyssa will try to establish contact. She may get a response. She may not. But then she'll introduce you, Angie, and you can say what's on your mind."

"Remember that ghosts are just people," Jason put in. "Talk to her directly and politely."

"Okay," Angie said. "I guess I'm as ready as I'll ever be." She shook her head. "I still don't understand how you guys can do this all the time."

"Go ahead, then, Lyssa. You begin," Jason said.

Lyssa sat up a little straighter on the couch. "This is Lyssa," she said in a clear, polite voice. "We spoke once before. There's someone with me who would like to speak to you, Mrs. Cavanaugh. Her name is Angie Larson. She's the young woman living in your house."

"I'm getting a little EMF change, but not much," Jason murmured in a low voice. "Go ahead, Angie."

"Hello?" Angie said. She cleared her throat. "My name is Angie, and I...I don't know how to do this," she whispered to Lyssa. "I feel so stupid. How do I know if she hears me or not?"

"You're doing fine," Lyssa said. "You might not know. Lots of times, we don't get an answer. That doesn't mean we stop trying. Just keep at it."

"Some things have been happening lately that really scare me," Angie went on. "I don't know whether you're making them happen or not. But maybe you can make them stop.

"I'm sorry if you're upset that I'm living in your house," Angie continued. "Your house is really beautiful. I can see why you love it so much. I promise that I will take really good care of it. Can we find a way to live here together? It's just for a year. Then Ellen will come back..."

She took a deep breath, held it for a minute, then let it out.

"I think that's all I wanted to say."

They waited a good ten minutes. But there was no answer.

"Okay," Jason said. "Let's call it a night."

After her attempt to talk to Eloise Cavanaugh, Angie went back to bed in the spare room. The TAPS team continued investigating throughout the night. There were no other incidents.

Now it was a bright, sunny morning. Lyssa and Jason stood on the front porch.

"You're sure about this?" Jason asked Lyssa.

The equipment van and SUVs were all loaded up. The TAPS team was heading back to the office to review the evidence they'd gathered. All except for Lyssa.

"I'm sure," Lyssa answered. "I promised not to leave Angie alone. At least not until we can figure out what she should do."

Jason nodded. "I think we're all convinced that there's paranormal activity in this house—and it could be dangerous. Be careful, Lyssa."

"I will be," Lyssa promised.

Jason walked down the steps and got into one of the waiting SUVs. The team drove off.

Okay, Lyssa thought as she turned back to the house. *Now it's up to me.*

The day passed quietly. Lyssa and Angie didn't talk much. *We're both waiting for the same thing,* Lyssa thought. *Nightfall. When the spirit of Eloise Cavanaugh comes out. When the nightmares get real.*

Nine o'clock came and went. Then ten and eleven. It seemed to Lyssa that she could feel some kind of pressure building in the house. Like steam in a pot ready to blow its lid.

"I'm sorry, Angie," she finally said. "I have to get some sleep. Besides, we've both got to go to bed sometime."

"It's all right," Angie said quickly. The two were sitting in the kitchen, drinking mugs of cocoa. The living room was much more comfortable. But neither Lyssa nor Angie really wanted to spend any time there. Not with Eloise's portrait staring down at them.

"I'm tired, too," Angie admitted. "I'm just so afraid to go to sleep. I wish I knew whether or not I got through to Eloise Cavanaugh last night."

Together, the two young women climbed the stairs. Lyssa's feet felt like lead weights. Angie would sleep in her own room tonight. There wasn't much point in her moving to the spare bedroom. Eloise had proved she could—and would—find Angie anywhere.

"I'll leave my door open so I can hear if you call out," Lyssa said. "If the slightest thing happens, you give a yell and I'll come running."

"No problem. I'll scream so loud, the rest of the team will be able to hear me back in Rhode Island," Angie said. Her lips curved upward, but the smile didn't quite reach her eyes.

"Great," Lyssa said. "I'll see you in the morning."

Angie turned away and walked down the hall to her bedroom. Lyssa stood at the top of the stairs and watched her go.

Sweet dreams. That's what Lyssa's mom always said.

"Sweet dreams," Lyssa whispered, but what she really meant was, *Please, no dreams at all.*

"Lyssa! Lysssaaaa!"

A bloodcurdling voice screaming her name jerked Lyssa wide awake. She bolted upright, her heart hammering. She hurled back the covers and swung her feet over the side of the bed.

"Hold on, Angie, I'm coming!" Lyssa shouted.

She raced down the hall toward Angie's room.

Then she saw something that made the hairs on the back of her neck stand straight up. Angie's bedroom door was opening and closing all by itself.

It slammed shut so hard, the pictures in the hallway bounced on the walls. Then it flew back open.

Lyssa skidded to a stop just outside Angie's bedroom door. In the quick glimpses she got when the door was open, Lyssa saw Angie lying on the bed. Her mouth was open in a silent scream. Her arms stretched straight up, with her palms flat. *As if she's trying to push someone away!*

Was last night's dream coming true? The dream of Eloise leaning over her, about to close her hands on Angie's throat. About to strangle her...

Slam! Crash! Slam! Crash! Angie's door pounded open and closed. Lyssa tried to leap into the room, but each time the door slammed shut in her face.

Lyssa stood, frozen, in the hall. Cold sweat trickled down between her shoulder blades. Her stomach churned with panic. If she didn't come up with something soon...

The portrait! she thought.

Eloise Cavanaugh was the key to what was going on inside this house. And the portrait just might be the key to Eloise Cavanaugh.

Lyssa turned and sprinted back down the hall. She took the

171

stairs two at a time. Once she reached the main floor, she dashed into the living room.

I've got to get Eloise's attention, Lyssa thought. *Get her away from Angie. Make her leave Angie alone.*

Lyssa dragged a footstool over to the fireplace. She climbed up onto it. Seizing Eloise's portrait by its heavy gold frame, Lyssa yanked the painting right off the wall.

"I've got your portrait, Eloise!" Lyssa shouted. "And I'll tear it apart, I swear I will, if you don't *stop this right now!*"

At her words, the house went wild. The window shades banged up to the top of the frames. The living room sliding doors began to slam open and closed. The television came on, sound blaring full blast. Lights flickered on and off. Magazines from the coffee table flew up and through the air straight at Lyssa.

Lyssa held the portrait out in front of her like a shield. She stood on the footstool like a statue on a pedestal.

"I mean it, Eloise!" she yelled. She tightened her grip, fingernails digging into the back of the canvas.

"Keep it up and your portrait is toast. But I'll make you a bargain. Leave Angie Larson alone. *Let her go right now!* Let her come downstairs to tell me she's all right, and I'll put the portrait back. Then I'll talk her into leaving your house. She will leave and never come back!

"Do we have a deal or not?"

Lyssa heard what sounded like a hurricane wind. The next second, two of the tall windows shattered. Sharp pieces of glass rained down all over the room. Lyssa gave a shriek of alarm, but she didn't let go of the portrait.

The wind ripped through the room. It toppled chairs, sending one crashing into the coffee table. Then, with a whooshing sound, the logs in the fireplace caught fire.

The fire crackled and danced as the wind fed it. Lyssa watched in horror. Instead of going up the chimney, the fire was reaching out, into the room. Any second now, the whole house would go up in flames. But Lyssa didn't move.

Then it all stopped. The window shades and doors were still. The wind died. The flames in the fireplace shrank to a red glow.

Lyssa stayed on the footstool. She gripped the picture frame so tightly, she could no longer feel her fingers.

"Angie! Angie, are you okay?" she yelled.

Silence.

Then she heard a *thump* from upstairs, followed by the sound of running footsteps. A moment later, Angie appeared in the entrance to the living room. Her eyes were two wide pools of fear. Her hands were at her throat.

"Are you okay?" Lyssa asked.

"Okay," Angie managed to gasp out.

"Here's the deal," Lyssa said. "I promised I would put the

portrait back and that we would leave—if she let you go. But we have to go tonight. How fast can you pack your things?"

"Already on it." Angie whirled around. Lyssa heard her footsteps again, pounding up the stairs this time.

Lyssa's knees began to shake. Slowly, she turned around and hung the portrait back on the wall. Then she climbed down from the footstool and sat on the couch. She stayed there, staring up into Eloise Cavanaugh's icy blue eyes, until Angie came back downstairs to say she was ready to leave.

"You got a postcard, Lyssa," Jen said a couple of weeks later as she brought in the TAPS mail. It was a bright summer day. The sky was blue. The sun was shining. Everything seemed so bright and alive.

"A postcard," Lyssa echoed. "Who sent it?"

"See for yourself," Jen answered with a smile. She handed Lyssa the postcard. There was a beach scene on the front. Lyssa turned the card over.

"Hey," she said. "It's from Angie Larson."

Jason looked up from his desk. "What does she say?"

Quickly, Lyssa scanned the few sentences on the postcard's back. "She says she's doing well. No more dreams."

"That's a relief, I'll bet," Grant commented.

"And she's never going back to that house?" Jason guessed.

"Angie says she's moving to a new house next week."

"I'm glad things are working out for her, but I still think what you did was pretty risky," Grant said.

"I know it was risky," Lyssa agreed. "But it was the only thing that I could think of."

"You know what I always say," Jason said with a smile. "Working for TAPS is a dream come true."

"Yeah, it's a real nightmare," Grant said, and the whole team laughed.

GHOST TOWN

Layne Stevens took off his black flat-brimmed hat and fanned himself. The sun was setting, but here in Tombstone, Arizona, it was still sizzling hot. Layne watched as dust swirled around the last group of visitors leaving the O.K. Corral. Nearly everyone has heard of the historic gunfight at the O.K. Corral. There have been books and movies about the famous shoot-out between Wyatt Earp and the Clanton gang in the old Wild West. But Layne got to watch it happen every day, up close and personal.

Layne played Wyatt Earp in a show about the gunfight. Hundreds of visitors came each week to see it. Layne and a crew of other actors would stand across from each other with fake guns in their holsters, waiting for the right moment to draw them. Then Layne would look left and right and see the actors playing Wyatt Earp's two brothers, Virgil and Morgan. He felt as if he were in a real standoff. His eyes would focus on the outlaws facing him, and his fingers would twitch, ready for bullets to fly at any second. And then *pop pop pop*! He would hear the guns. As the smoke cleared, some of it would get in his eyes, making them tear. The whole fight lasted only thirty seconds.

After the show the visitors were free to walk around the little town. They took pictures and went into the stores, which, like the rest of the O.K. Corral, looked the way they did on October 26, 1881, the day of the gunfight.

When five o'clock rolled around, Layne would round up everybody and send them on their way home. After that, he would go into each building, making sure no one had been left behind. He took his time going in and out of each building as the sun dipped behind the mountains. He never found anybody hanging around after the tourists had left.

At least, not anybody alive.

Lately Layne had been seeing things around the O.K. Corral after everyone had left. Movements in the corner of his eye, shadows behind windows, bright flashes of light in back of buildings...things he couldn't explain.

He hadn't told the other employees about it. He was worried no one would believe him. He thought they would make fun of him, because they all knew how wrapped up he got playing Wyatt Earp. But he knew what he saw.

So now, on evenings like this one, after the visitors had all left, Layne felt strange. He wondered what he might see.

Or what might be seeing him.

Layne watched the last car filled with tourists drive off and started his nightly rounds. He looked in the alleys between the buildings, filled with long shadows and lizards scurrying for cover. Then he went into the hat store, the telegraph station, and the jailhouse, searching all over and calling to anyone who might have been left behind. There was nothing out of the ordinary in any of those places, but Layne couldn't shake the strange feeling. It was like his senses were extra-sensitive. Little birds chirping in the brush seemed as loud as a car horn. The dust in the air clung to his skin, making it feel rough as sandpaper.

The last place in that part of town he had to check was the stables. On the side facing the street, there was a tall brick wall with a rickety gate that surrounded a corral. In the center of the corral was a shack with old, dusty windows.

Layne opened the gate and stepped inside the corral. The ground was very dry from being baked by the sun. He could feel the hard dirt through his boots. A bead of sweat ran down his forehead.

Layne walked around the corral and then made his way to

the shack. He put his hand on the hot metal doorknob and was about to open the door when he stopped. He heard a faint noise. Then it got louder. A gloomy howling sound was carried on the wind. After a minute it went away.

Probably just a coyote out there, he thought.

Layne stuck his head into the shack and looked around. A long cobweb fluttered in the corner of the room. Nothing else.

He left the shack and walked toward the gate. Out of nowhere he heard that sad coyote cry rise again. It was much closer this time and even louder. It sounded as if it was right behind him.

"Anybody here?" he called out.

He spun around, and suddenly his pulse throbbed in his neck and his throat choked up. A twisting pain shot through his stomach. Squinting at him through the window of the shack was an old man in a flat-brimmed hat, just like his.

The man snarled.

Immediately Layne ran to the door and threw it open. The floorboards squeaked under his feet. The gust from the door caused the big cobweb to break free from the wall and drift down to the floor. As it fell, the cobweb reflected light from the window. It looked like a cloud floating through the sky. Layne felt dizzy. His eyes darted to each corner of the room. He looked to his left and right. But he was alone. There was no one there.

Layne took a deep breath and stepped back out of the shack.

He inched toward the window, getting so close his nose almost touched the glass. He raised an arm and clinked his fingernail on the dusty window. It made a flat pinging sound.

It must have been my reflection, he thought. *It's just too hot out. I need to get some water.*

He slowly backed out of the gate and made it to Camillus Fly's photography shop. In the back there was a gift shop, which was very popular with visitors. There were also vending machines with bottled water. He walked to the back of the shop, passing the cap guns and pictures of Native Americans in tribal clothing. He liked looking at all the historical things at the O.K. Corral.

But sometimes the old pictures gave him a funny feeling—especially the black-and-white picture of Camillus Fly's wife, Mary, that hung behind the cash register. She had a broad smile and thick curly hair. Even for such an old picture, Mary's face was very clear. On the way out, Layne stared at it for a minute. He thought that if it weren't for the ruffly dress, Mary would look like someone he would like. She was pretty. The idea that people were much the same one hundred or two hundred years ago was strange in a way. They had the same brains and probably thought about the same things. Layne imagined himself going back in time and talking with them. That would be awesome.

Layne got his water and then went to the door. He had an

itch in his nose. A second later he sneezed. He took a big breath in through his nose. He smelled a strong aroma of flowers, like fancy perfume. It obviously hadn't come from outside. There were no flowers there. He stood by the door and gave the room another look.

"Hello?"

No answer. The smell grew stronger. He turned his head and looked at the picture of Mary. The smile on her face was so wide, it was as if the picture had been taken in the middle of a funny joke. Her eyes were so shiny, they seemed real. He felt as if she was looking right at him.

"Mary?" he whispered.

For a moment he thought the picture was going to answer him. He stared at it, his eyes making out the grainy details. Were her lips moving maybe just a little? The longer he stared, the thicker the silence in the room became. Soon it felt like water was clogging his ears. He shook his head quickly. *Snap out of it, Layne,* he told himself. He stepped out the door and moved on.

Layne was almost done for the night, and then he could go home. All he had to do was make sure no one was in the saloon.

There was a change in the air. The temperature had dropped just a little. And there was something else different. A faint sound. But not like before. He recognized this one.

As he approached the saloon, it became even clearer. Piano notes rang through the air. A lively, jangly tune was coming out of the saloon. It was so loud and fast, Layne thought whoever was playing must have been really hitting the keys hard.

Layne was cautious walking up the steps to the swinging doors. Whoever decided to hang around the town after hours was in for a surprise. Layne wanted to make sure they didn't hear him sneak up on them.

Layne pushed the doors open wide and was about to head straight to the piano when he froze. He stared at the instrument in shock. He saw an old piano and an empty piano bench. No one was playing, but the piano kept banging out the tune, louder and faster.

The music pounded in Layne's ears. He couldn't escape it. He felt dizzy, as if he were falling down a well.

Layne turned back toward the door. He wanted to get out of there, but what he saw next stopped him.

There at the bar was a man with a long, pointy beard. The man was calmly sipping from a glass. He turned his head and looked straight at Layne. Then, as if he had never been there at all, the man disappeared like a puff of smoke. A second later the last note from the piano still rang in the air.

Then the only sound was Layne's scream.

Lyssa sat in the front seat of the TAPS van as Jason drove through the Arizona desert. Living in Rhode Island, she was used to seeing water. The scrubby brush and mountains were new to her, but she liked the change of scenery. The air was crisp and clean. But she didn't like the extreme heat. The air-conditioning in the van wasn't working, so they all had opened their windows. With the wind blowing in her face, she could barely hear Mark talking to her over the walkie-talkie from the other van.

"Can you refresh my memory on what happened at the O.K. Corral?" she asked. "Everyone knows there was a gunfight, but..."

"Sure," Mark said. "Back in the old West, there really was no law. Well, there *was* law. But there weren't that many police officers to make sure people followed it. It was a very wild and violent time. Tombstone was the wildest town of all. That's where Wyatt Earp and Doc Holliday settled and became peace officers — what we now call the police.

"Back then, Tombstone was a boomtown. A lot of people came out there to try to make their fortune mining silver. And there was also lots of money to be made selling cattle. Unfortunately, plenty of dishonest people came to Tombstone, too. Gambling cheats, train robbers, bank robbers. But the shoot-out at the O.K. Corral was about cattle thieves. People would drive other people's cattle away from pastures and then sell them for a lot of money. The worst of these cattle thieves was the Clanton gang, run by a man named Ike Clanton. The cattle-robbing problem was so bad that ranchers had to hire watchmen to try to protect their cattle. But even that didn't stop the Clanton gang. They were tough. Few people could stand up to them."

"Get to the exciting stuff!" Jen chimed in. "Why did the shoot-out happen?"

"Oh, right…the shoot-out. Well, one day Ike Clanton rode into town with his gang. Wyatt Earp, his brothers, and Doc Holliday ordered them to give up their guns. They lined up across from each other. Much closer than you would think. They were only a handful of feet apart. But the gang refused to give up their weapons. And that's when the shoot-out happened. The whole fight lasted under a minute, and at the end, three members of the gang were dead. Three of the lawmen were shot, but not badly hurt."

"But the violence didn't stop there," Mike added. "A few weeks after the gunfight, Virgil Earp was attacked by a hidden shooter. He lost his arm because of it. And then, three months later, Morgan Earp was shot in the back by men hiding out in an alley. And within a year, two of the surviving Clanton gang members were also shot dead—one in another gunfight and one while stealing cattle. Those old cowboy movies don't exaggerate all that much. It really was a very violent period of history."

Lyssa looked ahead of her. At first she thought she was seeing a mirage. Wavy, dark shadows moved on top of the road in the distance. But after a minute she realized they were approaching a town. She turned to Jason.

"Is that Tombstone?"

"That's it. That's where we're headed," Jason said. Then he added, "The town of Tombstone has a nickname. They call it 'the town too tough to die.'"

Lyssa laughed. "I guess we're going to find out all about that!"

They parked and entered the town. Lyssa saw wagon wheels and wooden barrels along the old street. Horses were tied up to railings. Donkeys were braying underneath trees with twisted branches. Most of the buildings had long balconies that looked out into the street. Lyssa felt as if she had just stepped back in time. People were even walking around in long duster coats and big cowboy hats. One man with a bushy mustache caught sight of them and walked over.

"You must be from TAPS," he said.

Jason and Grant stepped forward.

"Layne?"

He stuck his arm out and shook their hands.

"Around here folks call me Wyatt Earp. At least during the

day. That's who I play for the visitors. But yes, you can call me Layne."

The team introduced themselves. Lyssa was impressed with how realistic the town was. Everything down to Layne's sheriff's badge seemed to fit. She made a comment about it, and Layne took it off his chest and handed it to her. It was heavy in her palm.

"That's a real badge from the eighteen eighties," he said. "Of course, it's not Wyatt Earp's. But we try to keep this place as authentic as possible. Unfortunately, you just missed the performance. We act out the gunfight every day."

"That's too bad. This place is amazing," Jen said.

"Normally the shoot-out is the most exciting part of the day. But lately things have been getting more interesting after the park closes up."

Lyssa handed back the badge.

"What are some of the reports people have been making?"

"Well, I haven't heard a whole lot from the visitors. Once in a while someone will come up to me and say they heard a weird noise, or smelled pipe smoke in an area with no one else around. Lately, though, I've been experiencing some things that I have trouble explaining. You don't know how happy I am that you all agreed to come. I really thought I was losing it. Follow me. I'll show you the town."

Layne took them on a tour of the little town, pointing out

where all the strange things he'd seen had happened. When they got to the saloon, Layne showed them where he saw the man sitting and pointed to the piano across the room.

"Are there any trapdoors, or anything like that someone could have used to escape?" Lyssa asked.

"Nothing like that. I saw both the man here and a man in the shed just vanish into thin air."

"Was it the same man?"

Layne shook his head.

"They wore similar clothes but were different people. And they had different expressions on their faces. It's strange—I only saw them for a few seconds, but I got a real sense about what those people were like."

"How so?"

"The one in the corral was angry. He had beady eyes, and he was scowling at me through the window of that old shack. But the one in the saloon seemed to be more mellow. He had this calm expression on his face."

"I see. Did either of the men say anything or interact with you in any way?"

"No. They were just sort of there. And then they just faded out."

Lyssa kept her cool, but Layne's claims were very exciting. "And did you recognize them at all?"

Layne seemed shocked.

"I don't think anyone here would be trying to play a trick on me..."

"No. I mean from a picture. There are photos hanging all over Tombstone from that time period. Maybe one of them seems familiar. Do you think you would recognize the real Wyatt Earp if he were standing in front of you?" she asked.

Layne thought about that for a minute. "Yes, I think I would. But I didn't recognize either of those men." Layne straightened his shoulders and took a step back. "Well, everything will be closing up soon, and I have to get back to the visitors. Why don't you have a look around and explore? Once everyone has left, I'll meet you back here."

"Sounds like a plan," Jason said.

Layne took a few steps, then stopped. He turned his head. "Oh, and one more thing—most people think the gunfight happened in the corral itself. But it didn't," Layne explained. "It happened around the corner, next to Camillus Fly's photography shop. Wouldn't want you to waste your time looking for ghost gunfighters where there wouldn't be any."

The sky was deep red when the last visitors' car drove off. Layne met up with the TAPS team and gave them keys to all the buildings. Then he said good-bye for the night and left the

TAPS team to investigate. After he left, Lyssa stared out into the desert. It seemed peaceful, but it also felt lonely. Aside from the sound of a small airplane flying overhead, the desert was completely quiet. In the twilight, the cacti looked like people buried waist deep in the ground.

Jason and Grant brought the team together.

"It's going to get dark soon," Grant said. "Which means the temperature is going to drop, too. It can get very cold at night in the desert. Make sure you all keep warm and keep in contact. Jason and I will set up the Command Center in the gift shop. There's plenty of space in the back. Jen and Lyssa, why don't you check out the corral itself? And Mike and Mark, you guys check out the saloon. Good luck, everyone."

Lyssa helped Jen gather their equipment. As they walked toward the corral, Lyssa stopped for a moment. She could see the first stars coming out above the mountaintops. There was still just enough light left in the day to see the street in front of her. No lights in the windows, no sounds of people, no life. The wooden buildings all around her made her feel as if she were living in the past. She shuddered. She felt a little lost standing there, as if the place didn't really exist.

A few wispy clouds glided across the crescent moon. Two bats whizzed by overhead, looping up and down. There was no need for Jason or Grant to make the call to go dark. The darkness of night fell over Tombstone as if someone had turned off a switch. Lyssa pushed open the gate to the corral.

"Let's take some readings outside first and then check the shack," Jen said.

"Good idea."

Lyssa took out the digital thermometer and began walking slowly around the corral. Jen was close by with the infrared camera. The reading on the thermometer was steady, at eighty-two degrees. After about ten minutes, the temperature dropped by a degree.

"See anything, Jen? These readouts are totally normal."

"Nothing yet. The rocks are still much hotter than the rest of the ground, but that's normal, too. They retain the heat from the sun."

Lyssa began walking toward the shack. She thought of Layne's story about the man in the window. It was so creepy, the way he said the man disappeared like smoke. She looked down at the thermometer. The readout said it was fifty-four degrees.

"Jen! Come here, quick."

Jen rushed over.

"Do you feel anything?" Lyssa asked.

"No, why?"

"You're not cold?"

"Not at all; it's still way hot out."

"I just looked at the thermometer. The temperature dropped over twenty degrees."

Jen scanned the area with the IR camera. But there was nothing out of the ordinary.

"Do you think it could have been the wind?" she asked.

"No way. There's barely a breeze."

Lyssa looked up at the shack. It was only a few yards away. The door was slightly open. She felt herself drawn toward it.

She stopped in front of the door. The thermometer reading was back to normal. She turned it off. Then she turned on the video camera.

"It's pretty cramped inside," she said to Jen. "I'll go in first."

She opened the door. It slanted at a funny angle and was hard to open.

"Hello?"

It was much hotter inside the shack. Lyssa stood in front of the window where Layne said he saw the man and focused her video camera. Then she sat down cross-legged on the floor with the camera pointing *at* the window. The wooden planks were rotting. She could smell the earthy scent of the ground underneath.

"Is anybody with me here tonight? Please say your name."

No answer.

"Do you work at the corral?"

She waited ten seconds in silence. A spider hung off a strand of silk in front of her face. She batted it away and refocused.

She recalled a detail from Layne's story. He had said the man was angry, that he was scowling at him.

"Can you see any robbers out there? Is there anyone trying to steal cattle from the corral?"

A split second later she heard a shriek from outside.

"Lyssa!"

Lyssa jumped up and rushed outside, where Jen was pointing the IR camera straight at the shack.

"Were you just standing in front of the window?"

"No. I was sitting on the floor. Why?"

Jen got right up to the window. She put her hand to it.

"It's the same temperature as the air..."

"Jen! What's going on?"

Jen showed Lyssa the monitor on the IR camera and rewound the tape. Lyssa watched the dark blue image of the shack. Then a ball of intense red light flickered.

"Whoa. What was that?"

"A big hot spot flashed on my screen and then was gone. Did anything happen while you were inside?"

"No," Lyssa said. "I was sitting on the floor. I held the camera and asked questions. But I didn't get a reply. Then you called out. I didn't see a thing."

"What were you asking?"

"The usual...if there was anybody present, if they worked there. Then I asked if there were any robbers. That's right when you called out to me."

"The IR camera registered heat. But there's nothing there... No electricity, no water pipe...nothing that could cause a spike in temperature."

Jen stared at Lyssa without a sound. Lyssa could tell she was puzzled, trying to think of the next step. Finally Jen's face softened.

"Let's look at your footage. There was no reason for that heat to show up out of the blue. Maybe your footage will show us where it came from."

Lyssa played back the last few minutes of her tape. She heard her own voice asking the room if there was anyone trying to steal cattle. Lyssa didn't know what to expect next.

Then she saw something.

"Jen, did you see that?"

"No. See what?"

Lyssa rewound a few seconds, then hit play. The camera was focused on the window. From where Lyssa was sitting, she had a straight shot out of the window. If she looked closely, she could even see the fence in the background. Then, out of the blackness, a sparkle of light shone, like a diamond being dangled on a string. It lasted for only half a second.

"What *was* that?" Jen asked.

"We'll have to look at the footage more closely in the morning. But I think I have an idea of what that was..."

"What?"

Lyssa had no way of knowing for sure, but she had a strong hunch.

"The night watchman," Lyssa said.

Mike and Mark stood in front of the bar in the saloon. The front doors were swinging half doors that didn't go all the way to the floor or the ceiling, so air flowed in freely from the outside. The door moved back and forth slightly with the small breeze. The lone streetlamp cast down a white light that crept in through the huge open windows. Mike shivered and rubbed his hands together—the desert temperature at night was considerably cooler than in the daytime. He looked at the mirror behind the bar and saw the reflection of the empty street through the windows.

"I didn't think to bring a winter coat to Arizona in June," he joked to his brother. Mark laughed and gave the bar a pound.

"We better keep moving to stay warm, then. Let's rock and roll."

Mike spun to face the room and took out the EMF detector.

"The saloon has four basic sections: the bar, tables for eating, a few card tables over there, and the piano and stage," he said. "Layne experienced the activity here by the bar and by the piano. So I say we split up. This place isn't too big. Are you sure you won't get lost, little bro?"

"I think I can handle it, old man," Mark replied. "I'll stay here at the bar and use the audio recorder. You check out the piano."

Mike went across the room to the piano. As he sat down at the piano bench, the old wood gave a groan under his weight. Mike hadn't played piano much since he was a kid. But sitting in front of one now made him feel almost like he was at a recital—a little nervous and excited. He closed his eyes. He could hear the creak of the door. He started to imagine the way the saloon sounded back in 1881: people talking loudly, the clink of glasses, the music of the piano.

After giving the piano a close look, he realized it was a player piano—the kind that plays on its own without a person hitting the keys. Of course Layne didn't see anyone playing it! Mike knew a bit about how these pianos worked. There was a sheet of paper inside the piano that rolled around and around, hitting little tabs that struck the keys from inside. He slid open the little door so he could see the inside of the piano. But there was no paper roll.

Mike turned on his flashlight and looked deep inside the

piano. He stuck his hand in, touching the cool metal. Something felt funny. The metal pieces just sort of hung there. He took his hand out of the compartment and looked at the piano keys. He held his finger over one of the keys and pressed. There was a dull thud.

He began hitting all the keys on the piano, but no notes came out. The piano was completely busted. There was no way it could have made any music.

He got up and turned on the EMF detector. He slowly waved it over the keys, getting a steady reading. Then he moved the EMF detector over the bench. Suddenly the reading spiked. He repeated the movement, but the reading stayed at the same level.

Mike looked under the bench, searching for an electrical outlet, a light socket for the nearby stage...anything that could create an electromagnetic field. But there was just dust.

Jason and Grant sat in the gift shop in the back of Camillus Fly's photo shop, monitoring the investigation.

"It's getting pretty late," Grant said. "I think it's time to wrap things up."

Jason agreed and made the call over the walkie-talkies. Then they began to pack up the Central Command Center. They put all the monitors and computer equipment into sturdy boxes and began bringing them to the front of the store.

On the second trip to the front, Grant stopped to look around at the key chains and postcards that were displayed near the cash register. Something seemed out of place. Something was different than before.

His eyes burned a little. A sharp scent filled his nose.

"Jason, come check this out."

Jason walked over. "What's up?"

"What is that? Flowers?"

Jason looked confused. Then his face lit up.

"Yeah...Oh, man, that is thick. It smells just like my grandma's house. Where is it coming from?"

They looked all over—behind the register and in the racks of T-shirts. Jason found a stepladder and inspected the air-conditioning vent. But the smell wasn't coming from there.

"This is really weird," Grant said. "The smell just came out of nowhere."

He looked up. His eyes caught the gaze of a woman in a photograph hanging above the cash register. There was something amazing about the picture. Her eyes pulled him in. He walked toward it. And as he got closer to the picture, the flowery smell got stronger.

"It's coming from over here," he told Jason.

Soon he was only a few inches away from the woman's face. It was so real he felt like she was really there. Then as quickly as it had come the scent disappeared.

He turned to Jason.

"It's gone," Grant said.

"Like a fan just blew it all out the window," Jason said.

Just then the lights flickered. A moment later the room was plunged into darkness.

"What just happened?" Jason shouted.

"The lights went out!"

Quickly, Grant turned on his flashlight. He ran to get a camera and started snapping pictures of the room. He took twenty in a row of the area near the photograph of the woman. Then, a few seconds later, the lights came back on.

"That was something," Jason said.

"Yeah, but *what*?" Grant asked.

In the morning, the first thing the team did was review the audio that Mark and Mike recorded in the saloon. The team listened, but all they heard was Mark and Mike asking questions. No EVPs. No piano music.

"I'm disappointed," Mike said. "I just figured with everything leading up to this, the music from a broken piano and the high EMF reading...It all led me to think we would catch something on the audio."

"You can't predict what you're going to catch," Grant said. "But how can music come from a broken piano? That's a real find."

"I agree," said Lyssa. "There's no other explanation as to where the music came from."

Mike nodded.

"I guess you guys are right," he said. "Even without an EVP, it *still* adds up to something paranormal."

Next, the team looked at the footage Lyssa and Jen took. They synced up the recordings and played them both frame by frame. The hot spot appeared on Jen's film the exact same instant the light appeared in Lyssa's footage.

"Whoa!" Mark exclaimed. "Look at that! It came out of nowhere!"

"It's definitely not attached to anything," Mike said. "It's just a glowing ball...See, it even moves up and down slightly."

"And you're absolutely sure there was nothing that caused the reflection? Not a flash on the camera, anything like that?" Jason asked.

"There wasn't anything," Lyssa said. "Jen and I looked everywhere. But I have a theory. Layne said the man had beady eyes, that he looked angry. And then I remembered something Mark had mentioned. He had said the cattle ranchers hired watchmen, whose job it was to make sure no one stole their cattle. In the shack, I asked if there were robbers around. That's when we saw the flash. I think the spirit could be a night watchman. Do you guys think it's possible?"

"Sure, it's possible," Jason said. "But without doing more investigating, I don't know if we can prove that. But looking at what you got here, there's clearly something paranormal going on."

Finally, Grant looked at the pictures he took of the gift shop. He stopped on one of the woman above the register. Even in the picture of the picture she looked real. There was just something very eerie about her face and the way she smiled.

"I think it's time we have a talk with Layne," Grant said. "He should know what we found."

When the TAPS team arrived back at Tombstone the next day, groups of visitors were just beginning to show up. The team found Layne near the saloon and waved to him.

"Good morning," Layne said. "I'm eager to hear what you found."

Lyssa showed him the footage of the shining light in the shack.

"We looked for every possible explanation," Jen said. "But we came up with nothing that could make this glow, so we have to conclude that something paranormal is happening."

"That's so strange," Layne said. "That's right where the man I saw was standing."

Then Mike told him about the broken piano.

"With all this evidence, I think we can say the saloon is haunted, too," Mike said.

"But there's one thing that happened I'd like to ask you about," Grant said. "Are there any electrical problems in the gift shop?"

"No. Because of all the tourists, we have maintenance crews working on the buildings at all times."

"Are the lights on any sort of timer?"

"Definitely not. I turn off all the lights at night."

"Do you sell any sort of perfume in the gift shop?"

Layne's eyes widened.

"Mary."

"Who's that?"

"The picture..."

Grant looked stunned. "What do you mean?"

"I thought it was all in my head..." Layne said. "The woman in the picture. Her name was Mary Fly. Her husband owned the photography shop. I've also smelled flowers in the gift shop. Especially when I'm near her photograph."

"That's amazing!" Grant said. "Both Jason and I had the same experience. It's what we call a phantom smell. It's very possible that Mary's spirit is present and shows itself by the scent of her perfume. And what's even stranger is as soon as we found the source of the scent, the lights went out for no reason."

"With so much different activity going on here," Jason explained, "I think the question isn't whether this place is haunted, but what other parts of the town have activity that we don't know about."

"From everything we've seen, this seems to be a residual haunt," Grant concluded. "The spirits have no idea they are in the modern world. They just replay their lives over and over again."

"Sort of like the shoot-out show," Layne said.

"Exactly."

The group said their good-byes and got back in the van. As they pulled out into the desert, Lyssa saw that cars full of tourists were passing by to check out Tombstone—a *real* ghost town.

"*There's something down there.*"

Twelve-year-old Cynthia Parker crouched by her bedroom window, staring down into the backyard. A full moon was slowly creeping up the sky. It shone through the bare branches of the woods just outside the back fence, filling the yard with strange shadows.

Cynthia's older sister, Amanda, peered over Cynthia's shoulder.

"I can't see a thing," she said.

"I heard it," Cynthia insisted. "I heard something moving around."

Every night, the same sound woke Cynthia, and every night

she ran to the window and stared down into the yard. But she never saw the creature making the sound. She just heard it: the deep, steady panting of some enormous animal.

"There's nothing down there," Amanda said, her voice sharp. "You can see that for yourself. There's no reason to get all freaked out."

"I didn't say I was all freaked out."

"But you are. I can hear it in your voice."

So what? Cynthia thought. She scrunched her shoulders so she wasn't touching Amanda. Anybody would be freaked if there might be something in his or her own backyard.

Something strange. Something that did *not* belong. It had to be some kind of wild animal. The nearby woods were filled with them. But Cynthia had never heard an animal that sounded like this.

"I'm going down there," she announced.

"No way," Amanda protested as Cynthia stood up quickly. "Mom's not home yet. You know she's working the late shift at the hospital this week. She'll ground me for a month if I let anything happen to you."

"Nothing's *going* to happen to me," Cynthia said. She started for the bedroom door.

"You don't know that," Amanda argued.

"Sure I do," Cynthia came right back. "You told me so yourself. There's nothing down there."

Before Amanda could stop her, Cynthia rushed out of the bedroom and through the house. She didn't slow down until she reached the door that led to the backyard.

Creeeaaaakkk.

Cynthia was trying to be brave. But just the sound of the back door sent a shiver down her spine. It reminded her of every horror movie she had ever watched: The door would squeak, and then the monster would jump out. But that was just in movies, right? There was no monster.

Was there? Cynthia had to know what was making the strange noise.

Still, she wished she hadn't come down here alone. Cynthia poked her head out the back door. The moon was higher and brighter now. The wind rattled the bare branches of the trees in the woods. The backyard was covered with dead leaves. They made a whispering sound as they blew across the dry grass.

Cynthia tightened her grip on her flashlight. It was a gift from Mom's brother, Uncle Dave, the king of all flashlights. He gave each of them one for Christmas every year.

Cynthia switched on the flashlight. She breathed a sigh of relief as the wide, bright beam of light sliced across the yard. She stepped out onto the back porch steps. She held the flashlight out in front of her, aiming the light at the chain-link fence that separated their yard from the woods.

That's where the sounds came from.

Cynthia lifted her right foot to go down the first of the porch steps—and heard the tiniest whisper of sound *behind* her!

Choking back a cry, Cynthia whirled around.

"Watch it," Amanda whispered. "And get that light out of my eyes."

Heart thundering, Cynthia lowered the flashlight.

"Are you *trying* to scare me to death?" she asked her sister. "Because if so, hey, really good job."

"I'm sorry, all right?" Amanda said. "I decided I couldn't let you go alone."

"Why not?"

There was a pause.

"Because you'd never let me go alone," Amanda finally said.

She turned on her own flashlight. Cynthia muffled a burst of crazy laughter when she realized her older sister had grabbed the biggest flashlight in the house.

"You really think there's something out there, don't you?" Amanda asked.

"Yes," Cynthia said. "I really do."

"All right," Amanda said. "Then let's go find it."

It was Cynthia's idea to walk together, arms linked, straight up the middle of the yard. Cynthia swept her flashlight to the right, Amanda, to the left. The lights the girls carried were powerful enough for them to see the corners of the yard.

But there was nothing to see. So far.

Dead leaves crunched underfoot. When her light hit the chain-link fence, Cynthia could see more dead leaves pressed up against it.

"The neighbors probably think we're nuts," Amanda said after a couple of moments.

"Not the Lutzes," Cynthia replied. The Lutzes lived on the corner. They had garden gnomes in their front yard. A lot of them. Mrs. Lutz even gave them all names.

Amanda grinned. "If Mrs. Lutz sees our lights, she'll probably think aliens are landing."

The girls reached the back fence and stopped.

"Now what?" Amanda asked. "There's no way I'm going any farther than the yard."

"Me, neither," Cynthia said. "You think I'm nuts?"

"Sometimes I do. Like now," Amanda said. She aimed her flashlight through the fence. They could see the woods just beyond the fence. They could make out a narrow grass path leading deeper into the dark woods.

"So we didn't see anything. We didn't even hear anything. Can we go back now?" Amanda said.

"I hear it every night. It has to be some kind of animal," Cynthia said. "I just can't figure out *what* kind. It's not a raccoon."

"How do you know that?"

"Easy," Cynthia said. "The garbage never gets knocked over."

"True," Amanda said. "Maybe it's—" Her voice dropped to a whisper. "What's that?"

"You hear it, don't you?"

Amanda nodded. "I hear something. Footsteps crunching the leaves? Loud breathing. It sounds *big*."

Cynthia listened closely. "It sounds nearby," she whispered. She stepped to the fence, shining her light into the woods. Slowly, she began to move the light along the line of trees.

"There!" Amanda cried.

At the edge of the trees, something caught the light. Two small round objects. They glowed an eerie red.

Cynthia took four quick steps back, then made herself stop.

"What is that?" Amanda whispered. "What *is* it?"

"Eyes," Cynthia suddenly said. Her heart was thumping as if it wanted to jump right out of her chest. She turned to her sister and said, "Do you see them? Right there. Red and glowing—like a monster's eyes."

Then the eyes winked out. When they appeared again, they were even closer. The eyes stared right at Cynthia. She could see the monster was just outside the chain-link fence.

"Oh my gosh," Amanda said. Cynthia could hear Amanda breathing really, really fast. "What kind of animal is it? Can you tell?"

"No. All I can see are its eyes. But they're too far off the ground to be anything small. Maybe it's a deer?"

"No," Amanda said. "If it was a deer, it would have run away by now. Deer always run if people walk toward them. These eyes—they're not moving away. They're watching us."

Cynthia had an awful thought—that the animal was not only watching them, but *hunting* them.

She moved the flashlight back and forth, shining it into the trees. Again the eyes winked out. As if the animal disappeared.

But then there they were again. The eyes were closer.

A lot closer.

Cynthia couldn't believe it. The eyes were now on their side of the fence! Whatever this animal was, it had jumped a high fence. And it was now in their own yard!

"Run, Cynthia!" her sister screamed. *"Run right now!"*

The girls spun around and sprinted back toward the house. The sound of her own breathing filled Cynthia's ears. She could hear Amanda sobbing as she ran beside her.

And behind them, getting closer with every step they took, was the creature. She could hear it panting. She could almost feel its hot breath on her neck.

We're never going to make it, Cynthia thought.

Then, totally without warning, there was a bright light in her eyes. She heard her mother's voice.

"Girls, what on earth?" she cried.

Cynthia saw a dark shape cut in front of the car headlights as her mother dashed toward them. She yanked open the side gate.

"Mom!" Cynthia sobbed out. "Mom, don't let it get us."

And then she and Amanda were in their mother's arms.

It was only later, when everything was quiet, after they'd told their mother what happened — and after she was safely tucked in her own bed — that Cynthia let herself think about what had happened that night.

She shut her eyes and forced herself to remember exactly what she saw in the yard.

Only then did Cynthia realize the truth. The thing that terrified her most of all. The thing she'd seen in the split second before she and Amanda turned to run.

The creature had been inside the yard with them. The eyes had come straight at them. But Cynthia still hadn't seen what the thing was.

I didn't see a body. I couldn't *see a body,* she thought.

What if the thing in the woods didn't have one?

"So remind me how you know these people again?" Jen asked as the SUV rolled toward its destination. Jen was up front with

Grant. Mike was sitting in the back. Jason, Lyssa, and Mark were in the second SUV, along with the equipment.

"I don't actually know *them*," Grant said. "But the girls' uncle, Dave Parker, was my college roommate. We keep in touch. His sister, Holly, called Dave in the middle of the night. She said her daughters saw something really strange in their backyard. They say they saw red glowing eyes that got closer and closer."

"Animal eyes can look red and glowing and scary," Mike spoke up from the back.

"Yes, that's true." Grant nodded. "But here's the strange part. This animal didn't seem to have a body. So naturally, when Dave called me, I told him we would be glad to help."

"Are we there yet?" Mike asked.

Grant laughed. "It is a long way," he admitted. "But at least it's a pretty drive."

Cynthia, Amanda, and their mother lived in northern Vermont in what was called the Northeast Kingdom. Canada was just twenty miles away, on the far side of the woods in back of the Coopers' property. Grant said it was where Holly and Dave grew up. Now Holly was back in her hometown.

It is *beautiful*, Jen thought. But it was also kind of bleak. In Rhode Island, where the TAPS office was, the leaves were still on the trees. Up here, the leaves were all gone. Jen could practically feel winter breathing down her neck.

She seriously hoped that was the only thing she felt. The case report had been, well, really strange.

"Turn off, just ahead," Grant said. "Get on the walkie-talkie to the other SUV, will you, Jen? Tell everybody to get set to roll."

"We're not making all this up, I swear," Cynthia said as soon as the TAPS team sat down.

"We're really not, I promise. We just can't explain it," Amanda added.

The girls' mother, Holly Cooper, sat in a nearby chair. It was no more than an arm's length away, Jen noted.

"I didn't see a thing," Holly admitted. "But I believe the girls."

"Okay, first things first," Grant said. "It's okay that you can't explain what you saw. That won't make us think you're making things up. People come to us with mysteries all the time. Trying to explain them is what we do. That's our job."

"Maybe it would help if you told us exactly what you saw," Lyssa said.

"Eyes," Amanda said simply. "We saw a pair of glowing eyes."

"Okay, eyes," Grant said. "What else did you see? Did it have a shape? A color?"

"No," Cynthia answered. "That's sort of the problem. We couldn't see anything except two glowing eyes."

"Was there anything else?" Lyssa asked.

"There's this funny sort of breathing sound," Cynthia said. "Like a really big animal panting. I've heard it before. The sound keeps me awake at night."

"Cynthia told me about the sound a couple of weeks ago," Holly said. "I admit I didn't think much about it. We *are* pretty close to the woods. There are all sorts of animals out there."

"What happened last night?" Jason asked.

"We heard the sound first," Cynthia began. "It was so dark out, we couldn't see anything. So I decided to go outside with a flashlight to see if I could figure out what it was. I shone the light into the woods. Then I saw the eyes."

"When that thing spotted us, it came right for us," Amanda added. "And we ran for our lives."

"Did it actually get into the yard last night?" Grant asked.

Cynthia and Amanda looked at each other.

"It felt like it did," Cynthia said. "But we didn't hear or see an animal jump a fence. But the eyes got closer and closer. Once I started running, I did *not* look back. Amanda didn't, either."

"Well," Jason said. "I think our first step is perfectly clear."

"Absolutely," Grant agreed. "We check out the backyard while there's still some daylight."

"Of course," Holly said. "I'll take you the same way the girls went. Out through the kitchen."

"I do have one more question, though," Grant said as he fell into step beside Cynthia.

"What?"

"Does your uncle Dave send you guys a flashlight for Christmas every year?"

Cynthia grinned. "How did you know?"

"He does the same for me," Grant said. "They're usually pretty awesome."

"In that case, you're going to love our collection. They're in the kitchen," Cynthia said. "Come on. I'll show you."

Several hours later, the team was assembled in the kitchen, by the back door. They finished their first sweep of the backyard before dark. Now the true investigation was about to start.

"I don't think all six of us need to be out back at once. We'll only end up tripping over one another," Grant began.

"The six stooges," Mike said under his breath.

Jen choked down a laugh.

"So Jen, Mike, and I will take the yard," Grant went on. "Jason, Mark, and Lyssa, you guys stay inside the house and monitor the activity from the girls' room. Jay and I want some readings from up there, since that's where they first heard the sounds. I want to know if anything pops in the house."

"I have audio and visual recorders in key locations throughout the house," Jen reported. "Also outside. There are a couple of cameras on the fence pointing toward the woods where the girls said they saw the eyes. A couple more are on the edge of the roof. We're covering as much of the yard as possible."

"Sounds good," Jason said.

Grant opened the door. "Okay, backyard team, let's go."

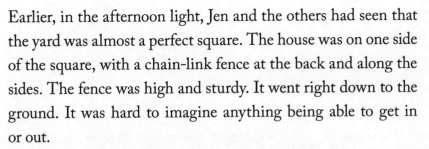

Earlier, in the afternoon light, Jen and the others had seen that the yard was almost a perfect square. The house was on one side of the square, with a chain-link fence at the back and along the sides. The fence was high and sturdy. It went right down to the ground. It was hard to imagine anything being able to get in or out.

Jen glanced behind her. The Coopers' house looked small and somehow lonely. She knew there were other houses in the neighborhood. But in the dark, the other houses all seemed very far away.

"Remember your positions," Grant said in a low voice. "I'm on the right. Mike, you're left. Jen, you're going straight up the middle. We'll meet at the fence. Maintain silence unless you're in trouble. We don't want to get confused by our own voices. Okay, let's move out."

Moving the flashlight slowly back and forth in front of her, Jen began to walk across the yard. Dried leaves crunched underfoot. A cold wind darted down the collar of her coat. She shivered.

The moon was no longer full. But it was still big enough to cast strange shadows across the yard. Jen squinted. The moon was actually making it more difficult to see. Everything looked weird, all wavy and stretched out.

Her flashlight beam danced across the leaf-covered ground, then lit up the metal of the fence. She caught a glimpse of the trees on the other side of it.

What was that?

Jen stopped walking. She wasn't sure, but she thought she heard something that sounded like a deep and steady panting. She opened her mouth to call out to Grant, then shut it again.

I'm not in danger, she thought. *Grant and Mike are close by.*

Jen leaned forward, stretching out her arm as far as it would go. She tried to make the flashlight beam go through the fence to the woods beyond. That's where she thought the sound came from.

I'm not close enough yet, she thought.

Jen took a deep breath, then kept on going, one step at a time.

The night seemed different now that Jen had heard something she couldn't identify. It was full of sounds. She heard the wind whispering through the trees in the woods. Bare branches hitting against each other. The crackle of dead leaves as they blew across the yard. And then another sound. Something on the ground, moving through the leaves.

Jen jumped back as something strong—and soft—pushed against her shoulder. Then she heard a rustling sound at her feet, and a high-pitched scream cut through the night.

She bit back her own cry. Her arm struck out—but there was nothing in front of her.

"Jen!" Grant was by her side. "Are you all right?"

Jen nodded. "I felt something. It touched my shoulder. It was"—she couldn't explain it—"soft?"

"Like feathers?" Grant asked. He shook his head in disbelief. "I saw it. It was the wing of the biggest horned owl I've ever seen."

"And it just caught the biggest rabbit I've ever seen," Mike added with a shudder. "That's what made the screaming sound."

"Poor rabbit," Jen said. Her heart was still racing, and the hand that held the flashlight was shaking. She tried to make her voice sound normal. "Do you think that's what the girls saw? An owl's eyes?"

"I don't know," Grant admitted. "But I don't think owls make panting sounds. And I heard panting before."

"Me too," Mike admitted.

"Me three," Jen said. At least she wasn't the only one who heard the strange sound.

"I think we should keep searching," Grant decided. He and Mike went back to their sides of the yard.

"Right." Jen shone her flashlight in front of her. She wasn't going to let herself get spooked. Great horned owls were a little scary. But they weren't monsters.

Jen had only taken a few steps before she heard the strange panting sound again. She approached the fence. She swung the flashlight. The beam moved across the diamond pattern of the chain-link fence.

What's that?

Jen froze. Just outside the fence, something caught the beam of her flashlight. Caught it and *reflected it back!*

Two glowing red eyes. There was no mistaking them.

The eyes were round. They looked big to Jen—about the size of quarters. In the light of her flashlight, the eyes gleamed bloodred. They looked exactly like what the girls described.

And they were staring right at Jen.

"Guys," she called out. Her voice sounded funny, even to her own ears. "I think I've got something."

Instantly, Grant and Mike swung their flashlight beams in Jen's direction.

"What is it?" Grant asked. "What have you got?"

"Whoa," Mike said. "I can see it now. What *is* that?"

"Eyes," Jen said. "Just eyes. Just like the girls said."

"We've got to move in closer," Grant said. "See if we can

figure out what we're dealing with here. But go slow. We don't want to spook it. Frightened animals can be very dangerous."

Jen began to walk forward, still shining the light out in front of her. Abruptly, she saw the eyes wink out. Then they returned again. Winked out again.

"Whatever it is, I think it's moving," she said. "Maybe turning its head from side to side?"

"Like it's trying to track us," Grant said, his voice low.

As if Grant's words had been some sort of signal, the eyes stayed still. They were gazing straight ahead at Jen once more. Then, slowly but steadily, *they* began to move toward her.

Jen's heart shot straight up into her throat.

It's coming right at me!

"Stop!" Grant commanded. "Jen, Mike. Stop right where you are! We still don't know what we're dealing with. Don't get too close."

One. Two. Three. Four.

Jen counted silently as the thing outside the fence got closer and closer. Her arm ached with the effort she was making to hold the flashlight steady. She felt a trickle of icy sweat creep slowly down her spine.

"But what *is* it?" she asked again in a low voice. "It's so close. Shouldn't we be able to tell what it is by now?"

"I would think so," Grant said. "Unless maybe its fur is dark."

Totally without warning, the eyes seemed to shoot forward.

They were right outside the fence now! As if whatever was out there had taken a giant leap closer.

Jen couldn't help herself. She stepped back with a cry.

"Jen!" Grant was at her side in an instant. "Are you all right?"

"I'm fine," Jen gasped out. "It's just— *why can't we see it?*"

"It's definitely still out there," Mike said. "I think the fence stopped it. But I didn't hear anything hit. If anything hits that chain link, it would make a noise."

The eyes were moving again now. Back and forth, right outside the fence.

"What's it doing?" Jen said.

"Pacing," Grant answered shortly.

"Big cats do that," Mike said. "Could it be a mountain lion?"

"Mountain lions have light-colored coats," Grant said.

"What about a wolf?" Jen suggested. "We're pretty far north."

"We've got to identify what we're dealing with," Grant said. "But now I'm thinking only one of us should try and get closer. Lots of animals pace when they're frightened. Maybe all of us getting closer at once wasn't such a good idea."

"I'll go," Jen offered. "I saw it first. And I feel like it's been staring at me all along."

"You're sure?" Grant asked.

Jen nodded, though her stomach was all tied up in knots.

"I'm sure," she said.

"Be careful, Jen," Grant warned.

"I will," Jen promised.

Slowly, carefully, she began to walk toward the fence once more.

"It's okay. It's all right. I won't hurt you," Jen murmured as she walked. Closer. Closer. Closer. "I just want to see what you are."

She was almost at the fence, holding the light straight out in front of her. Grant and Mike's flashlights were shining to the left and right of her. But all she could see were those round, red eyes. They had stopped moving. They were right on the other side of the chain-link fence, gazing right at Jen.

Like whatever it is, is waiting for me, Jen thought.

And then, all of a sudden, the eyes were gone.

Jen's heartbeat pounded in her ears. As if from very far away, she could hear Grant and Mike yelling. But Jen couldn't understand the words. All her focus was directed at just one thing.

The eyes.

Where were they? Where did they go?

Then Jen heard the strange, deep panting sound again. This time it was right behind her.

The creature was *in the yard!*

Jen spun around. The beam of her flashlight swung crazily. For a moment, she thought she caught a glimpse of Mike's terrified face. Then her light found the eyes. Red and glowing, they stared right at her.

The creature stood between Jen and the house.

Grant and Mike had stopped yelling. Except for the sound of the wind in the trees and the frantic pounding of Jen's own heart, the night was absolutely silent.

Jen tried to swallow, but she couldn't. Her throat was too dry. The glowing eyes moved closer. And closer.

This was all wrong. Most wild animals fled when humans got close to them. They didn't jump a fence to come after you.

Unless you were their prey.

Jen backed up. One step. Two steps—until she felt the cold metal of the chain-link fence press against her back.

She heard the panting sound again. She felt the animal's hot breath. Jen couldn't help what she did next. She reached her hand out to touch the creature.

She only touched air. There was nothing to touch. No fur. No head. No body.

And then Jen knew. The reason she couldn't see or feel the body was because the creature didn't have one.

It's not an animal. It's a ghost.

Slowly, hardly daring to move, Jen took a step sideways to the left. The burning red eyes also moved to the side. And then slowly, relentlessly, they began to move toward her.

The ghost had her trapped!

"Grant," Jen said urgently. "Whatever this thing is, it's coming straight toward me. I've got the fence at my back. I don't know what to do."

"Stay calm, Jen," Grant said at once. "Don't make any sudden moves. I'm going to try to distract it. If you see the eyes turn away from you, run toward Mike."

"Will do," Jen said. *Hurry!* she thought.

"Here. Over here!" Grant cried out.

Jen could see him waving his arm back and forth. For a long moment, the glowing eyes stayed steady, staring at Jen. She held her breath.

"Here!" Grant cried again. He moved the flashlight beam in fast, tight jerks. The light danced wildly. The eyes turned toward Grant. Jen heard a deep-throated growl.

"Go!" Grant shouted.

Jen sprinted toward the light of Mike's flashlight. She felt a strange current of ice-cold air move past her.

Then, nothing. The night around her was perfectly still. Perfectly calm.

"Whoa," Grant said.

"What happened?" Jen gasped out.

"The eyes vanished," Grant said. "Whatever that thing was, it's gone."

"Please tell me that we got some of what happened in the backyard," Grant said several hours later. The TAPS team was gathered in a motel room. They wanted to review the evidence right away.

"I've been going over the video from outside," Mike said. "Take a look." He tapped on the keyboard and the laptop screen went dark. A moment later, three flashlight beams appeared.

"Okay, that's us," Grant said.

The TAPS team watched in silence for several moments. Jen realized she was holding her breath.

"There!" Mike suddenly said. He pointed at the screen. "Right there. You can see the eyes. They're as spooky on-screen as they were in person."

Jen kept her attention on the center flashlight beam. *That's me*, she thought. She watched as the light moved closer and closer to the fence and to those gleaming red eyes.

Totally without warning, the eyes seemed to rise in the air. They sailed over the fence, then came down on the other side.

"Wow," Jason said. "That's incredible."

"How tall is that fence, would you say?" Mark asked.

"At least five feet," Grant replied.

Mark scratched his head. "What kind of an animal can jump a fence that high?"

"That's the million-dollar question," Jason said. "A mountain lion or a bobcat could do it. And maybe a wolf. Bears can climb trees."

"But it wasn't a normal animal," Jen said. "It was some kind of paranormal being."

Things were happening very fast on the playback now. Jen watched herself make a sudden movement, then come to a screeching halt. And those eyes...

"You're sure it was paranormal?" Jason asked.

"I'm positive," Jen said. "The eyes were practically staring into my face. They looked like headlights, they were so bright. I could feel its breath. But when I tried to touch it—there was nothing there. The next second, it was as if the eyes went right through me. That creature wasn't normal, Jason. It was definitely some kind of ghost or spirit."

Mike hit a key and the laptop screen went dark.

The next morning, the TAPS team returned to the Coopers' house. But they didn't go inside. Instead, they headed for the woods behind the fence.

"What do you think is going on?" Jen asked Grant as they walked through the bare trees.

The path near the Coopers' yard went straight for a while. Then it branched off. The TAPS team divided up into the same groups as the night before: Jen, Grant, and Mike in one, Jason, Lyssa, and Mark in the other.

"Have you ever investigated an animal haunting?" Jen went on when Grant didn't reply. "Whatever was out there—I *know* it didn't have a body. So where does that leave us?"

"With a ghost," Mike replied. "There are lots of stories about animal spirits and ghosts. They've been around forever."

Jen stepped carefully to avoid a big tree root that stretched across the path.

"Grant still hasn't said anything," she commented. "He's hoping I won't notice."

Grant smiled. "I don't know any more than you guys do," he reminded her. "But I think your conclusions are right. I think we've pretty well debunked the idea that this is a living animal."

Grant's walkie-talkie suddenly came to life. "This is Jason to Grant. Come back. Over."

"Grant here. What's up, Jay? Over."

"Double back and follow the second path to our location," Jen heard Jason's voice say. "I think we've found something."

"Wow, check it out," Mike said about twenty minutes later.

He and Jen and Grant were staring at a small, wooden building in a clearing. Its tar paper roof had holes in it. A few boards were missing from the front door.

"It's an old cabin of some kind," Jen said. "It's practically falling apart."

"Hey," Grant said as Lyssa, Jason, and Mark stepped into the clearing. "What did you guys find?"

"We're not sure," Jason admitted. "That's why I wanted all of us to look at it together. Lyssa's already taken some pictures. We'll let you guys go in first. We've got some strange readings here. I think something's here, inside the cabin."

Jason pushed open the door. It sagged on old, rusty hinges that made a sound like something screaming in pain.

Jen stepped inside first. The cabin's floor was made of dirt. On the far side, across from the door, there was a window. Jen could see jagged pieces of glass sticking up like broken teeth. There wasn't any furniture, only a rusted metal tube that looked like a stovepipe from an old wood-burning stove.

Jen stepped all the way in, pausing for a moment to let her eyes adjust to the dim light. The cabin felt small and cramped. Had someone actually lived here? There was barely enough room for a table, a chair, and maybe a bed. And the smell—

The air had a strange smell. Like rotted leaves...and something more. As if something got trapped here and never got out.

Jen had a bad feeling about this place. Something had died here, she was sure of it. She wanted to run outside, back into the sunlight.

But she couldn't move. She just stared at the floor. There was a big pile of bones just a few steps from where she stood. Jen felt as if a piece of ice just slid down her back. Was this the creature whose spirit had come after her last night?

"Grant," she said, trying to keep her voice calm. "I think you're going to want to see this."

Jen stepped out of the way so Grant could get a closer look. After a couple of minutes, Jason and the others crowded in, too. The TAPS team filled the small, dusty space.

"Do you know what it is?" Jen asked.

"Whatever it was, it was big," Jason answered.

No kidding, Jen thought. Bones of a huge rib cage curved up into the air. The skull was long, the teeth enormous. And there were large bones that were clearly legs.

"I don't think it's a mountain lion," Grant observed. He pointed to the head. "See, the head is too long. I think a cat's skull would be shorter and flatter."

"Could it be a wolf?" Lyssa asked.

"I suppose it could be," Grant said. "We wondered about that last night. But why would a wolf come inside a cabin to die?"

"To get out of the cold?" Mike asked, his tone only half joking.

Grant shook his head. "Wolves are too wild for that. There's got to be a connection between this place and the animal."

"Maybe it was injured," Lyssa suggested. "With just the bones, there's no way to tell."

"I wonder how long it's been here," Jen said.

Grant frowned. "There's no way to tell that, either. Not by just looking at the skeleton, anyway. We would have to send the bones to a lab."

Jason turned on his flashlight. "Let's make sure there's nothing else in here."

For the next half hour the team searched the cabin, inside and out. But aside from the bones and the old stovepipe, there was nothing to find.

"All we know is that a big animal died here," Jason said at last.

"And," Jen added, "we've got a pretty good idea that its spirit is still around."

"An old cabin?" Holly Cooper echoed an hour or so later.

The TAPS team had gone straight from the woods to the Coopers' house. They told them what they found.

"Oh, I know," she said. "It must be the old Maguire place. People always called it a hunting lodge."

"Do any of the Maguires still live around here?" Grant asked.

Holly shook her head. "No. They moved away years ago. Right after…" Holly sat up a little straighter, as if she had been poked by a pin. "Wait a minute. Oh my gosh. You don't suppose…"

"What?" Jen asked.

Holly turned to Grant. A frown creased her brow. "You're absolutely certain those bones aren't human?" she asked.

"*Mom,*" Cynthia and Amanda said at the same time.

"The four legs rule out human," Grant replied. "We're just not sure what kind of animal it was. From what we saw, I'd say we found the remains of a wolf, or maybe a very large dog."

All of a sudden, the frown on Holly's face smoothed away.

"Of course," she said. "Edgar Maguire's dog.

"Edgar Maguire was my grandfather's age," Holly went on. "He was kind of a local legend. Always prowling around in the woods, even in the wintertime. One year, he went out during a storm—the worst storm of the year—and never came back. Everyone around here searched and searched. But they never found him. To this day, I don't think anybody knows what really happened."

"And..." Cynthia prompted. "Come on. Don't be so mysterious. Jeez, Mom."

"I don't mean to be," Holly answered with a smile. "If somebody I know would stop interrupting..."

Amanda gave a snort of laughter.

"I could get to the part where Mr. Maguire had a dog. I think its name was King. He went everywhere with Mr. Maguire. I remember King seemed absolutely huge, big as a wolf. But then, I wasn't very old at the time. Everyone thought that dog was with Mr. Maguire when he disappeared. No one ever saw either of them again."

"Maybe the dog survived the storm," Jen said softly. "And it came back to the cabin, looking for its master."

"You think the skeleton in the cabin might be King?" Cynthia asked.

"I'm still not sure what I think," Grant admitted. "Is there a vet in town?"

"Of course," Holly said. "I can give you the address." She got up.

"But if you found bones, shouldn't we bury them?" Cynthia asked. "I mean, even if it isn't Mr. Maguire's dog. I'd want somebody to do that if I lost an animal."

Amanda nodded. "Maybe that's why the ghost came to us. He was trying to let someone know that he needed help."

"I think burying the bones is a great idea," Jen said. "If a human body isn't buried properly, sometimes the spirit will wander. I don't see why it should be any different for a dog."

"Where do you think the dog should be buried?" Grant asked.

"Right outside the cabin," Cynthia said at once. "That was his home. I think King's ghost was roaming around, looking for his master."

"The cabin is where they stayed when Mr. Maguire went

hunting," Amanda added. "That's where the dog waited for him. I think that's where King would be at peace."

Holly came back into the room. She handed Grant a slip of paper. "That's the number for the vet," she said. She put an arm around each of her daughters. "I heard what you girls suggested. I think that sounds like the right thing to do. Then maybe King's ghost will be able to rest."

"I'm glad to hear that," Grant said. "Hey, you, too, man. Talk to you later. Tell Holly and the girls we all say hi."

Smiling, Grant hung up the phone. He turned to the rest of the TAPS team. Everyone was sitting at their desks, staring at him. It was about a week after the investigation at the Cooper home.

"That was Dave," Grant said. "As if you couldn't tell. He said he just talked to Holly. Everything is quiet. There have been no more sightings of the ghost dog. Looks like burying those bones near the cabin finally laid the old dog to rest."

"That's good news," Jen said.

Grant nodded. "It is."

"I wonder what happened to Edgar Maguire," Mike said.

"I've been wondering about that, too," Grant admitted. "Maybe we'll never know. And maybe his bones are out there someplace, waiting to be found. Maybe one day, we'll get a call."

At just that moment, the telephone rang.

"Oh, man," Mark exclaimed as Lyssa picked up the phone. "Now *that's* what I call spooky!"

"The Atlantic Paranormal Society," Lyssa said. "How can I help you?"

RUNAWAY GHOST

New Hampshire, 1925

There's no going back now.

Frank Thompson paused on the steep stairs of Bryant House. He craned his neck, staring into the darkness. His breath came in short, quick gasps. Sweat trickled down his back, hot and sticky. The air around him felt thick, as if he were trying to breathe through a towel. Frank could hear rain drumming on the roof overhead.

He wasn't supposed to be up here. Nobody was.

But Frank had never been very good about following the rules. That was how he'd ended up in Bryant House in the first place.

Bryant House. It sounded like some fancy hotel. Frank figured the name of the place made all the parents and guardians who put kids there feel better about what they did.

It didn't help the boys inside very much, though.

Bryant House was named after its founder, Silas Bryant. But Bryant House was no hotel. It was much more like a prison. Boys were sent here "for their own good." And nobody who went into Bryant House ever came back out unless Silas Bryant said so.

Frank Thompson was going to change all that. He was breaking out of Bryant House. Tonight. Right now. He couldn't stay here. Not now that he knew Mama was so sick.

She needs me, Frank thought. *And all I've ever done is let her down.* That was something else that Frank was going to change. He'd take care of Mama. He would make everything all right again.

Once he got out of Bryant House.

Frank continued to climb the stairs, careful to walk on the balls of his feet. He tested each step before he put his full weight on it. He didn't want the steps to creak and give him away. When he arrived at the top of the stairs, Frank paused to catch his breath once more. He was in good shape, but having to go quietly was starting to wear him down. He didn't want to get caught. He *couldn't* get caught.

Frank reached up, standing on his tiptoes, stretching his

arms as far as they would go. He wasn't very tall. Other boys picked on him because of his height. But Frank was a fighter. Nobody picked on him these days, at least not more than once.

There! His pulse racing with excitement, Frank found with his fingers what he was searching for: the outline of the trapdoor that would take him to the attic at the very top of the house. The attic had four windows, one on each side. You could see them as you walked around the outside of the house.

All Frank had to do was climb out the window closest to the big old maple tree that stood on the right side of the house. But the roof was steep. And it was made of slate. It would be slippery because of the rain. If Frank wasn't careful, he could fall and break his neck.

That would make Tyrant Bryant happy, he thought. *One less boy to worry about.*

Frank's searching fingers found the rope that would open the trapdoor. He pulled. Hard. The trapdoor swung open with a groan. The rickety set of steps swung down. Frank put one foot on the first rickety step and tested his weight.

The step creaked a little, but it held him. So he took another step. And another.

A few minutes later, he was in the attic. Frank bent down and heaved the trapdoor closed. There was no sense in leaving it open. There was no way Frank was going back. He was only going out.

He paused for a moment to get his bearings. Because of the windows, even at night, the attic was not as dark as the hall. Frank could make out vague objects scattered throughout the room. Old furniture and trunks. The trunks might contain something valuable. Maybe there was something he could sell once he was on his own. But he couldn't take time to investigate now. He fought down the temptation to explore.

He had to keep going. He had to get out of Bryant House.

Any minute now, it would be time for bed check. The warden would walk up and down the rows of beds and see that his bed was empty. The alarm would be raised. A search would be started. Frank wanted to be far away from the house before any of that happened.

Frank turned to the right and made his way over to the window. It was raining harder now. He could see the rain bouncing off the slate roof.

He turned the lock at the top of the window. Then he knelt down to push the window up. It didn't move. The window was stuck shut!

No! Frank thought. *No.* He could feel adrenaline rushing through his veins. What if the warden and the others were already looking for him? Frank didn't want to think about what would happen to him if Tyrant Bryant found him in the attic.

I have to get away. I have to get away now! Frank heaved with all his might. With a screech, the window shot up.

Frank quickly straddled the sill, sticking one leg out into the downpour. He had spent a lot of time outside in the last few weeks doing yard work on this side of the house. So he knew exactly what he had to do now.

The roof outside the attic was very steep. The only way to get down it was to slide. At the bottom, the roof flattened a little, becoming less steep as it leveled out to cover the right wing of the house. If Frank could make it to that section of the roof, then he could walk—very carefully—over to the maple tree, leap into its branches, and climb down to the ground.

And then he would be free, *free*, FREE!

Frank turned to face into the attic. He swung his other leg outside onto the roof. Clinging to the sill, he stretched himself out to his full length. Rain pounded down onto his body, dripped down into his eyes. Frank was sopping wet in an instant.

He let go and began to slide.

Fast! Too fast!

Frank's body whooshed down the wet slate of the roof like ice skates over a smooth, icy pond. Frank put his hands down flat, desperate to try anything that could slow him down.

Whack! Thump!

He landed on the lower section of the roof so hard he saw stars. Frank felt a sharp pain shoot up his left leg.

No! he thought. *NO!*

If he hurt his leg, he wouldn't be able to run.

Slowly, Frank rolled over. His left leg was throbbing with pain. Carefully, Frank touched his calf. It hurt worse than anything he had felt in his whole life, but he didn't think it was broken. No bones were sticking out.

Keep going, he told himself fiercely. *Don't stop now.*

Slowly, Frank got to his knees. Then he carefully stood up. Sharp pain shot through his whole body as he put his left foot down. He picked it up quickly, then windmilled his arms as the sudden change made him lose his balance for a moment.

The tree. I have to get to the tree, he thought. *Even if I have to crawl.*

Frank dropped back to his knees. Rain dripped down his face and ran off the bottom of his chin. The rain bounced up from the roof and into his eyes. But Frank was determined. He began to crawl on his hands and knees along the roof, toward the big maple tree.

Almost there, he thought. *I can make it. I can make it!*

What was that?

Were those sounds below voices? Yes. He could hear voices shouting. Calling out his name.

No! Frank thought. *No!* It was too soon. He was supposed to have been far away by now. So far that nobody would ever catch him and lock him up again.

The maple tree loomed in front of him. His left leg screaming in agony, Frank got to his feet. He had to do it. There wasn't any other choice.

He bent his knees and jumped.

At the last second, his left leg gave way. Frank felt something go *snap* as he pushed down with all his might. He screamed in agony and fear as he tumbled through the air. Not into the branches of the maple tree the way he'd hoped. But out into the cold and rainy night. Now the only direction he could go was down, down, down.

And the only thing to meet him, the last thing Frank would ever know, was the cold, wet ground.

Present day. On the road.

"Hey, Jen. What's up?" Grant said into the speakerphone. He and Jason were together in one of the TAPS SUVs. They were returning from out of state. The rest of the team were in the office.

"Where are you guys?" Jen's voice filled the car.

Jason checked the GPS, since Grant was driving. "We're still in New Hampshire, near Concord," he said. "We should be back at the office by the end of the day. What's up?" Jason repeated Grant's question.

"We just got this unusual phone call," Jen explained. "We

talked it over and decided it was one you guys should know about. It's in New Hampshire, pretty near Concord, as a matter of fact."

"Really. What do we need to know?" Grant asked.

"Yeah," Jason said. "Fill us in."

"Well, first off," Jen said, "our client claims she's been stabbed by a ghost."

"Who's there?" a low voice asked.

Jason and Grant were standing on a wide front porch. But it was so overgrown with bushes and trees that the porch seemed small and gloomy.

And dark, Grant thought. *This actually* looks *like a haunted house.*

"It's Jason Hawes and Grant Wilson," Jason said. "We're here from The Atlantic Paranormal Society. You called our office this morning, ma'am."

The front door opened a crack. A pair of eyes peered out.

"I'd like to see some identification, please," the quiet voice said.

Jason and Grant got out their driver's licenses and held them up. There was a moment of silence while the person inside looked them over. Then the door opened a little wider, just wide enough for the two men to fit through.

"Please, come inside." They stepped through the front door into a narrow hallway. "I really do thank you for coming so quickly," the woman said as she led them down the hall.

Just as Grant had expected, the hall was dark. But when the trio reached the kitchen, he got a surprise. The room was bright and cheerful. Brightly colored bowls of different colors sat on open shelves.

There were two big windows with cheery yellow curtains. The curtains were pulled back to let in the sunshine. Through the windows, Grant could see a neat and tidy backyard. There were flower beds filled with purple-and-white petunias. Vegetable beds grew lettuce and tomatoes. A crab apple tree filled with bright red fruit stood just outside the kitchen door.

"I didn't mean to sound like you weren't welcome," the client went on. Like her kitchen and garden, the older woman was neat as a pin. Her face was lined with wrinkles, but her eyes were blue and bright.

"But I can't be too careful. A woman like me, all on her own. My name is Abigail McGrath. But then your staff would have told you that, I suppose."

"We're pleased to meet you," Jason said. "And we understand your concerns. We want you to feel comfortable. Would you like to tell us what's been going on? The staff member who called us said you believe you've been hurt by a ghost."

"Yes," Mrs. McGrath said calmly. "I was."

She turned around. Now both Jason and Grant could see a white bandage on one shoulder. Mrs. McGrath patted the bandage.

"This happened just last night. I've been worried and upset before, of course, but this...well, this was simply the last straw. I knew I had to call someone. Whatever's going on inside this house, the time has come for it to stop.

"I've lived here for more than fifty years," Mrs. McGrath continued in her quiet voice. "First with my husband, Leo, then on my own when he died. I've never had a bit of trouble until just lately."

She gave a quick shudder. As if to distract herself from bad memories, she went to the cupboard and got down three cups. She poured coffee and carried them to the table, then brought milk and sugar and finally a plate of cookies.

Grant watched Abigail McGrath as she moved around the kitchen. His eyes took in the details of the room. He got so busy doing this that he jumped when Jason laid a hand on his shoulder.

"Check out the top of the fridge," Jay said in a low voice.

Grant nodded. "I know," he whispered back.

On top of the fridge was a big piece of wood with half a dozen knife handles sticking out of it. *A knife block,* he thought. *That's what people call it.*

"You keep your knives on top of the refrigerator?" Grant asked as Mrs. McGrath finally sat down.

"Oh, yes," she said calmly. "I know it must seem odd, but my niece has a young son. That boy loves to climb. Would you believe I actually found him swinging from the chandelier above the dining room table once? I forgot to push one of the chairs in, and he climbed right up on it. From there he got onto the table, and after that—"

She broke off with a smile. "Anyhow. I didn't want to run the risk of his getting into the knives. So I keep the knife block on top of the fridge. I figured it would be out of reach way up there."

"Makes sense to me," Jason admitted. All of a sudden, he grinned. "You know, *my* mom claimed I swung from the dining room chandelier when I was a boy. I always figured she was making it up. Guess I'm going to have to call her up and apologize."

"Maybe you should have joined the circus," Grant suggested.

"I thought I had."

"You boys sound just like brothers," Mrs. McGrath commented. "How nice."

"Mrs. McGrath," Grant said, his expression serious now, "will you please tell us what happened last night?"

"I went to bed about eleven, like I always do," she said. "All day long, I was kind of jumpy. I think it was all the noise from down the street, where they're tearing down the old Bryant House. It was a reform school—what we used to call a home for wayward boys."

Mrs. McGrath paused.

"Wayward," she said quietly. "Such an interesting word, don't you think? They weren't bad boys. Not all of them. They just didn't fit in, and so they got locked up."

She gave herself a little shake, like she was waking up from a dream.

"I'm sorry," she said. "Where was I?"

"Last night," Grant prompted.

"Oh, yes. That's right. Well, I went to bed, but I couldn't sleep. I kept hearing all these noises. Like somebody was banging around inside the house. I didn't really want to get up. Night is when all the bad things happen."

"Like what?" Jason asked.

"Well," Mrs. McGrath said quietly, "just last week, I heard a noise in the living room. When I got there, all the books were pulled out of the bookshelves. When I went to put them back, one came flying through the air and hit me on the head pretty hard.

"The next night, while I was making a cup of hot chocolate before bed, the burner on the stove I was using went out. But all the other ones came on full strength. The oven door banged open and closed.

"I went out to the living room. I didn't want to get burned. When I went to sit in my favorite chair, I felt a pair of hands on my shoulders. They pushed me down, hard."

"All that sounds pretty scary," Grant said.

"Well, yes," Mrs. McGrath said. "It was." She looked at Grant and Jason for a minute. Her blue eyes moved from one face to the other. "I don't know how you were raised," she said, "but I was raised to solve my own problems. I don't like to ask for help. But after last night..."

Her voice trailed off.

"But anyway, last night I heard a noise, as I said," she continued. "The noise came from the kitchen. I was afraid to get up. But I told myself I had to do it. I refuse to be afraid in my own home.

"So I got out of bed and went down the hall. The kitchen was completely dark. And that was strange. I keep a night-light on in every room to help me find my way around.

"I was just stepping into the kitchen when something pushed me from behind. I stumbled across the room and ran face-first into the fridge. Then I felt two hands turn me around. They pushed me back against the fridge a second time. Something hit my head so hard I saw stars, and I felt a sharp pain in my shoulder.

"I think I must have fainted. The next thing I remember, I was sitting on the ground. I got to my hands and knees and crawled across the room to turn on the light.

"That's when I saw the knife block on the floor. But there was just one knife out of the block. The blade was pointing straight at me. I *was* afraid then. Afraid that I'd been harmed by whoever is haunting this house. That's when I knew I had to have help. I can't go on like this. Something has to be done. Can you help me?"

"Okay," Grant said later that night. "Let's go over the setup."

He and Jason were talking in low tones in the entry hall. Mrs. McGrath was already in bed. Except for the hall light above Grant's and Jason's heads, the rest of the house was dark. Mrs. McGrath promised not to come out of her room unless she felt she was in danger.

"We don't have a camera with us, so it's audio only. There's a voice recorder on the kitchen counter and one in the living room, as well."

"But we'll each be wearing our own recorders," Jason put in. "I'll have an EMF detector. You'll have a flashlight. That way, each of us will have one hand free."

"Right." Grant nodded. "I'm thinking maybe we should start in the living room, then work our way to the kitchen. There have been occurrences in both places, according to Mrs. McGrath."

"Right there with you," Jason said. "Let's make it happen."

"Okay," Grant said. "And we're going dark in five, four, three, two, *one*."

He hit the hallway light switch. The light went out, and the house was plunged into total darkness.

"This is Grant," Grant said several moments later. He was marking a level for the voice recorder. "Jason is with me. We're heading to the living room now."

He switched on the flashlight. A thin white beam sliced through the dark.

"Entering the living room," Grant continued.

"EMF readings low and steady," Jason reported.

"Roger that."

Grant walked slowly into the room. He shone the flashlight around. To the right was a giant stone fireplace with built-in bookcases on both sides. All the books were right where they belonged.

"I'm going to try to make contact," Grant said.

"Go for it."

Grant cleared his throat. "Hello? My name is Grant, and with me is Jason. Is there anybody else here with us?"

Grant paused. He and Jason stood back to back in the middle of the living room. Grant faced toward the street now. He swept his flashlight beam slowly back and forth. He knew Jason was doing the same with the EMF meter right behind him.

"Reading is coming up a little," Jason said. "I've got four lights now."

"If you're here, we'd really like to meet you," Grant continued. "We're trying to understand what's going on in this house. If there is someone here with us, can you give us a sign?"

"Whoa," Jason suddenly said. He pivoted quickly so he and Grant were standing side by side. "Super-big spike." He held out the EMF meter so Grant could see it. The EMF meter was reading eight lights, almost as high as things got.

"Well, that rocks."

"What now?"

"Well, I'm thinking we should—"

All of a sudden, Grant felt Jason's hand squeeze his arm. Hard.

"What's that?" he said, his voice low and urgent. "Over by the window. Do you see what I'm seeing?"

Grant looked. He felt a cold shiver slide down his spine.

In front of the house was a big streetlight. It made a glow through the curtains even when they were closed. In the center of the window, directly in front of Jason and Grant, was a big black mass. An enormous shadow.

"I'm going to try something," Grant said quietly.

"Right with you, bro. Go for it," Jason replied.

Grant stepped left. Jason moved also. The dark shadow shifted so that it stayed right in front of them. The two men stepped back to their original locations, and the shadow moved, too.

"That answers that," Grant said. "I'd say we're definitely dealing with something intelligent. I'm going to try to make contact again."

He opened his mouth to speak. Before Grant could so much as make a sound, the shadow swooped toward him.

"Look out!" Jason cried.

Jason and Grant dove in opposite directions. The shadow kept on coming. It went straight to Grant. He tripped over a footstool and fell over backward.

And then the shadow was on top of him.

Icy cold swept over Grant. It seemed to him that he could feel two strong hands on his chest, pushing and pushing. It pinned him down on the floor!

Grant couldn't see. A dark mist covered his eyes. He thought he could hear Jason calling his name, but he couldn't be sure.

Then, just like that, it was over. The shadow was gone. Grant could see and breathe once more. Instantly, Jason was at his side. He helped him sit up.

"Grant," Jason said. "Talk to me, buddy. Are you all right?"

"I'm okay. I'm okay," Grant said. He took a couple deep breaths. "But I need a minute here. That was pretty wild."

"The EMF meter was lit up all the way to the top!" Jason said. "Something major definitely just went down."

"Tell me about it," Grant said with a short laugh. He got to his feet. He took a few more deep breaths. "Okay. Better now. Well, I think that answers the first question. There's definitely an entity inside this house."

"Next stop, the kitchen," Jason said. "Come on. Let's go check it out."

Quickly yet carefully, Grant and Jason walked toward the kitchen. They paused in the doorway. Grant flicked the flashlight around the room. Everything was right where it belonged. Pale moonlight shone in through the windows, giving the room an eerie glow.

Grant moved the flashlight beam so that it lit up the top of the refrigerator. The knife block was in its usual place. It just didn't have any knives. Grant and Jason took them out earlier in the day. The two wanted the scene to be as close to the night of Mrs. McGrath's attack as it could be, but knives were nothing to mess around with.

Better safe than sorry, Grant thought.

"We're entering the kitchen," Grant heard Jason whisper behind him.

Grant stepped across the threshold.

One ... two ... three ... four ...

Grant realized he was counting his steps silently as he walked across the room. So far, everything was quiet. But the air felt funny, like it was filled with static electricity. Grant could feel the back of his neck prickle. The hair stood up all along his arms.

"What's the EMF reading?" he asked Jason.

"High," Jason said. "But that could just be the appliances. The kitchen's full of them."

"Let's head toward the fridge," Grant said. "Let me know if the reading changes."

"Will do," Jason said. "Whoa... *Ouch!*"

Totally without warning, Jason stumbled back. Grant felt a blast of cold air sweep by him. He spun around.

The dark shadow hung in the air between him and Jason, cutting the two friends off from each other. Grant couldn't even *see* Jason, the shadow was so dense and dark.

"Jay!" Grant cried. "Are you all right?"

"It's okay. I'm okay," Jason answered at once. "Something pushed me back, and I think I just got *slapped*."

"Oh, man," Grant said. "That is absolutely wild!"

"My name is Jason," Jason said. "Grant is with me. We don't mean you any harm. We just want to understand who you are. Did you once live here? Was this house your home? If the answer is yes, open the cupboard above the sink."

Jason paused. All of a sudden, Grant realized he was holding his breath. He let it out slowly, without a sound. The shadow continued to hang in the air between them. The kitchen was intensely cold.

"We want to understand why you're here," Grant spoke up. "We want to help. Are you angry or upset about something? Is that why you're in this house?"

The shadow moved. Once again, Grant felt strong hands push against him, hard. He fell back several steps, then got his balance. Then he was pushed back again.

Wham!

Grant smacked into the refrigerator. The back of his head whacked against the freezer door. Running totally on instinct, he raised his arms to protect the top of his head, just as the knife block came hurtling down.

Crash! Thunk!

The heavy wooden knife block banged against the floor.

"Grant!" Jason cried.

But Grant couldn't reply. He was too busy trying to catch his breath.

The dark shadow hung in the air in front of him. Then, very slowly, it began to fade out. It grew thinner and thinner until Grant could see Jason through it. Then, like fog disappearing when the sun comes out, the shadow was gone.

Grant looked down. The knife block was right in front of him. He shone the flashlight on it. Where it landed, there was a big dent in the floor.

"Wow," Jason said as he walked over. "Would you take a look at that? I'm glad that dent's not in your head, buddy."

"Yeah," Grant said. "You and me both." He blew out a breath. "Okay, so. What we both experienced has convinced me. There is definitely an entity in this house. The question is, did it intentionally injure Mrs. McGrath?"

Jason thought for a moment.

"You just had an experience that was almost identical to hers," he finally said. "You both got pushed back against the fridge. *Hard.* That's what made the knife block fall off: the impact of a body hitting the fridge. *You* didn't get cut, because we'd removed the knives ahead of time."

"But if we hadn't done that," Grant filled in, "chances are very good I would have been cut, too. Which means we can debunk a deliberate stabbing, but *not* an attack. I *was* pushed. I could feel hands on my shoulders."

"So the questions are who pushed you and Mrs. McGrath, and why?"

"I'd say some research is in order," Grant said. "The entity in this house is one angry spirit. We need to find out why."

"So, let's review what we've got on the McGrath case," Grant said. "I want to get this wrapped up so Mrs. McGrath can go back home."

Grant and Jason were back in the TAPS office. Neither of the

TAPS founders felt good about leaving Mrs. McGrath alone. Her niece lived in a nearby town, and she'd been meaning to visit, so Jason and Grant encouraged her to go. She was there now, waiting for the results of the TAPS investigation. Jason, Grant, and Mark were going over evidence in the conference room.

"Why don't you go first, Mark?" Grant suggested.

"There's not a lot to go on," Mark reported. "I found records for the house, of course. But aside from when it was built and who built it, there's not much there. No reports of unusual incidents over the years. No deaths, violent or otherwise. The only thing that seemed at all like it might tie in is that the house was built by a man named Silas Bryant."

"Bryant," Grant said. "How come that sounds familiar?"

"That's the interesting part," Mark replied. "In the early nineteen hundreds, Silas Bryant founded a school for what we'd now call troubled youths. Specifically, boys."

"Bryant House!" Jason exclaimed. He turned to Grant. "Mrs. McGrath mentioned that, didn't she?"

"She did," Grant agreed. "She said they were tearing the old place down."

"I did some research about Bryant House itself," Mark continued. "Apparently, old Silas Bryant was a pretty strict guy. His nickname was Tyrant Bryant. Several old newspaper articles I read mentioned boys trying to run away. One of them actually *died* trying."

"That *is* interesting," Jason said. "Did you find out anything about him?"

Mark checked his notes.

"His name was Frank Thompson," he said. "Apparently, he had some bad news the afternoon before he tried to break out. His mother was seriously ill. So Frank tried to bust out. That night, there was a big rainstorm. The newspaper mentions it because the storm went on to cause flooding in the town. Anyhow, what they think happened is that Frank climbed out an attic window, slipped on the steep slate roof, and fell off. He died that same night."

"That could explain why he's so angry. I guess he wants to get back at Bryant—or anyone living in his house," Jason commented.

"Okay," Grant said slowly. "But why wait until now? Mrs. McGrath said she'd lived in that house for fifty years. Things only started happening recently."

"Maybe it's connected to Bryant House itself being torn down," Mark proposed. "Did you guys pick up anything that might help explain things on the voice recorders?"

"You know, I think we just might have." Grant nodded. "A couple of words came through pretty clearly. They didn't make too much sense on their own. When you put them together with Frank Thompson's story, maybe they do make sense."

He tapped a few keys on the laptop to cue up the sound.

"Let's listen to it again. This is from when we were in the kitchen. Right before the block came flying."

Grant hit a key, and Jason's voice filled the room.

"We don't mean you any harm. We just want to understand who you are," Jason's voice said.

There was a strange sound, like something scratching against the microphone. Then a hushed voice.

"*...no more...*"

"Did you once live here?" Jason's voice continued. "Was this house your home?"

Again, they heard that strange sound of static, followed by the voice. This time, the voice was more insistent. It sounded as if it was frustrated that no one understood it.

"*...no more...NO MORE!*"

And then there was a sound of footsteps, followed by two big thumps and a heavy crash. Grant turned off the playback.

"That sound is me...smacking into the fridge and then the knife block falling down."

"Wow!" Mark said. His eyes were wide. "All of that is totally wild. Those words are really clear. And for the record, I'm glad you're in one piece, boss."

"Me too," Grant replied.

"What do you suppose the words mean?" Mark asked. "No more what? No more being shut up in Bryant House?"

"Or maybe, if this is the spirit of Frank Thompson, he's ready to pass on. Maybe he means no more being among the living," Grant suggested.

"So what do we tell Mrs. McGrath?" Jason wanted to know.

"I think I have an idea about that," Grant said. He stood up. "First, let's call Mrs. McGrath and have her meet us at the house. Then we can talk about a plan on the drive."

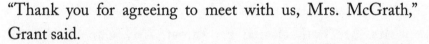

"Thank you for agreeing to meet with us, Mrs. McGrath," Grant said.

It was late that afternoon. Grant, Jason, and Mrs. McGrath were once more seated in her sunny kitchen. Mrs. McGrath's niece, Jackie, was there, as well. Jay and Grant told Mrs. McGrath about their plan.

"You really think this will work?" Jackie asked now.

"To be quite honest, we have no idea," Grant admitted. "Sometimes, we just have to do what makes the most sense to us and hope for the best. Now is one of those times."

"But if the entity in this house is a restless spirit that actually wants to be at peace, we think this is a good approach," Jason added.

"I agree," Mrs. McGrath said in a firm voice. She patted her niece's arm. "And besides, I have to do *something*. This is my home. I have no intention of leaving it."

"Okay, then," Grant said. He stood up. "Let's give this a try. But I suggest we try to make contact in the living room." He smiled at Mrs. McGrath. "I don't know about you, but I'd like to be as far away as possible from that knife block."

A few minutes later, they were all settled in the other room. "Okay, Mrs. McGrath. Ready?" Jason asked.

Mrs. McGrath nodded. "Yes, I'm ready."

She and Grant sat side by side on the couch. Jason and Jackie sat just opposite.

"Go ahead, then," Grant said.

Mrs. McGrath cleared her throat. "My name is Abigail McGrath," she said in her calm, quiet voice. "I am speaking to the spirit in this house. I think your name might be Frank Thompson. There's something that I want to tell you, Frank."

"Keep it up," Grant murmured. "You're doing fine."

"This is *my* house," Mrs. McGrath went on. "It doesn't belong to Silas Bryant anymore. He can't hurt you. He can't make you do anything you don't want to do. He can't keep you a prisoner anymore.

"I don't know what you did to get locked up in Bryant House, and I don't care. I'm sure that, in your heart, you're a good boy. I know your mother was ill, Frank. I'm sure you wanted to help take care of her. If you want to leave, you're free to go.

"But if you decide to stay, we have to get along. This has been my home for more than fifty years. I'm not going to be scared away from it now.

"I think that's all I have to say. I hope you are listening. I hope you understand."

"Great," Grant said quietly after Mrs. McGrath had finished. "You did that really well."

"But how will we know whether it's done any good?" Mrs. McGrath asked.

"Well," Jason began.

Pop! Pop! Pop! Pop! Pop! Pop! POP!

At that moment, all the lightbulbs in the house began to explode. The sound of the shattering glass echoed throughout the house. Mrs. McGrath cried out and clapped her hands to her ears.

Pop! Pop! Pop! Pop! POP! POP! POP!

With a shower of sparks, the overhead light in the living room burst. Pieces of jagged glass rained down.

"Look out!" Grant cried. He dove toward Mrs. McGrath, trying to protect her. "Keep your head covered!" he cried. "Keep down!"

"It's all right," Mrs. McGrath panted. "I'm not hurt." She took her hands down from her ears as the house fell silent. "I'm fine. But let's hope that's the last trick Frank Thompson ever plays."

"Let's hope so!" Grant said. "You're sure you're okay?"

A few hours later, Jason and Grant prepared to leave. They were happy to say that the house had been quiet.

"Are you sure you feel okay staying here?" Jason asked.

"Yes, I'm fine," Mrs. McGrath reassured him. "This is my house. I'm staying."

"We'll keep in touch," Jason said. "Please let us know if anything else happens."

"And be careful," Grant added.

"I will. I promise."

"I just got off the phone with Mrs. McGrath," Grant said a week later. "Everything is back to normal. She said she repeated her message to Frank for a couple of days, just for good measure. But after the lightbulb explosions, all the activity in the house has stopped."

"I'm glad to hear everything worked out," Jason said. "I have to say I think Mrs. McGrath was a pretty cool client."

"You can say that again," Grant agreed at once. "She actually said she thought it was a good thing all those old lightbulbs got broken. It gave her the chance to go out and buy those new, longer-lasting, more energy-saving ones!"

"Do you think the spirit in that house really was Frank?" Jason asked.

Grant shook his head. "We'll probably never know. But whoever it was, I think we helped it move on."

"What's up next?" Grant asked.

"Boy, you sure believe in getting right to the *point*, don't you?" Jason said.

"Ouch!" Grant said with a laugh. "Don't mention anything pointy or sharp to me for a while, okay?"

"*Don't stick around. Don't stay in the lighthouse after dark.*"

Pete Abernathy stood at the base of the St. Augustine Light-house. He looked up. *Right,* Pete thought. *As if I have a choice. I have to go into the lighthouse. It's my job.* The lighthouse was so tall, he had to lean backward to see the top. The surrounding park was closed for the night. Pete had already checked every-place else—visitor center, restrooms. There was only one place left to lock up for the night: the lighthouse itself.

It was the one place he didn't want to be after dark. But now it was dark, and Pete didn't have a choice. He was the caretaker at the lighthouse. Going into the lighthouse after dark was his job—his first real job. What difference did it make if he was afraid?

Okay, make that totally freaked out.

Get moving, he told himself. *The sooner you go in there, the sooner you can come back out.*

Besides, old Mack, the caretaker who trained Pete, didn't say not to go *into* the lighthouse after dark. He only said not to stick around. No way was Pete going to stick around.

The St. Augustine Lighthouse wasn't a working lighthouse anymore. It was now like a park. Lots of tourists visited the site, but only during the day. It was scarier at night.

He opened the heavy door and stepped inside. It was cool inside the lighthouse. Everything on the bottom level looked fine. There were exhibits explaining the history of the lighthouse. The big panel of light switches was right by the front door. For a moment, Pete was tempted just to turn them off and go right back out the door.

He didn't, though. He had to be sure that he was the only living soul in the St. Augustine Lighthouse. He walked to the spiral staircase and began to climb.

One hundred and forty feet up. Round and round and round. Pete's feet clanged against the metal steps. His footsteps echoed inside the great hollow tube of the lighthouse.

Nine landings until the tenth level at the very top. Pete knew because he counted them every time he climbed the stairs.

Almost there, he thought. He passed the ninth landing. Everything was quiet. Everything was still.

Of course it is. Why wouldn't it be? Pete thought. *Because,* his mind answered. *Because sometimes I hear things.*

Pete forced himself not to think about those sometimes. Right now, it was quiet. Everything was just the way it should be.

Five minutes later, Pete was at the top of the lighthouse.

Quickly, he made a turn around the big light. It wasn't on, of course. It was just for display now. Then Pete headed for the door that led to the observation platform outside. Going out onto the narrow deck was Pete's least favorite part of locking up.

But he had to do it. He had to make sure nobody was out there. He stepped outside and walked along the deck, which circled the very top of the lighthouse. He was so high up that he was afraid to look down.

But it was all clear.

Pete breathed a sigh of relief. There was nobody in the lighthouse but him. He could go back down.

He stepped back inside. He locked the door to the observation deck and gave the padlock an extra tug. Just yesterday, when Pete opened up in the morning, he found the padlock unlocked. And Pete was *absolutely sure* he'd locked it the night before.

Clang. Clang. Clang. Clang. Clang. His footsteps echoed on the metal stairs as he hurried down.

Too fast. Don't go too fast, he thought.

If he went too fast, he might lose his balance and fall. Pete clutched the curving rail, trying to steady himself. All of a sudden, he felt dizzy. He imagined himself falling—tumbling down, his screams echoing through the lighthouse.

Keep on going. Keep on going. Don't look down.

Five landings above him, four below. Pete was more than halfway down now. All he had to do was keep going. Keep looking straight ahead. It was a quiet night.

"Help me..."

There were just two words. No more than a whisper of sound. But Pete heard them, clear as the sound of a bell. The sound came drifting down from the top of the lighthouse—where he'd been standing just a few moments before. Impossible. He had just checked, and he knew for sure that no one was there.

No, he thought. *Not again. Not tonight!*

Pete began to run.

Clang. Clump. Clang. Clump.

His feet pounded on the metal stairs. He was taking them two or three steps at a time. Pete's fingers slid along the rail as he bounded down the stairs. He no longer cared about falling. All he cared about was getting out of the lighthouse.

Don't stick around...Don't stay in the lighthouse after dark. That's what Mack had said.

Two more landings to go now.

"Help me!" the voice above Pete cried once more. *"Help me!*

Help me! Help. Help. HELP!" The voice got louder. Did that mean it was getting closer?

And then, finally, Pete reached the bottom. He was going so fast that he couldn't stop himself. He skidded off the stairs and crashed into the curved wall of the lighthouse. Pain shot through Pete's shoulder. He ignored it and kept on going. He ran straight to the door.

Beside the door was a panel of switches that controlled the lights. Pete seized the handle of the door with one hand and yanked it down. He swept his other hand across the switches, turning them all off at the same time.

"HELP ME!" the voice in the lighthouse screamed.

Pete pushed on the door with all his might. And then he was outside. Staggering out into the cool autumn air. The door closed with a crash behind him.

Pete stood for a moment, sucking air, leaning against the door to the lighthouse. In front of him, he could see the path that led to his cottage. The path was made of oyster shells. They glowed an eerie white in the darkness.

Like bones, Pete thought. He shuddered. He took two steps, then stopped cold.

High above his head, from the observation platform, came the sound of a woman crying. She was sobbing as if her heart would break.

That's when Pete Abernathy began to run.

"So, we're investigating a lighthouse. How cool is that?" Mike Hammond said.

"Extremely," Jason answered with a smile. He gave Grant a poke on the arm. Grant was driving one of the TAPS SUVs. Jason sat beside him, with Mike in the backseat. The three had been traveling all day, heading to St. Augustine, Florida.

"How soon till we get there?" Mike asked.

"Yeah, how much longer?" Jason chimed in.

"About another hour," Grant said. "Hold your horses, guys."

Mike laughed. "You sound just like my mom. She always did the driving on long car trips. And her favorite thing to say was..."

"'Don't make me stop this car!'" Mike, Grant, and Jason all said at exactly the same time. Then they all laughed.

"Okay, okay, enough road trip fun and games," Grant said after the laughter died down. "Let's get down to business and review what we have so far. That way, when we hit the lighthouse, we'll be ready to roll."

"Okay, Mom," Mike wisecracked as he opened his backpack and got out a folder. Then he pulled a small flashlight out of the bag and switched it on.

It was just Mike, Grant, and Jason for this investigation. The rest of the team were back at the TAPS office.

"The caretaker's name is Pete Abernathy," Mike read out

loud. "He's reporting activity inside the lighthouse. Shadows, footsteps, voices. He says he's been experiencing them off and on for about three weeks now."

"Which is about how long he's worked there. Is that right?" Jason asked.

Mike nodded. "Yeah, that's right. He's a pretty young guy—just out of school, I think." He looked at his notes again.

"The lighthouse at St. Augustine isn't a working lighthouse anymore," Mike went on. "There's a visitor center next door and exhibits on the ground floor of the lighthouse. Then it's quite a climb to the top. According to Mark's research, St. Augustine is the eighth-tallest lighthouse in the entire country."

"Sweet," Grant commented. "What else?"

"So, Pete's been on the job almost a month," Mike continued. "He says the last caretaker warned him that there was some strange stuff going on. The old caretaker said *he* was told the same stuff when he was new—about thirty years ago. Pete thought the guy was joking."

"Does he still think that?" Jason asked.

Mike looked up from the papers. "No," he answered quietly. "Not anymore."

About an hour later, Grant pulled the SUV into a parking lot. "Looks like this is it," Jason said. A lit sign read ST. AUGUSTINE LIGHTHOUSE. Not that it was really necessary—there was no way anybody could miss the lighthouse. It shot straight up into the sky. Jason, Grant, and Mike had been able to see it long before they got there.

"Wow!" Mike said as Grant brought the SUV to a stop.

It's one thing to read that a building is tall, Mike thought. *But seeing it in real life is something else.* The St. Augustine Lighthouse was painted white. Wide, black stripes curved around and around it. *It looks like a giant barber pole*, Mike thought.

At the very top was a glassed-in area where the light shone out of. At the bottom was a little red house.

As Mike, Jason, and Grant got out of the SUV, a young man came toward them from the front of the lighthouse. He was wearing a St. Augustine Lighthouse cap, a khaki shirt, and pants.

"You guys from TAPS?" he asked.

"Absolutely," Jason answered with a smile. He shook the guy's hand. "I'm Jason, and this is Grant and Mike."

"I'm Pete," the guy said. "I'm the one who called you. Thanks a lot for coming."

"Our pleasure. Trust me," Grant said. "We're really looking forward to investigating the lighthouse."

"Why don't you come into the visitor center?" Pete suggested. "There's a meeting room in there. We can all sit down. I'll tell you what I know."

The team settled themselves around a table in the visitor center as Pete began to talk about the lighthouse.

"The lighthouse was built in the late eighteen hundreds on

the site of an old watchtower," Pete explained. "It was built to warn ships away from something called Crazy Bank. It's a weird sandbank that would appear, disappear, then reappear again in a different place. Super-dangerous for ships."

"That *does* sound crazy," Mike said. "I've never heard of anything like that before. I have a question. Aren't most lighthouses closer to the water? This one seems kind of far away from it."

"It is." Pete nodded. "The shoreline has changed a lot since the lighthouse was built. The tide affects it a lot. The lighthouse is far away from the ocean *now,* but when it was built, it was right on the water."

"I see," Mike said. "The lighthouse was finished in 1874."

"Right," Pete said. "Some really bad things happened when it was being built. The man in charge of building it lived nearby. He had a wife and three young daughters. Two of the girls were killed in an accident.

"Some people around here say that the man's wife and the daughter who didn't die in the accident haunt the lighthouse. People claim they've heard their voices at the very top of it."

"So what do *you* think about all this?" Jason asked.

Pete Abernathy sighed. "If you asked me that a month ago, I would have said it was all a lot of nonsense," he said. "Stories like that are great for bringing in tourists. But does stuff like that actually happen in real life? No way. That's what I used to think. "

"And now?" Mike prompted.

"Now I'm not so sure," Pete admitted. "Since I've been here, I've had some pretty strange experiences. Sometimes, when I lock up at night, I swear I hear a woman's voice. Last week was the clearest so far. It totally creeped me out. That's why I decided to call you guys."

"Has anybody else seen or heard anything?" Grant asked.

"Yes." Pete nodded. "One of the things the caretakers do is keep a log, sort of like a ship's captain does. When I started having weird experiences, I wrote them in the log. I felt kind of silly, but I felt I had to. Then I got to wondering if other caretakers did the same.

"They did. There are reports going back a long time. And just before I decided to call you, I had a group of campers on the grounds. They claimed they heard a woman sobbing all night. The sound came from the top of the lighthouse. I don't think it's just me. I'm not making this stuff up."

"I'm sure you're not," Jason said. He stood up. "And you've definitely given us lots to go on. Why don't you take us over to the lighthouse, and we'll get set up."

"Sounds good," Pete said. Mike could hear the relief in the caretaker's voice. "What do you want me to do after that?"

"Get a good night's sleep," Grant said. "And leave whatever is going on inside that lighthouse to us."

"All set?" Jason asked about an hour later. He peered over Mike's shoulder to look at one of the laptop screens. The team had set up a command center on the lighthouse's ground floor. The laptop Jason was staring at was showing pictures from a camera at the top of the lighthouse.

"All set," Mike said. "I wish I had more cameras. It would be great to have one on each landing."

"How many landings are there?" Grant asked.

"Nine."

"Dude," Jason said. "I don't think we even *own* nine cameras."

Mike laughed. "I know, I know. I just said it would be nice, that's all."

"So what *have* we got?" Grant asked.

"Three cameras," Mike answered. "One on the upper level set to cover the top of the stairs and one on this level pointing up through the stairwell. I also have one on the fifth level. That's halfway up. We should be able to see most of the stairs that way."

"Excellent," Jason commented.

"I have voice recorders in all those locations as well. We'll each have our own portable recorders, of course. And flashlights."

"Great work," Grant said. "Sounds like we're good to go."

"Be careful on the stairs," Mike warned. "I got dizzy a couple of times going up and down during my setup. Also, the stairs make a lot of noise. Go slow and steady so we can hear the voices—if there are any."

"Gotcha," Jason said.

He walked over to the lighthouse door. Beside it was the panel of light switches.

"Everybody ready?" Jason asked.

Mike and Grant nodded.

"Okay, then, this is it," Jason said. "The investigation of the St. Augustine Lighthouse starts now. We are going dark."

"This is Mike," Mike said in a low voice. He was setting a level for his personal voice recorder. "Climbing up the stairs with Jason and Grant."

Mike was first in line. He was the most familiar with the lighthouse because he did the setup.

"Wow," said Jason, who was right behind him. "In this place, going dark really means *dark*."

"You know it," Grant spoke up. He was behind Jason. "But see where the windows are?"

He pointed up to the first of four tall windows along the lighthouse's face. "I think it's a little brighter up there."

"It must be the lights of the town shining in," Mike said.

The three climbed in silence for several moments. Around and around and around. Mike moved carefully, on the balls of his feet. He tried to make as little sound as possible. Even so, the team's footsteps seemed to echo through the lighthouse.

"We're on the fifth landing," Jason said.

That's five more to go, Mike thought. He leaned over the railing. He looked up, trying to see all the way to the top of the lighthouse.

Then he looked down.

Big mistake! The second he looked down, Mike realized just how high up he really was.

Below him, the metal steps of the staircase spiraled down, down, down. Quickly, Mike shifted his gaze to his own feet. That was even worse! The steps were sturdy metal, but they were open mesh. A diamond pattern, sort of like a chain-link fence but smaller. Beneath his feet, Mike could see dark, open air.

If he stepped wrong, would he fall all the way down? What if the stairway just collapsed? It was very old, after all. Mike felt dizzy. Sweat broke out all over his body. It was getting hard to breathe. It felt as if a giant hand were wrapped around his throat.

"Guys," he croaked, "I think I'm having some weird reaction to the height. I might need to stop or—"

"What's that? *Did you see that?*" Jason broke in. His voice was urgent. He put a hand on Mike's arm. Mike turned to face Jason, who was pointing to the landing two levels up.

"What?" Grant demanded. "What did you see, Jay?"

"Something just moved in front of the window on the landing," Jason said. "I saw a black mass come in front of the light. You're closer, Mike. Look up there and tell me what you see."

Mike took a deep breath. He wasn't dizzy anymore. He was too excited. He stared upward, aiming with his flashlight.

"It's totally dark up there," he said. "I can't see a thing."

"That means it's still there!" Jason whispered fiercely. "It has to be in front of the window, blocking out the light."

"Okay," Grant said. "Try making contact."

"Is there someone here with us?" Jason called out. "If there is, could you give us a sign? Can you move away from the window?"

"I have an idea," Grant said quietly. "Shine your light on the stairs above that landing, Mike. I'll shine mine between here and there. Jay, you climb. If anything moves either up or down, our lights should catch it. Maybe we can get a better look at what we're dealing with."

"Got it," Jason said. "Okay, here I go."

Jason squeezed past Mike and began to climb. Mike watched the way Jason's flashlight moved as he circled around and around. He was almost to the next landing now.

"Anything?" Grant whispered from right behind Mike.

"Nothing," Mike whispered back. "No movement that I can see."

"Who are you?" Grant called. "Are you the woman who needs help? Are you a child?"

"Whoa!" Mike cried. "Movement! I've got movement. Going up. It's heading for the top of the lighthouse, Jay! Go. Go. *Go!"*

"I see it!" Jason exclaimed. "Holy cow! It looks like a woman in a long dress."

Jason sprinted up the stairs, taking them two and three at a time. The lighthouse echoed with the sound of his steps. The spiral staircase shook with the force of his climb. Mike and Grant clung to the rail.

"I see it!" Mike heard Grant say from right behind him. He added his light to Grant's, trying to see what Jason was chasing. "I see it, too, now. That definitely looks like a woman's long skirt. She's moving so fast! We should help Jay. Come on."

Mike raced several steps up. Then he stopped so suddenly that Grant crashed into him.

"What is it?" Grant demanded. *"What?"*

"Shhh," Mike said. "Wait a minute. Listen. Jason! Don't move."

From the very top of the lighthouse, he heard it again. The barest whisper.

"Oh my gosh," Grant said. *"Do you hear that?"*

"I hear it." Mike nodded.

"Help me ... help me!" a woman's voice sobbed.

Then it stopped. The St. Augustine Lighthouse was silent once more.

"What do we do now?" Mike asked.

"We go up," Grant answered. "All the way to the top. That's where the sound is coming from."

Slowly, step by step, Mike, Grant, and Jason continued up the curving stairs. Mike kept his eyes focused upward. His ears strained for the slightest sound. The team was seven levels up now. Just three more and they would be at the top of the lighthouse.

"I gotta tell you guys, that was pretty incredible," Jason said quietly. He was in the lead now. "Did you see how *fast* that thing was?"

"*She*," Mike said. "I definitely saw a woman in a long dress."

"Me too," Grant said. "And she was running up those stairs like somebody's life depended on it."

"Somebody's might have," Jason said. "Could she be the mother of the girls who died?"

"No way to know at this point," Grant answered. "It's certainly possible."

"We should try to make contact again," Mike said.

"Okay," Grant said. "Go for it."

"Hello?" Mike called out.

His voice seemed to bounce off the walls of the lighthouse. Slowly, carefully, the team continued to climb. Eight landings now. One more and they would be at the tenth level, where the lighthouse light was.

"Is there somebody here with us? We think we saw you just now, going up the stairs. And we think we heard your voice. We think we heard you ask for help. We'd like to help you, but we don't know how. Can you tell us? Can you help us help you?"

In front of him, Mike saw Jason hold up a hand. All three TAPS team members stopped walking.

"What?" Grant said, so softly Mike could barely hear him. "What is it, Jay?"

Jason didn't answer with words. Instead, he leaned out over the edge of the stair rail and looked up. Mike and Grant did the same.

At the very top of the lighthouse, a pale face gazed back down. Long blond hair streamed over her shoulders. Her ruffled skirt flowed through the railings on the staircase. Mike couldn't see her features clearly, but he was sure he saw a pair of dark eyes, gazing downward.

Mike's breath stopped in his throat. He felt as if he had taken a quick punch to the gut. "I cannot *believe* I'm seeing this!" he breathed.

"Look!" Jason suddenly said. He reached back and seized Mike by the arm. "Look at that! Do you see that?"

Jason aimed his flashlight. There was a hand on the railing. Like the face, it was pale and white. Mike could actually see the fingers curl around the rail.

Then, totally without warning, the hand moved. It slid along the rail so fast it was a blur.

"She's coming!" Jason shouted. "Guys, she's coming straight at us!"

Mike felt a surge of energy. He pushed past Jason and began to climb up to meet the ghost!

Jason and Grant followed close behind. They reached the ninth landing. Mike was traveling so fast he skidded around the corner. He clutched at the rail, desperately trying to keep his balance.

"Can you see her?" Grant called out.

"Not yet," Mike called back. "But I'm almost to the top."

Flash!

A bright light flooded the top of the lighthouse. Mike cried out and covered his eyes.

"What *is* that?" he cried. "What's going on?"

"I don't know," Jason replied. He leaned over, resting his hands on his knees as he sucked in air. Then he straightened up and looked around. "Wait a minute. Check this out," he said.

He pointed to a light attached to the curve of the lighthouse wall.

"That light must be a motion sensor. We set it off. Well, I guess that's it, guys. Whoever that woman is, she's gone now."

"She may be gone *now*," Mike said, "but I definitely saw something. We were not alone. There's an entity inside this lighthouse."

"I can't wait to see what you've got," Pete Abernathy said the next morning.

He and Mike were sitting at Pete's table in the visitor center. Jason and Grant stood behind them. Mike had a laptop and an audio recorder all set up, ready to play back both images and sounds from the investigation.

"Let me start by saying that this is one of the most remarkable cases we've ever encountered," Mike said. He glanced back over his shoulder. "I'm sure Jay and Grant agree."

"Absolutely," Jason said.

"I'm going to start with the audio," Mike went on. He pressed the play button on the audio recorder. Instantly, the room was filled with sound.

"That's us, running like crazy up the stairs," Mike filled in.

"Shhh. Wait a minute. Listen. Jason! Don't move," Mike's voice cried.

The sound of footsteps halted abruptly. There was a moment of eerie silence. Then a new voice. One so low it was almost impossible to make out.

Pete leaned toward the recorder. "That's exactly what I heard the other night!" he said. "That woman, begging for help. I can't believe you actually recorded her. That is totally wild."

"We thought so," Grant said as Mike turned off the recorder. "But we're not done yet. Go ahead, Mike."

"We set up several cameras inside the lighthouse," Mike explained. "One of them was aimed straight up. What you're about to see took place at the top level."

Mike pressed a button on the laptop, and the screen came to life. It was very dark. But the spiral stairs were clearly visible.

"Okay, now watch right *here*," Mike said. He leaned over and pointed to the screen.

At the topmost level, a pale form appeared. It leaned over the railing, as if staring down. Then it made a sudden, swooping motion down the spiral stairs. It rounded the first corner and disappeared.

"Oh my gosh!" Pete exclaimed. "That's incredible. It's going so fast!"

"And there's another thing," Jason said. "Play it again, will you, Mike?"

"Sure thing," Mike said. He recued the footage, then played it again.

"See where that is?" Jason asked. He leaned over and pointed to the screen. "That's the very top level of the lighthouse. We were about two levels down. We went running up there after that thing. Right before we hit the top level, our movement triggered the motion-sensor light.

"The figure we saw *moved*," Jason continued. "It moved *fast*.

You just saw that. It was right up at the top level. And its movement didn't trip the sensor light. But just a few minutes later, when we ran up there, we did."

Pete was silent for a long moment. "So you are saying that this woman didn't set off the motion sensor, because she isn't a human with a body. Is that what you mean?"

"Yes, that's what it seems like to us," Jason said.

"Well," Pete replied, "you have just officially made a believer out of me, guys. I seriously expected you would come in this morning and tell me it was all my imagination. I sure didn't expect anything like this. But what do I do now? What about my visitors?"

"We've been talking about that," Jason admitted. "From what you've told us, these paranormal sightings aren't new. People have been having unusual experiences in and around the lighthouse for quite some time."

"Yes." Pete nodded. "That's right. For years now."

"But there haven't been any accidents, right? No visitor has ever been threatened or harmed?"

"No. No accidents." Pete nodded again, more firmly this time. "I know that's correct. I checked the records myself."

"Then I think that's your answer," Grant said. "Whatever's going on inside that lighthouse, whoever the entity is, she means you and your visitors no harm."

"It could even be what we call a residual haunting," Mike

filled in. "In a residual haunting, the spirit isn't aware of the 'real' world at all. It's just repeating the same actions, over and over again. Sort of like an endless loop. The spirit is literally stuck in time.

"It may be upsetting for you—particularly if the ghost is the mother of those two little girls who died. But she probably doesn't even know you're there."

Pete was silent for several moments.

"So it's really true," he said. "I'm the caretaker of a haunted lighthouse."

"Well, that was definitely one for the record books," Mike said as Grant pulled the TAPS SUV out of the St. Augustine Light-house parking lot.

"Absolutely." Jason nodded. "And I thought Pete handled the whole situation really well."

"I think so, too," Grant agreed. "I wouldn't be surprised if he starts including information about the spirit on his tours of the lighthouse."

"There is just one thing, though," Mike said.

"What?" Jason asked.

"Anybody but me notice that the weather down here's a whole lot warmer than in Rhode Island?"

"That's a no-brainer," Grant said with a laugh. "Of course."

"I don't suppose you'd consider relocating the office," Mike said.

"Nice try," Jason said.

"Oh, well," Mike said. "You know what we say."

He leaned forward, extending one hand in a fist. Jason reached back and gave Mike the traditional TAPS fist bump.

"You bet I do," Jason said. "On to the next one!"

The GHOST HUNT Expert Guide

by

Jason Hawes and
Grant Wilson

Introduction

Ghosts, spirits, apparitions, haunts. There are lots of different names for them—and lots of information and *mis*information about them. As ghost hunters, our job is to find out the truth. Finding paranormal evidence is exciting. But so is finding normal reasons for what people think is paranormal. We call this debunking claims.

But you know that. You've read our cases, and you've seen us on TV. Now it's time for you to join us and become an expert ghost hunter. You don't need all the fancy equipment we use. All you need are this guide, a good brain, and an open mind.

Maybe you've had an experience with the paranormal yourself. Maybe you have already done some investigations on your own. Or maybe you're just curious and want to learn more. Either way, we'll help you start your own investigations. Ghost hunting is a lot of fun. It's really thrilling to investigate a site that you think is haunted. But it's also hard work. Trust us. You can't believe everything you see. Read on to find out what you need to know to have a successful and safe ghost hunt investigation.

For those of you who have already done some ghost hunting, this guide features some special **Expert Tips**. Look for them in every section of this guide.

But first let's see just what kind of ghost hunter you are. On the next page is your first test case. Answer the questions and see how you would react on a TAPS case. Don't worry if you get a lot of wrong answers. This test is just for fun—the test that counts is at the end of this guide.

Ready? You're on the case...

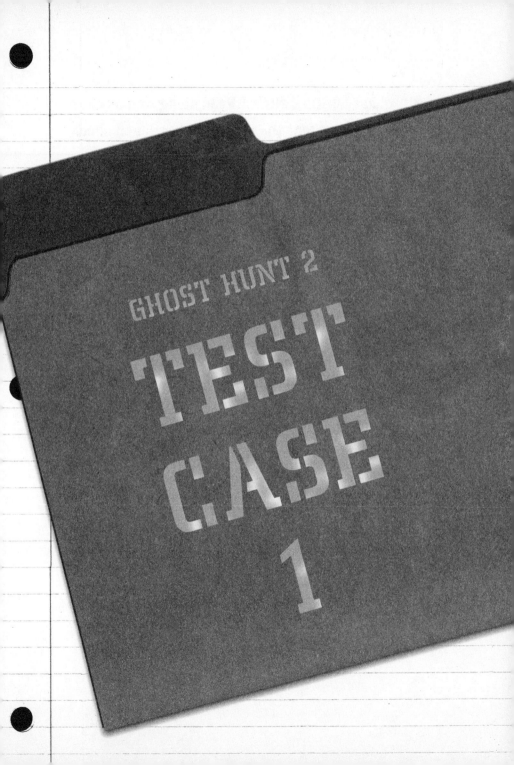

GHOST HUNT 2

TEST CASE 1

Test your ghost hunting skills! Read along and answer the questions throughout the investigation. Then check your answers to see how you did. Good luck!

The sun is setting over Camp Elk River, and you've just finished unpacking your bags. Your counselor calls all the bunk mates together and says that as a way to get to know one another, your cabin will go camping that night. You toss your flashlight and some clothes into a duffel bag and head out into the woods.

After making some s'mores, your counselor begins to tell a ghost story. The tale is about a lost soldier who was injured in a bloody battle many years ago. And now his ghost roams the woods—these very woods you are sitting in—trying to find his way home. Each night, he appears with his lantern, making his way through the forest, warning his fellow soldiers about the advancing army.

"You think that's a true story?" you ask the camper next to you.

"Nah… probably just trying to scare us. But it would be real cool if it were true."

"Yeah, you're right," you say. But in the back of your mind, you remember that there was a major battle in the Revolutionary War not too far away from the campgrounds.

1. **You decide the story could be true because it fits the description of a...**

a)   **Demonic haunting**

b)   **Intelligent haunting**

c)   **Residual haunting**

d)   **Poltergeist**

Suddenly in the distance you see a dim orange light flicker. It sways a little bit, like someone holding a lantern. It floats for a second, then disappears. You get a little freaked, but you keep your cool.

Yet there is still something strange in the air. Over the scent of the burning campfire, you can smell something else. It's a strong odor—almost like kerosene from an old lantern. A gust of wind picks up, blowing the campfire in all directions. After a few moments, the wind dies down. Again, you see a light flicker about a few hundred feet away. The light is moving back and forth. Your counselor is wrapping up his story, but you hear a different noise in the background: a very faint voice.

2. **You think whatever is going on out there is probably...**

a) **Nothing paranormal; it's probably just another group camping out**

b) **Swamp gas**

c) **A ghost with a lantern**

d) **A lost hiker with a flashlight**

Your counselor finishes the story and puts out the campfire. Everyone goes into the tents. You get comfortable in your sleeping bag, but right as you are about to fall asleep, you see something strange through the side of your tent. You know your counselor put the campfire out, but it looks like there's a different fire now.

3. **The dim flicker you saw is now brighter. It looks as if it's moving toward the campsite, straight to your tent. You decide to...**

a) **Shine your flashlight back at the light, hoping to scare away whatever spirit is there**

b) **Look outside the tent to see what's there**

c) **Roll over and go to sleep**

d) **Do research the next day in the camp library about the soldier in your counselor's story**

You unzip the tent flap and look outside. At first you don't see anything. Then out of the corner of your eye, you see that orange light shining in the total opposite direction from where it was before. You quickly move your head to get a better look, but right when you fix your eyes on it, the light vanishes. You wait a minute or so, but nothing happens. So you zip the tent flap closed, and soon you drift off to sleep.

The next morning you ask your counselor if there were any other cabins camping out last night. He says there weren't. Then you ask him if he saw anything weird. He mentions that he saw a bright light. But he didn't think much of it.

A few days later, after dinner in the mess hall, your cabin has some free time. You decide that light you saw was just *too* strange. You want to investigate it.

4. **You have enough room in your backpack to bring only four pieces of ghost hunting equipment, so you decide to take all the following pieces:**

a) **Thermometer, compass, camera, set of extra batteries**
b) **Compass, camera, flashlight, set of extra batteries**
c) **Camera, flashlight, walkie-talkies, set of extra batteries**
d) **Flashlight, thermometer, compass, set of extra batteries**

You go out into the woods to the same spot where the campfire was the night before. It isn't too far from the cabin, only a bit off the trail.

5.   **By the time you find the spot, the sun is setting. The first thing you do is...**

a)   **Call out to the spirit**
b)   **Look for markers of a burial ground**
c)   **Sit down where your tent was and wait for the spirit to show itself**
d)   **Take a few pictures of the area**

Darkness is falling pretty quickly, so you turn on your flashlight. You decide to use your compass as a simple EMF detector. You know that if the compass spins around instead of pointing true north, something odd is happening in the electromagnetic field of the area. That could mean a spirit is present.

Looking at the compass, you see that the needle is spinning all over the place. Quickly you look around. But there's nothing. The woods are totally quiet. You don't have much time, since you have to be back to your cabin by the time it gets dark.

6. **The next thing you decide to do is...**

a) **See if you are wearing or carrying something, like a watch or belt, that could be affecting the compass**
b) **Stay out all night until something shows up**
c) **Take as many pictures as you can because something must be out there**
d) **Pack it in and go back to your cabin**

Then you call out to the spirit.

"Hello?" you say. "If there is a spirit here, I would like to help you. Show me a sign you are here."

7. **You take a few steps forward and wait a few moments. When you look back down at the compass, it's stopped spinning. Is that the sign you asked for?**

a) **Yes, the spirit responded to your asking for a sign by stopping the compass needle**
b) **No, the compass should spin faster if a spirit is present**
c) **Maybe, it's not 100 percent proof one way or the other**
d) **No, if it was the spirit, the orange light would be back**

You snap a few pictures and go back to your cabin. You think it's best not to tell anyone what you've been up to until you have a chance to go over the evidence. So you hang out with your bunk mates until lights-out.

The next morning, you check out the pictures you took during the investigation. Scanning through the images, one image in particular catches your eye. Between two trees, there seems to be a shadowy figure. You zoom in. You can even sort of make out what looks like an old-fashioned gun, a musket, strapped to the figure's back.

8.   **This looks like a great piece of evidence! But before you can be sure, you must...**

a)   **Check it against other pictures to see if the figure appears in them**

b)   **Look at the image from different angles to make sure you aren't matrixing**

c)   **Look for other things in the picture that may indicate the paranormal**

d)   **All of the above**

After giving the picture a hard look, you think the figure is real. This is way exciting.

9.   **You decide to...**

a)   **Tell your counselor not to camp out at that spot anymore because it's dangerous**

b)   **See if anyone else in your cabin is interested in ghost hunting and set up a ghost hunting team**

c)   **Go back to the spot alone for more investigation**

d)   **Write home to your parents, and tell them to send you a better camera**

The next night you go back out to the site with a few of your friends. Everyone is excited about the investigation. You start by studying that picture of the figure that you thought looked like the soldier. You find the exact spot where you took it and look straight ahead. Your friend points out that a knot in the tree next to a weird branch is actually what's in the picture—definitely not a spirit. Bummer, you were matrixing after all. Your mind was making you see a soldier because of what you had heard about the site. But there's still more to be done.

You take out the compass and start checking the area again. You walk around a bit until you look down and see the needle spin. You call two friends over to check it out quickly. They are amazed by what they see—until one of your bunk mates looks up and sees an electrical wire leading toward camp directly overhead.

"Do you think that could be doing it?" he asks. "Maybe something with the electricity…"

"Yeah," you say. "It's too much of a coincidence." You remember that the last time the compass stopped spinning, you had walked a few steps forward. So you try it again, and sure enough, when you get away from the wire, the needle points directly north.

"So far, we've debunked most of the evidence," you say. "But what about the light? I know what I saw. It looked like someone holding a lantern."

"That could've been anything," your friend says. "Maybe something from the cabins. Who knows? But I think we can call this case closed."

"It's getting dark," another friend says. "We should go back."

You start down the trail leading back to camp, but suddenly all three of you stop cold. A flicker of light twinkles around some trees in the distance. A barely audible voice is carried on the wind. You can hear it say, "Run! They're coming! They're coming!"

"It's the lost soldier!" you shout.

Quickly, you and your team run toward the direction where the voice is coming from. As you get closer, you see the orange light appear. Now you all run as fast as you can.

But when you reach the light, you are disappointed. Your counselor is waiting for you there, smiling and holding an electric lantern.

"Sorry, guys. It's a Camp Elk River tradition. Each year, we tell the story about the lost soldier and walk around with the lantern to scare the new campers."

"So you were walking around with the light the whole time?"

"Well, the other counselors helped while I was telling the ghost story."

"And you pretended to be the ghost calling out, 'Run, they're coming'?"

"Huh?"

"That voice we just heard. That was you, too, right?"

"No, I didn't say anything…"

Just then, your counselor's face turns white. The hairs stand up on the back of your neck. You can hear the voice now, louder, yelling, *"Run! They're coming!"*

ANSWERS

Question 1: You decide the story could be true because it fits the description of a...

Answer: c) Residual haunting

All the indications point to a residual haunting—a spirit doing the same thing over and over again, never changing what it does or interacting with people.

Question 2: You think whatever is going on out there is probably...

Answer: a) Nothing paranormal; it's probably just another group camping out

Swamp gas might be a common explanation for strange-looking lights... but you're camping in the woods, not at a swamp. You've got to be aware of your surroundings. And even though the ghost story might be a little creepy, you can't just jump to the conclusion that something paranormal is going on. All those weird things could just as easily be another group of campers. Think about it. The orange light and the smell could be from a torch for bugs; the voice could be another counselor. And a sudden wind is not that unusual.

Question 3: The dim flicker you saw is now brighter. It looks as if it's moving toward the campsite, straight to your tent. You decide to...

Answer: b) Look outside the tent to see what's there

At this point you should probably check out what's going on. Answers *a* and *d* both assume that the light is definitely a ghost, but you'd never actually know without looking. Remember, a ghost hunter always needs to walk toward the area where they think something paranormal is going on. If you chose answer *c*, you may not be cut out to be a ghost hunter—sometimes we're up all night!

Question 4: You have enough room in your backpack to bring only four pieces of ghost hunting equipment, so you decide to take all the following pieces:

Answer: b) Compass, camera, flashlight, set of extra batteries

A thermometer won't really help you out in the woods. It's mostly used for finding cold spots inside a room. In the open, there are too many variables to accurately use it. You also won't need the walkie-talkies, because you're going out alone.

Question 5: By the time you find the spot, the sun is setting. The first thing you do is...

Answer: d) Take a few pictures of the area

Sometimes simple is good. There's a lot going on in the woods—birds and other animals, branches moved by wind—and shadows can often play tricks on a person. Taking a few pictures while it's still fairly light out is a smart idea.

Question 6: The next thing you decide to do is...

Answer: a) See if you are wearing or carrying something, like a watch or belt, that could be affecting the compass

Remember—your first job is to debunk a claim. Staying out all night will only get you in trouble, and who knows if there's even anything out there? Taking pictures is not a bad idea, but before jumping to a conclusion about what's going on in the woods, you need to see what's up with the compass.

Question 7: You take a few steps forward and wait a few moments. When you look back down at the compass, it's stopped spinning. Is that the sign you asked for?

Answer: c) Maybe, it's not 100 percent proof one way or the other

It *is* a strange coincidence that the electromagnetic field changed when you asked the spirit a question. If a spirit really was present and close to you, it's true that the compass would spin faster. But just because that didn't happen when you asked for a sign doesn't mean a spirit wasn't there. You will need more evidence. It might also seem logical that the light would be back as well, but spirits can take many different forms. So just because the light isn't there doesn't mean that a spirit isn't present.

Question 8: This looks like a great piece of evidence! But before you can be sure, you must…

Answer: d) All of the above

Always remember—look for the simplest explanation first. A shadowy figure in the woods? That could be a hundred different things. But if you rule out all those possibilities, you might have some strong evidence.

Question 9: You decide to…

Answer: b) See if anyone else in your cabin is interested in ghost hunting and set up a ghost hunting team

If you think you have a strong piece of evidence, then you definitely need to go out and collect more. And the best way to do that is with a team. Remember, two (or three) heads are better than one—and also safer.

REVIEW

If you got the questions mostly right, that's great. You're on the right track to being a ghost hunter. If you got a few questions wrong, that's okay, too. Just turn the page and you'll find everything you need to know.

Every case is different. Over the years, we've investigated cases with all types of hauntings. All our investigations are different from each other. But paranormal investigators, like us, say there are four basic forms of haunting. We're going to break them down for you here. Use this information in your own investigations. With enough evidence, you can usually piece together what kind of haunting is going on.

INTELLIGENT HAUNTING

When most people think of ghosts or hauntings, they usually imagine an intelligent haunting. Most of the ghosts from scary stories and movies fall into this category. In these cases, the spirit is aware of its surroundings and can move around freely. The spirit may also interact with people. In movies, ghosts are often shown to have super-speed or to be strong enough to move heavy objects. But in our experience, spirits are usually limited in what they can do. For instance, a spirit might move an object to get attention. But most of the time, it will be able to move only very light objects.

Spirits in this situation can be friendly—like Paul O'Leary in the story "Play Dead"—or disruptive—like Eloise Cavanaugh in "It's Just a Dream." It depends on the reason why they are haunting a location. They may be haunting a place because it was once their home. They may be searching for an object they don't want to leave behind. Or they may be trying to communicate something important to the living. It's also possible they are looking for a particular person. And then there are some who just can't accept the idea that they have died. Whatever the reason, they are here, and usually they do not want to leave.

POLTERGEIST

A poltergeist haunting will start off with knocks and bangs. The furniture may start to move around by itself. The activity will become more and more intense. Eventually a poltergeist may show itself—sometimes just by making voice sounds—other times by appearing as a full-bodied apparition.

We have personally seen chairs slide across the floor and beds shake. Objects can even fly across a room. Poltergeist hauntings are loud and rowdy. In fact, that is how this type of haunting got its name. *Poltergeist* is actually a German word that means "noisy spirit."

Most of the time, a poltergeist haunting is connected to a single person. It may seem that most of the activity doesn't happen unless that certain person is present, and usually the activity appears to stop when that person leaves the home. Often, but not always, the person is a child. It is thought that a person's energy can affect spirits, resulting in a poltergeist haunting. So a very stressed person could be causing the haunting without knowing it.

In most poltergeist cases, the spirits will disappear without any warning. The haunting may stop within a few days. Other times it may take years. And you may never know the reason why it happened. Most people are just happy to see the spirit go.

RESIDUAL HAUNTING

This is the most common form of haunting. We see it often, especially at historical sites like Alcatraz or Tombstone. In this type of haunting, the spirits are completely unaware of their surroundings. They don't see the people around them. They are in their own world and their own time. In fact, the spirits are *caught* in their own time. That explains why people often make claims that they've seen a ghost wearing old-fashioned clothing, like the ghost in "Restless Spirit." These spirits repeat an action over and over again, in the same place every time. The haunting may occur every night or every week or even every year, like in "Cries in the Night," where the spirits relived their shipwreck every year.

The event being repeated is always something that was important to the spirit when it was alive. It can be an everyday activity or it can be an event that was very sad or painful. We've had cases where we hear screaming or crying. We often find out the site was the scene of violence or death. That was what we had thought when we heard the woman in the St. Augustine Lighthouse. In many cases, the spirits have no idea that there are now live people in the house.

There is very little you can do to get rid of this form of haunting. We have found that the best thing is simply to make the family who is living with it understand what is going on. They aren't in any danger. The spirit means no harm and will just continue to do whatever it's doing no matter what.

DEMONIC HAUNTING

Demonic hauntings are very, *very* rare. They are caused by an inhuman entity. These spirits are nasty. They are like the evil spirits you see in movies. We have heard of cases where people have been thrown through the air and even attacked. But so far these claims have not been proven.

We have debunked several hauntings that looked like demonic hauntings. We had a case where a boy woke up with cuts and bruises and his parents thought he was being attacked by spirits. But we found out that he was doing it to himself—while he was asleep. He was like a sleepwalker and had no memory of what happened when he was asleep. But he was actually scratching himself.

Some people have reported that during a demonic haunting, there is an awful odor, like decaying flesh or sulfur, and the air in the room feels hot and thick, like fog. We have also heard reports of a growling sound coming with the odor. We once investigated a case like this. We smelled the nasty odor and we heard the growls. But we didn't find a demonic spirit—the growls and the odors came from the homeowner's dog! Turned out the dog had a "digestive problem" that was causing the rotten odor. Get what we mean? Of course you do!

THE
TAPS
METHOD

You know ghost hunting is exciting. We live for the moment when we "go dark." But you also know that our method is based on trying to *debunk* the claims. We try to rule out every explanation until the only thing left is the paranormal. As Jason once said: "If you set out to prove a haunting, anything will seem like evidence. If you set out to *disprove* it, you'll end up with only those things you can't explain away."

So in a way, our job is not to *find* ghosts, but to *not* find ghosts. Whenever people hear a rattling sound in their home and call us saying they have a ghost (we call these reports **claims**), we check the air-conditioning system in the house first to make sure it isn't what's making the sound. If someone sees strange lights, we check to make sure they aren't just headlights from passing cars. If we can prove the claims are not paranormal, then we say we have **debunked** the claims.

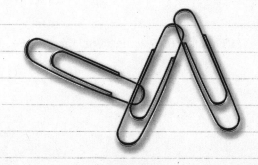

Even though we have investigated hundreds of cases, every TAPS investigation follows the same steps:

1. **The Interview**

2. **The Sweep**

3. **Setting Up the Command Center and the Equipment**

4. **Collecting Evidence**

5. **Research**

6. **Analyzing the Evidence**

7. **Conclusions**

Let's quickly review the steps, the way we always do with our team.

STEP 1: THE INTERVIEW

Getting a new case is the best part of our job. When someone calls us with a story about seeing a ghost, we're ready to pull an all-nighter to catch a glimpse of it. But you know there's work to do first.

You need to get the story. That's what we call the interview. A good interview can tell you what to look for and where to look for it. The point is to get as many details as possible. Remember, we always ask specific questions to get the best results. You don't say "So what happened?" You need to ask questions that will give you exact answers, like these:

- When was the first time you heard or saw the paranormal activity?
- Where exactly were you when it happened?
- What did you see or hear?
- Did the spirit move at all?
- Was there anyone else with you?
- Did you both experience the same thing?
- Were objects moved, or did the spirit try to communicate?
- Does this activity happen only in one spot or throughout the house?

Once in a while we come across someone who is trying to trick us. Maybe that's happened to you... It's best to find out if someone is just messing around early on so you don't waste time that could be spent investigating a real claim.

☑ when was the first time you heard or saw the paranormal activity?

☑ where exactly were you when it happened?

☑ what did you see or hear?

☑ Did the spirit move at all?

☑ was there anyone else with you?

☑ Did you both experience the same thing?

☑ were objects moved, or did the spirit try to communicate?

☑ Does this activity happen only in one spot or throughout the house?

Expert Interview Tip:
Spotting a Lie

Sometimes we get a call and everything is just right—exciting claims, historical location, people who seem trustworthy. All the pieces are adding up, and we are eager to investigate. And then when we show up at the site, something feels *off*. Maybe there is a stack of books on the paranormal or a Ouija board that "just happens" to be left out. Or the people seem more excited than troubled. But we just get a weird feeling that maybe we aren't getting the whole truth. This may happen to you. What do you do?

Get to the bottom of it fast. Ask a lot of questions until you get the whole story. Ask the interview questions we gave you, and then keep going. Get super-detailed. Make sure it all adds up. For example, your friend Eric says he saw a spirit while he was eating a midnight snack. Ask him what he was eating. If he can't remember, that could be a clue that something isn't right.

Look people right in the eye, and watch their body language. If the people you are interviewing can't look you in the face or if they keep fidgeting or if they blush, they may be lying to you. Then just stare right at them, and ask them straight out if they are lying. Their reaction will tell you the truth.

STEP 2: THE SWEEP

We do most of our investigations at night, but we always start with a daytime tour of the site. We call this part the sweep because we spend this time looking for what we call false positives. Remember, that's our term for things that seem paranormal but are, in reality, just normal.

Use this handy checklist to help you when you walk through your site.

SITE SWEEP CHECKLIST

Be sure to look closely for these things:

- **Old pipes, radiators, and air ducts** can make scary noises.
- **Water leaks** can cause noises and creepy dampness.
- **A house settling** can make creaky sounds and can make floors uneven, which can result in falls or weird feelings.
- **Mice, rats, raccoons, and other critters**—even termites in the walls—cause noise and scratching, and they can move in the dark.
- **Cracks in the windows** create drafts and drops in temperature.
- **Blinds or shades that blow in the wind** can make banging noises.
- **Bad insulation** can create a cold spot on a wall.

Expert Sweep Tip:
What's Behind the Walls?

It might be easy to run through a sweep too quickly. After all, you are excited to do an investigation. But you need to stay focused. Here's an important tip: Imagine what's behind the walls.

Having an idea of the layout of a house can be very important in an investigation. We're plumbers, so we have a lot of knowledge about how a house is built. We know what is behind the walls that could be making noises. But you don't have to be a plumber to figure these things out. You just have to pay close attention. Sometimes, a buzzing sound can be caused by electricity. In that case, look for an electrical outlet nearby. If you don't see one, look on the other side of the wall in the next room.

Water running through pipes can sometimes sound weird. But if you know where the sinks and toilets are, you can figure out if pipes are nearby. By keeping an eye out for those types of things, you will be training yourself to debunk first. And you'll be less likely to miss something important when you do your investigation.

STEP 3: SETTING UP THE COMMAND CENTER AND THE EQUIPMENT

Before we go dark, we need to get organized. You know that we don't just walk through a house without knowing where to meet up afterward or deciding who goes where. We set up the Command Center so the team knows where to meet and regroup during the night. On a TAPS investigation, we set up monitors so the team members can check out the action in the whole house at the same time. We can also see where the other team members are.

When it comes to setting up equipment, make sure to have all the hot spots covered by a team member or two and from all angles, if possible. When you set up, look for conditions that could cause false positives. (Look at the sweep checklist for help.)

Expert Setup Tip:
Setting Up Outside

Not all investigations take place indoors. Think of the "Ghost Town" story. Lyssa and Jen experienced a cold spot outdoors. And even though Lyssa was inside the shack, Jen was the one who caught the video evidence from outside. So no matter where you are investigating, you still need a Command Center.

Make sure it's an easy place to find. If for some reason you get split up or your walkie-talkies stop working, you will be able to meet up quickly that way. If you're in a place where there are a lot of buildings, choose to set up near the tallest one or one that is lit up—that way you'll be able to see it from far away. If you're in a more open space, you should make sure to stay within shouting distance of the Command Center. If your teammates at the Command Center can't hear a shout, then they are much too far away from the investigation. Other than that, your Command Center setup should be similar to the one you use when indoors.

But remember one important thing: Bring lots and lots of extra batteries. Nothing will end your investigation faster than not being able to use your flashlight.

STEP 4: COLLECTING EVIDENCE

Between the hours of 11 PM and 4 AM is when most spirits appear, so that is when you should investigate. It takes a lot of energy for a spirit to appear, and it is easiest during these hours. Think of it like this: If you were to turn on a flashlight during the daytime, you would hardly notice the light. But if you were to turn it on in the dead of night, the light would shine brightly. Before starting an investigation, remember to get permission from your parents and the owners of a site first. And always investigate with a partner. You see more and you enjoy it more—and it's safer.

When you come across activity that you think might be evidence of a spirit—like a strange noise or a cold spot—you need to walk *toward* it. It's natural that your first instinct might be to back away. But instead, you should walk slowly but steadily into the area. What you're trying to see is if the activity gets more intense as you get closer. If you walk toward it and the activity just goes away a second later, it might be nothing.

As a ghost hunter, what you need most of all are your eyes, your ears, and your brain. There are some things that no gadget can capture. There are things going on in a room that just cannot be recorded with any piece of equipment. But there are some basic inexpensive tools that we always like to use.

Audio recorder: TAPS prefers one with an external microphone, so you won't pick up the sounds of the recorder itself.

Video recorder: We set up cameras in hot spots where activity has been reported, and we also carry handheld cameras to record what we experience.

Compass: A compass can be used as a basic EMF detector. The needle will spin around if the electromagnetic field of an area changes. This could mean a spirit is near, but it can also mean it's close to a magnet or metal. Wave the compass very slowly in a circle to see if there are minor changes in the electromagnetic field. Don't move too quickly, to avoid a false positive.

Flashlight and lots of batteries: The flashlight is a no-brainer. But why the batteries? This might not seem very important, but believe us, it is. Spirits will use any available energy source to manifest—including draining your camera or flashlight batteries.

Digital thermometer: (Note: Use an ambient thermometer—one that measures the temperature of the whole room, not just the spot where it's pointed.) A digital thermometer is a very common tool in ghost hunts. Use it to look for warm spots or cold spots. A cold spot might mean a spirit is drawing energy from the room, using the warmth from the air to manifest. Of course, once you find a cold spot, the next thing you should look for is a natural cause. **Don't forget to use your checklist from the sweep.**

Walkie-talkies: Use these to keep in touch with the rest of your team.

☑ Digital camera
☑ Tape recorder
☑ Walkie-talkies
☑ Flashlight
☑ Thermometer

MAX-MIN THERMO

MAX-MIN   RESET
OUT   MAX-MIN   RESET
                  IN

In order to be scientific about an investigation, TAPS does use other equipment that can accurately measure things. Keep in mind, though, that you don't need all our high-tech stuff to do a good investigation. There are advances in science and technology all the time, so we are always looking for new equipment that will help us.

Here is a list of some gear we use. You can find more in the glossary at the back of the guide.

EMF detector: This measures the force given off by electrical charges. Scientists call this force the electromagnetic field. We do *not* use EMF detectors to *prove* there are ghosts. We use them to see if there is a sudden increase in the electromagnetic field. A sudden increase *could* mean a spirit has entered the area. It could *also* mean that you walked in front of an object with a high electromagnetic field, like a large appliance. So you have to be careful.

Some people are very sensitive to electromagnetic fields. A strong electromagnetic field can make them feel sick or dizzy. Sometimes it gives people a creepy feeling, which can make them think there are paranormal things happening. When we find high EMFs, we often tell people to have an electrician fix the electricity in the house. If the creepy feelings go away, we can debunk the claim.

Geophone: Scientists use this device to study earthquakes. A geophone detects vibrations. We use it to try to pick up the vibrations made when spirits walk.

Ion generator: An ion is a particle with either a negative or positive electrical charge. An ion generator makes the air electrically charged. Paranormal investigators think the charged air makes it easier for ghosts to try to show themselves.

IR illuminator: We use this camera attachment, which shoots out invisible infrared light into a room, to make the IR function work better.

K-II meter: Like the EMF detector, this detects the electromagnetic field. A light blinks to show how strong the field is. TAPS teams have tried using K-II meters to communicate with spirits. We ask yes-or-no questions. If the spirit wishes to answer "yes," it can use energy to change the magnetic field and cause the light to blink. If the answer is "no," the light stays off.

Laser grid: This piece of equipment shoots out lasers (a laser is a very focused beam of light) into a grid of bright dots arranged in a pattern. All a person sees are little red dots on whatever the laser grid is pointed at. If a spirit walks in front of the laser grid, the dots will disappear as if they are blocked by the entity.

Thermal camera: A special kind of IR camera. Thermal cameras collect visual information about heat and cold. They make warmth and coldness visible and can see what regular camcorders can't. We use them to detect cold spots and warm spots—and to watch for changes in temperature, which could mean a spirit has entered a room.

Gathering Audio Evidence

Say you're investigating a house for strange noises. As you go through the house, you will hear all sorts of normal sounds. Don't forget to **tag** all those sounds. Just say "The floor creaked under my foot," or whatever the case may be. These investigations can take all night, and you might forget something insignificant like that when you are listening for EVPs later. It's important to be careful because you want to be sure your electronic voice phenomenon is real.

Sometimes the sounds you hear explain what the spirit is looking for. Remember the spirit in "Lost in the Lake"? We heard "Find me," and eventually he was found.

So how do you get ghosts to talk? You start by talking to them. Remember, spirits were once alive and deserve the same respect you'd give any person. Don't start off by asking questions like "How did you die?" or "Why are you haunting this house?" Instead, ask simple questions, such as "Who are you?" or "What are you doing here?" or "What do you want?"

After each question, wait ten to twenty seconds. It takes time for a spirit to gain enough energy to respond.

Collecting Video Evidence

A regular camcorder is a great tool for a ghost hunter. You can watch the whole investigation over again second by second and not miss a thing. You can even slow time down to study every part of an important moment. This helps when you're not sure whether what you're seeing is actually evidence. Is that black thing just a shadow… or a black mass? Most camcorders also have a night vision camera, which is perfect for a ghost hunter walking around in the dark.

Professional ghost hunters like us also use thermal cameras. They're great for debunking a site. Some thermal cameras are so strong that they can pick up the heat of a mouse in the wall. If it were not for these IR cameras, you'd never know it was the little mouse all along making those creepy, scratchy noises.

Expert Evidence Tip: Experiment

If you do think something paranormal could be happening, be creative. Try to think of an experiment you can do that would debunk the strange thing going on. For instance, if you hear a funny sound that's near an air duct, have a teammate try to re-create the noise by standing at the other end of the duct and calling down to you. Metal tubes can make a voice sound really garbled. If you see a flash of light, think about where it could be coming from. Then see if you can duplicate it with your flashlight. If you see a door slam for no reason, go over to it and open it and see what happens. It may just be hanging at a funny angle.

STEP 5: RESEARCH

Doing research about a site can bring your investigation to the next level. If all your evidence adds up and your research backs it up, you might have a real haunting on your hands. We spend a lot of time looking up information about our investigations. We try to find out who lived in the house and what they did there. If an area or a town has a lot of history, there will be a lot of great information to find.

But we know you know this from reading about us and watching our show: Always do the research *after* you've investigated the site.

Have you ever passed someone drinking a soda and then five minutes later you're dying for a Coke? That's because the idea of drinking a soda was planted in your head. The same thing can happen if you do research before the investigation. If you show up at a site knowing that a famous singer died in the house, every faint noise will sound like someone singing to you. Or you may be so focused on trying to capture the singing that you overlook other important evidence. To be a good ghost hunter, you have to observe and take good notes. Then you can do research and come up with some conclusions.

Expert Research Tip:
Getting More Information

You've done a thorough investigation and have some convincing evidence—that's great. But what if you go do research and you come up short? The information you need just isn't there. If you're like us, the Internet is most likely where you started doing your research—and it is a great place to begin. You can find lots of information on almost any topic or location in a matter of minutes. But it's just a start.

There are a few other options. First, try your local library. Ask the librarian if the library has old articles that relate to your investigation. Many libraries have microfilm stations where you can look at very old newspaper articles. Some libraries have even converted the film to digital files so you can read them on a computer and print them out. You can also take out a few books on local history if necessary.

You could also do more interviews. Neighbors, senior citizens, and your teachers might have some information that could be important. Anyone with knowledge of the location would be a good source for your research. And you will be amazed by how much people enjoy talking about their town's history. It's one of the best parts of our job. We love making a connection to the past.

STEP 6: ANALYZING THE EVIDENCE

You have hours of videos and audiotapes. You've recorded everything. You've done your research. Maybe you've even experienced something you couldn't quite explain. Now it's time to study and analyze the evidence.

Remember, you need to be very careful when analyzing photographs or video footage. Is that white form a ghost? Or is it nothing? You need to look very closely. These normal things are often thought to be evidence of spirits:

- cold breath
- smoke or fog
- dust, rain, or bugs
- a finger or camera strap in front of the lens
- a reflection from the camera's flash or lens flare

Video evidence can be very convincing, but it can fool you, too. Here are some tips that will help you know the difference between real evidence and footage you shouldn't bother looking at again:

Never fast-forward during the first viewing. Yes, there are hours and hours of video to watch. Yes, it will be boring. Yes, there is a large chance that you will not find any evidence of the paranormal or ghosts. But do you really want to take the chance of missing something? An important piece of evidence might only be present in your footage for half a second. There's no way you would spot it if you were fast-forwarding.

Watch out for an out-of-focus picture. Some cameras, especially in dark situations, lose focus. This can make objects blurry. Blurry objects can look spooky. Is that a ghost hunched over in the background, or just a lamp? You could be fooled if the camera is out of focus.

Beware of matrixing. Have you ever looked at a cloud and thought it looked like your dog? It's human nature to make things seem familiar and understandable. It's something we all do. But ghost hunters like us, and you, have to be really careful about it. Let's say you have a photograph of a mysterious face in a window. You have to be sure that your mind isn't turning a random pattern of raindrops into a face.

Matrixing often happens when you have a picture with a lot of stuff in it. Pictures of tree branches or leaves, fields, or a room with a lot of furniture can fool you. If something in a photo looks like a ghost crouching in your closet, make sure it isn't just a pile of sweaters.

Expert Analysis Tip: Helping Spirits

Being a ghost hunter is not only about gathering evidence. There are real people involved—you and the person who called you—and sometimes a spirit is present as well. You know to be respectful when gathering EVPs. But what should you do if you actually get a message? What if the spirit is asking for help?

Often, a spirit just wants to communicate. Many of the EVPs we get are simply people stating their names. But sometimes a spirit will have unfinished business that is preventing it from resting in peace. This can be a tricky and stressful situation. Especially because when you finally hear the message, you will not be in the presence of the spirit anymore—you'll be at a desk going over all your evidence.

If the request is simple, you or your client should consider doing it. Almost like a favor to a friend. Or if it seems like the message is meant for someone else, you should consider delivering it to that person. Remember, as a ghost hunter, your job is to help everyone involved, including the spirit.

But you may get a message that's a little more troubling. If a spirit seems really lost or has a request that you just can't do, then you must let it go. You should try your best to help, but in the end, a spirit must find its own path to peace.

STEP 7: CONCLUSIONS

The best way to be sure your evidence is real is to work with your team. You need people with different opinions and different sets of eyes and ears. It's important not to count anyone out. If one person disagrees with you about the evidence, it could give you a whole new way of thinking.

Expert Conclusions Tip: Keep Investigating!

Even if you follow the TAPS procedures we just reviewed, we can't guarantee you will see a ghost. But you will learn a lot about how to do an investigation, and you'll have a lot of fun. If you don't see a ghost, don't give up! Keep a file on each case, even if you don't think anything paranormal happened. You'll find that, pretty soon, you'll have drawers full of case files. By now you know the whole point of being a ghost hunter is to find out the truth about the paranormal, and that can take some time. Look at us—we have investigated hundreds of cases, and we're still finding out new things all the time!

MORE EXPERT TIPS FROM TAPS

Ever since our first book, *Ghost Hunt*, came out, we've been getting more and more questions from kids like you who are doing their own paranormal investigations. We are going to share some of our answers here to help you have the best possible time on your ghost hunts. Keep reading to discover the answers to your most-asked questions.

Where do I look for ghosts?

A lot of readers asked us where to start their ghost hunt. Many people have the idea that they should head straight to the cemetery, because that's where all the dead people are, right? But think about it: How many people actually passed away there? Chances are, not many. So it's not all that likely a spirit will be connected to a graveyard.

Instead, try to find friends or relatives who think they might have a haunting on their hands. First listen to their claims, and then plan your investigation. If you don't know anyone being haunted, do some research about your town. See if there are any nearby public places that are known to be haunted. Many towns have old buildings that are said to hold spirits. But make sure you get permission to go inside.

Do you use special tricks to make ghosts appear?

We get asked all the time if we have a special method or technique to get ghosts to show themselves. If we could just make ghosts show up, we wouldn't have to hunt for them. But we do have a few tricks up our sleeves. Ghosts are unpredictable, so sometimes we try to surprise them. Casually snapping a picture over your shoulder might result in a great piece of evidence. It may sound strange, but it's worked for us. Also, we are usually very polite. But sometimes we do try to make the ghosts a little angry. In the Alcatraz case, we dared a spirit to come out.

How do you keep your cool?

Ghost hunting can get pretty scary. A lot of readers want to know how we keep our cool during an investigation. The truth is, we sometimes get scared, too. It happens to all of us. It would be weird if you didn't get a little freaked in the places we investigate. So it helps to always have a team member with you. With someone by your side, you automatically feel less scared. Also, we try to keep in mind that ghosts really aren't like how they are shown in movies. They're not out to get you. But if we do start to feel really scared, we just get out. There's nothing wrong with that at all. You won't be able to focus on the actual investigation if you're too scared.

How do you know when an investigation is over?

   We talk a lot about what to do during an investigation, but our readers have been asking us about how to end an investigation. The best thing to do is trust your gut. If you're getting a little bored because nothing is happening, quit and come back another time. Or if you have a very scary experience, go home. You can always come back.

I don't believe in ghosts. Where's the proof?

   First of all, it's not our job to prove ghosts exist. Our goal is to find out the truth and help people who have had scary experiences. But our advice to people with friends who don't know much about the paranormal is to take them along on a ghost hunt. We have often worked with people who don't believe in the paranormal. After all, for people who haven't seen it firsthand, the paranormal may be hard to understand. But this isn't a bad thing. It keeps us on our toes. We always want people to ask questions and point out explanations when it comes to evidence. We need to make sure our evidence is as good as it can be. But here's the bottom line: There's always room for doubt.

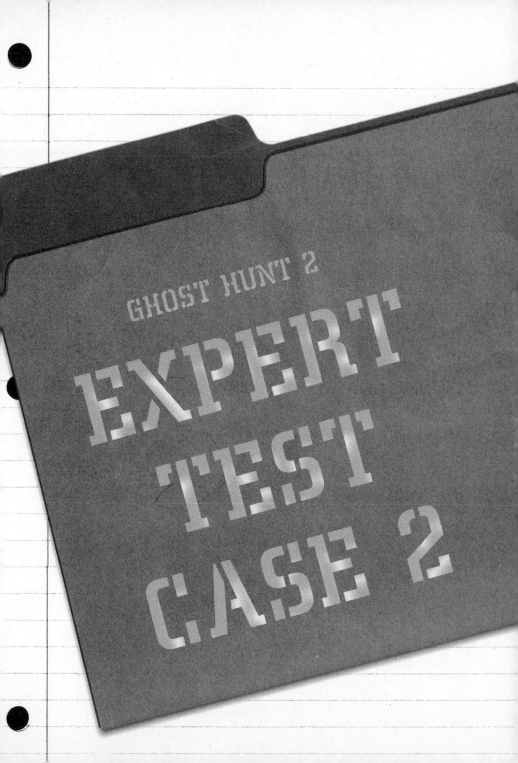

Your training is almost complete. We've given you lots of knowledge and tips you need to do a ghost hunt, so it's time for a real test. In this test, you will get a chance to join us on a TAPS investigation. You will be asked to go into a very scary site with the team. You will handle the gear, listen to and watch the recorded evidence, and help the TAPS team come to their conclusions.

Is the deserted, spooky Oakwood Academy haunted? You are about to find out.

Good luck!

INVESTIGATION AT OAKWOOD

"We just got a call from the groundskeeper at Oakwood Academy. He wants us to investigate," Jason tells the TAPS team.

"Oakwood Academy?" you ask. You may be the newest member of the team, but you're not going to be shy. "Do you mean the boarding school that closed down a few years ago?"

"That's the one," Grant says. "The school was open for almost a hundred and fifty years. Students complained that the rules were too harsh. There were always rumors about unexplained accidents. Were they really accidents? Then, three years ago, a student named Robert Miller fell down the stairs and died. After that, the school was closed."

"Why does the groundskeeper want an investigation? What are the claims?" you ask.

"Well, he says he can hear noises coming from the dorms. It sounds like kids talking to one another. He also reports hearing squeaking noises, like the sound of people jumping on beds. He's also heard footsteps running down the halls. He's even seen moving shadows in the hallways. The guy was pretty freaked," Jason says. "I think we should check it out. What do you think?"

1. You want to show the team what you've learned, but you don't want to be too eager just in case this isn't something they would investigate. After thinking it over, you say...

a) "Definitely. This place must be haunted because of the death of the student."

b) "Yeah, it might be worth it. I'm going to do some investigating first to find out more about the student who died. Then we'll decide whether to go."

c) "It sounds like something paranormal might be going on. If you think the groundskeeper is telling the truth about what he heard and saw, we should check it out."

d) "I don't think it would be worth it. Something doesn't add up to me. Wouldn't the ghost of a student just be near the stairs?"

The team decides to investigate. On the day of the investigation, you arrive at Oakwood Academy in the early afternoon. You meet briefly with the groundskeeper. Then you and the team check out the student dorms. This is part of the sweep. You are walking up the stairway near where Robert Miller fell when you stop cold. You hear a squeaky sound—like springs in a bed. You remember what the groundskeeper said about hearing the sound of squeaky beds.

"Grant, do you hear that?" you say.

"Yeah. It's really creepy. What do you think it is?" Grant asks the team.

2. **Your teammates have several suggestions. What do you think the team should do?**

a) **"Check out the hinges on the doors. Maybe a loose one is making the squeak," Lyssa says.**

b) **"Find the exact spot where Robert Miller fell. That might be where it's coming from," Mark says.**

c) **"It's a ghost. Run, dude!" Mike says.**

d) **"Try to communicate with the spirit," Jen says.**

Grant reminds you that it's most important to look for normal reasons for the sound. So the team follows Lyssa's advice. You all look through the stairwell, paying close attention to the windowpanes, the door frames, and the air ducts. Everything appears to be normal. You can't find anything that would make the squeaking noise, so you can't debunk it. But you're not ready to call it evidence yet, either. You make a mental note that it should be investigated more. Eventually you move on and finish sweeping the rest of the dorm.

It's getting pretty dark outside, so the team regroups. After setting up Central Command, you and Jason go to the main hallway in the dorms to set up equipment. This is where the groundskeeper heard the footsteps.

3.   **What piece of equipment should you use to find out if there really are spirits walking?**

a)   **EMF detector**

b)   **IR camera**

c)   **Ion generator**

d)   **Geophone**

You hand Jason the geophone. You know that it will pick up very tiny vibrations—like footsteps. Then you help Mike and Mark arrange the cameras. The sun has finally set, and the team goes dark.

You go up one floor and walk slowly with the EMF detector in your hand. The readout is pretty steady until you get to the study hall. At the door to the room, the EMF detector spikes way high. So you go inside to investigate.

Wham!

The door slams shut right behind your back. Your heart jumps into your throat. You take a minute to calm down. The room is totally still and completely dark. You flick on your flashlight and scan the room. Nothing is out of place. Then you look at the door. It's just a regular door. The kind you have to push closed. It's not the kind that shuts itself with springs. This is really weird. You think it's possible there is a spirit in the room. You want to try to make contact with the spirit. You decide to use the K-II meter.

4.   **You hold the K-II meter out in front of you, and you say...**

a)   **"Robert, is that you?"**

b)   **"If there is a spirit present, please come closer and make the lights on the meter blink."**

c)   **"Spirit, what is your name?"**

d)   **"Spirit, how did you die?"**

The K-II meter blinks. Your eyes open wide. You can't believe what you are seeing. You have actually communicated with a spirit. Or was it just an accident? You ask another question: "Did you go to school here? If you did, please make the light blink again." You can feel your heart beating as you wait for the response. It seems like forever, waiting for the colored lights to blink. Then, three seconds later, the light blinks again! Now you're sure there's something going on.

5.   **The next thing you do is...**

a)   **Turn on the audio recorder**

b)   **Ask another question**

c)   **Assure the spirit that you mean no harm**

d)   **All of the above**

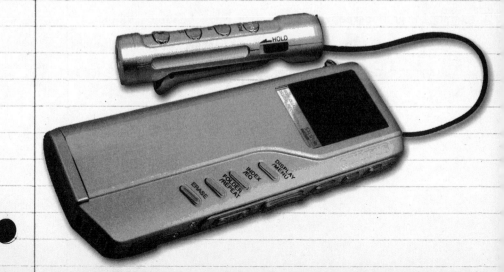

You're excited by the K-II meter results, so you keep asking more questions. But the K-II meter stays unlit. You think the slamming door and the response you got on the K-II meter may be evidence of something paranormal. But now nothing is happening in this room. You decide to move on.

You walk toward the students' bedrooms. As you get closer, you hear that squeaking noise again. You get on the walkie-talkie and ask Jason if he sees anything on the geophone. He says nothing is showing up.

By now you're at the first set of bedrooms. You keep walking. A strange smell fills the air. It's almost like wet wool. Suddenly, you see movement out of the corner of your eye. Just as you spin around, you see a shadow retreat into the room next to you.

You jump back and call Lyssa on the walkie-talkie for backup. Within minutes, she's standing next to you. You tell her what you saw.

"That's really interesting," she says. "Moving shadows is another thing the groundskeeper said he'd seen. I've got a hunch, though. Watch the door." She starts pointing her flashlight at different angles. She shines it at the wooden floor, at the walls, then sweeps it back and forth across the whole hall.

6. You think she must be...

a) Trying to catch the groundskeeper, who has been trying to play a trick on TAPS

b) Trying to re-create the shadow

c) Scaring off the spirit

d) Making it easier for the spirit to show itself

"Look, over there." Lyssa points at the next door down as she moves her flashlight back and forth. "Did the shadow look like that?"

"Yeah… sort of."

"It's possible you made the shadow yourself with your flashlight."

"Maybe. But it was *next* to me. Not in front of me."

You and Lyssa decide to investigate the bedroom. As you walk in, you notice the air feels stuffy. There are two beds at opposite ends of the room next to two desks. You can almost imagine the students doing homework at those desks.

Lyssa takes out the IR camera. She points it all around the room. The temperature is pretty steady, but when the light lands on the bed, she notices there are two small warm spots right in the middle.

7.   **They look like footprints. This means…**

a)   **You may have evidence that the squeaky noise was from a ghost jumping on the bed**

b)   **There is a spirit standing on the bed right now**

c)   **There are mice in the bed**

d)   **Your body heat is throwing off the IR camera**

You look closely at the bed. You look under the bed. You try to find an explanation for the warm spots. But there isn't anything. It seems you have evidence that something was standing on the bed. You stay in the room for about an hour, collecting video footage and audio recordings. Then you get a call over the walkie-talkie. It's Jason.

"Things have been pretty quiet for a while. Why don't we call it a night?"

"Sounds good," you say.

The next day, you start going over the evidence. You are listening to the audio recordings from the bedroom. Near the beginning of the tape, you think you hear something. You replay the tape a few times. It sounds like a boy's voice saying, "Quiet, he's coming."

"I'm not sure about that," Jen says. "I guess it would make sense… like a kid watching out for a hall monitor. But it doesn't sound like much to me."

"But what about the shadow and the IR camera image? We saw footprints on the bed. It all adds up."

"Maybe. But this audio recording just sounds like fuzz."

You listen to the recording a few more times, and you're still pretty sure it's an EVP.

8.   **There's more evidence left to go over, so you…**

a)   **Put the recording aside—for now**

b)   **Try to convince Jen that it's not just fuzz**

c)   **Take Jen's word for it and decide it's nothing**

d)   **Call the groundskeeper to see if he knows a story that will back up the voice**

At the end of the day, no one has found any hard proof on tape, other than the footprints on the IR camera.

9.   **After reviewing all the evidence one last time, the team comes to the conclusion that...**

a)   **There's not enough evidence to back up the claim that Oakwood Academy is haunted**

b)   **The groundskeeper was probably making the whole thing up**

c)   **Because of all the personal experiences, Oakwood Academy is probably haunted**

d)   **Robert Miller's spirit was trying to communicate**

"Everyone did really good work," Grant says. "But I can't help feeling like there's a piece missing."

"I know what you mean," Lyssa says. "There was so much going on, but I just wish we caught a little more of it on tape."

10. "Well, there are some things we can do," you say. You suggest...

a)   Doing research on Oakwood Academy's history
b)   Contacting the groundskeeper to visit Oakwood Academy again, now that you know where the hot spots are
c)   Using audio filtering equipment to try to clean up the EVP you think you caught
d)   All of the above

Turn the page to find out how well you did on the test case.

ANSWERS

Give yourself five points for every question you got right.

Question 1: You want to show the team what you've learned, but you don't want to be too eager just in case this isn't something they would investigate. After thinking it over, you say...

Answer: c) "It sounds like something paranormal might be going on. If you think the groundskeeper is telling the truth about what he heard and saw, we should check it out."

You shouldn't jump to a conclusion at the beginning of an investigation. You can't assume the place is haunted based on the groundskeeper's story. But you can't dismiss the whole case because something doesn't sound right to you. A person's spirit doesn't necessarily stay exactly where he or she died, so you can't predict what it will do. And as a general rule, you shouldn't do research before an investigation. If you are thinking only about the dead student, you could miss evidence that points to a new direction.

So if everyone seems to think the groundskeeper's story is possible and he's not trying to fool anyone, an investigation is the next step.

Question 2: Your teammates have several suggestions. What do you think the team should do?

Answer: a) "Check out the hinges on the doors. Maybe a loose one is making the squeak," Lyssa says.

Remember, the sweep is the time when you can most easily debunk something because you are in broad daylight. Always rule out the normal reasons first. Those squeaks could be coming from the door hinges. That's why answer *a* is right.

Question 3: What piece of equipment should you use to find out if there really are spirits walking?

Answer: d) Geophone

A geophone is a piece of equipment that will pick up on very slight vibrations. Scientists use it to predict earthquakes. It's the best choice if you're trying to see if you can pick up on a spirit's footsteps.

Question 4: You hold the K-II meter out in front of you, and you say...

Answer: b) "If there is a spirit present, please come closer and make the lights on the meter blink."

Answers *a*, *c*, and *d* all ask the spirit to answer questions. But you have decided to use the K-II meter here. You want the spirit to make itself known by making the light blink. The only questions you could ask would be yes-or-no questions. For example, you could say: "Is your name Robert? If it is, make the lights blink."

Also, *a* is not a good question, because the spirit could be Robert, but it could also be someone else. And *d* should never be the first question you ask. Would you like to answer that question first?

Question 5: Now you're sure there's something going on. The next thing you do is...

Answer: d) All of the above

If a spirit appears to be communicating with you, you should definitely keep talking! Getting a response on the K-II meter is great evidence. And having the audio recorder on at the same time might result in an EVP. But at the end, you need to make sure the weird electromagnetic field that the EMF detector and K-II meter picked up isn't from something normal, like electrical wires.

So the right answer is *d*—you need to do all of those things.

Question 6: She shines it at the wooden floor, at the walls, then sweeps it back and forth across the whole hall. You think she must be...

Answer: b) Trying to re-create the shadow

Weird shadows can be made by lots of things... even in a dark room. The moving shadow you saw could be a reflection from your own flashlight. It's important to make sure you aren't creating something that looks like evidence with your own gear.

Question 7: They look like footprints. This means...

Answer: a) You may have evidence that the squeaky noise was from a ghost jumping on the bed

This could be a real piece of evidence. If there is no other logical explanation, it seems to make sense that the "jumping on the bed" noise and the footprints could be related. If there was anything else there, like a full-bodied apparition or mice, you would see them. And your own body heat wouldn't register on the camera unless it was pointed right at you.

Question 8: There's more evidence left to go over, so you...

Answer: a) Put the recording aside—for now

You need to listen to everyone in the group. If someone doesn't think a recording is a piece of evidence, it's important to hear him or her out. However, you shouldn't just throw out evidence because someone disagrees. Put it aside and go back to it later.

Answers *b* and *c* both are a waste of time. And answer *d* is bad because you shouldn't ask someone to back you up just because you want the EVP to be real—let your evidence do that for you. By going over the rest of your footage and recordings, maybe you'll find something that will prove the EVP is real or debunk it.

Question 9: After reviewing all the evidence one last time, the team comes to the conclusion that...

Answer: c) Because of all the personal experiences, Oakwood Academy is probably haunted

The team experienced a lot. Weird noises, strange shadows, doors slamming—but you didn't get a lot of recorded evidence. Does this mean there are no spirits at the school? No. Spirits are not predictable. You can't expect to catch everything on tape.

In fact, there could very likely be some paranormal activity going on. If you have not been able to debunk those strange things you experienced, then that leaves the paranormal as an explanation. And even though you do have some evidence of spirits trying to communicate, answer *d* is not right, because you can't be sure it was Robert Miller. To be sure, you'll have to go back to the site and try to make contact again.

Question 10: "Well, there are some things we can do," you say. You suggest…

Answer: d) All of the above

Oakwood Academy has some pretty weird stuff going on. Just because you don't have rock-solid proof now doesn't mean you should give up. There's a lot to learn about such an old place, so research is definitely needed. You can also try to clean up the EVP—with TAPS audio equipment, you can try to filter out some of the white noise to clean up the recording. And definitely try to investigate again. With all that happened the first time, the place deserves a second investigation.

CONGRATULATIONS!
You did very well on your first **TAPS** case.
Check out your score!

- If you got 20 points or less, you might want to read through this guide one more time.

- If you got 25 to 35 points, you have the makings of a great investigator.

- If you got 40 points or more, you are an expert and ready to do your own ghost hunt! Awesome!

CASE CLOSED

GLOSSARY

Anecdotal Evidence: Evidence of an event that comes from people's stories.

Apparition: A spirit visible to live people.

Audio Recorder: A piece of equipment that records sound. Audio recorders can be digital or analog. TAPS uses mostly digital audio recorders.

Black Mass: An apparition in the form of a shadowy black mist.

Cold Spot: A specific area where the temperature is colder than the surrounding areas, or an area where the temperature suddenly drops. Many paranormal researchers believe cold spots are caused by entities drawing energy from the air, literally sucking the heat out of the air in order to appear.

Demonic Haunting: One of the four types of hauntings. A demonic haunting is caused by an inhuman spirit. They can be very nasty. Fortunately, they are very rare.

Digital Thermometer: A device used by paranormal investigators to detect cold spots or hot spots.

EMF Detector (Electromagnetic Field Detector): A device that records the electromagnetic field of an area (the force given off by electrical charges). Paranormal investigators use it as a tool to detect spirits either disrupting or creating electromagnetic energy.

Entity: A disembodied spirit.

EVP (Electronic Voice Phenomena): An audio recording of voices or sounds that, at the time of recording, were not detectable to the human ear.

External Microphone: A microphone attachment that connects to the audio recorder. Paranormal investigators use these to avoid picking up the sounds of the recorder itself. External microphones can be directional (picking up sounds from only the direction they are pointed toward) or ambient (picking up sounds of the whole room).

Geophone: A very sensitive device that "feels" vibrations on the ground and registers how strong the vibration is on a display of lights.

Ghost: See *Apparition*.

Haunting: The continued appearance of an entity at a specific location. There are four main types of hauntings: Demonic Haunting, Intelligent Haunting, Poltergeist, and Residual Haunting.

Hot Spot: An area where a lot of paranormal activity has been observed.

Infrared Camera (IR Camera): A device that uses infrared waves to see in the dark.

Infrared Illuminator (IR Illuminator): A camera attachment that shoots infrared light into a room, making the night-vision function work better.

Inhuman Entity: A hostile entity of non-human origins.

Intelligent Haunting: An entity that has some awareness of its surroundings. It may have some limited mobility and may be able to communicate.

Ion Generator: A piece of equipment that electrically charges the air.

K-II Meter: A device that uses blinking lights to rate levels of magnetic fields and frequencies. Some paranormal investigators believe it can be used to communicate with ghosts.

Materialization: The process of an apparition becoming visible. Materialization can occur quickly or over a period of time, causing the entity to appear either solid or indistinct.

Matrixing: The tendency of the mind to add details to images, making the images seem more familiar. It happens all the time, but it can cause problems when analyzing evidence.

Orb: A floating sphere, often white or bluish, that shows up in a photograph or video. An orb is a contained ball of energy. Some consider orbs to be evidence of paranormal activity. They are often confused with dust, bugs, or optical illusions registering on film or video.

Paranormal: Literally, "beyond normal." Something paranormal is an event or a phenomenon that is beyond what is normally experienced by humans—or what can be scientifically explained.

Paranormal Indicator: Evidence that may lead one to believe paranormal activity has taken place.

Paranormal Investigator: Also called a ghost hunter. A person who gathers information and evidence about paranormal activity.

Phantom Smell: An odor caused by a spirit attempting to make itself known. Common phantom smells include flowers, tobacco, and perfume. A phantom smell is only considered paranormal if it cannot be traced to a source.

Poltergeist: A ghost that moves objects to draw attention to itself. Banging sounds often accompany the movements. The phenomenon often revolves around an individual person.

Residual Haunting: One of the four main hauntings. An entity will replay a moment from the recent or distant past at the exact location where it happened. Usually the entity does not have any recognition of the living people watching it.

Sensitive: Any person with a sensitivity to the paranormal.

Thermal Camera: An IR camera that makes cold and heat visible.

VP (Voice Phenomena): Sounds or voices heard during an investigation that have no natural cause.

Warm Spot: Similar to a cold spot, a warm spot is an area that is hotter than its surrounding areas. Some investigators believe spirits using energy to show themselves create warmth, almost like a body does.

ACKNOWLEDGMENTS

We want to thank Jody Hotchkiss at Hotchkiss and Associates for making all these things possible. Without your guidance, none of this could have happened. Our thanks to Cameron Dokey for helping make our stories come to life. Special thanks to Jane Stine from Parachute Publishing; your faith in us has allowed us the chances we have today.

Thanks to Craig Paligian and Alan David from Pilgrim Films and Television for taking a chance on us in 2004 that allowed us to change the way the paranormal would be looked at from then on.

And to Rob Katz, who has proven to be a true friend and the best executive producer in the field. And thanks, too, to David Axelrod for his work on the *Ghost Hunt* Expert Guide and his other valuable contributions to this book.

And to Little, Brown; you have given us a chance to prove our love for what we do, and for this we are always in your debt.

JASON HAWES and **GRANT WILSON** have been avid investigators of the paranormal for more than twenty years and have investigated over two thousand claims of paranormal activity, helping families, law enforcement agencies, the military, and churches do both preliminary and extensive investigations. They are the bestselling authors of the books *Ghost Hunting* and *Seeking Spirits* for adults, and they are best known for their television show, *Ghost Hunters*, on Syfy and for being the founder and the cofounder, respectively, of The Atlantic Paranormal Society (TAPS). Jason Hawes was born in Canandaigua, New York, and now lives in Rhode Island with his wife and five children. Grant Wilson was born and raised in Providence, Rhode Island, where he continues to live with his wife and three boys.